Meetings at the Metaphor Café

– Robert Pacilio

Published by Robert Pacilio, with pre-publication technical assistance from **LOTON*tech*** (www.lotontech.com/publishing).

ISBN-13: 9781449514136
ISBN-10: 1449514138

This is a work of fiction. All the characters and events portrayed in this novel are either products of the authors' imagination or are used fictitiously with the exception of Mr. Jim Reifeiss and Mr. David Rosenberg, who appear in the novel with their permission.

To all teachers who teach to kids,
not at them.

Acknowledgements:

Meetings at the Metaphor Café is a work of fiction, but in many ways it is autobiographical. In 32 years in the service of teaching children, I have learned a great number of lessons; one of the most important is that collaboration and teamwork is a key to success. In that spirit I need to thank several people who made this novel possible. First and foremost, my editor Kathy McWilliams who, like me, is new to this business, but she often reminded me that there are no shortcuts to writing a novel and that my own "North Star" was the voices of the students, not the teachers. Teachers are in the "kid business" and we sometimes forget that it is their story that matters the most. Kathy always reminded me of that. Mark McWilliams, who has edited all of my readers theater and play productions, pushed me to use my own voice and not rely on the wonderful music that has inspired me in and outside of the classroom—notably, the life-affirming music of Bruce Springsteen and the E Street Band.

There are two characters in this novel whom I must thank—they are real people who give their time and energy each year to my real life classes on 9.11. David Rosenberg and Jim Reifeiss both allowed me to use their real names in this novel—what they say each year to my students is remarkable and moving—and I thank them for committing to young people. Mr. Rosenberg's shelter for homeless teenagers in San Diego is both real and needed in our cities.

Ms. Asal Mirzahossein is a graduate of U.C. Irvine, as well as Columbia's School of Education, and she helped me enormously to understand Persian culture and her reading of the manuscript was critical for me to make sure that I understood what happens outside the classroom walls to girls and boys whose lives are shaped by the events in Iran. My colleague Victoria Stewart, who is the most well-read math teacher I know, read this novel as I wrote it—in real time, as we were experiencing those events from the beginning of school to the day of graduation. I cannot thank her enough for her encouragement along the way.

The cover photography of Bob Bjorkquist is just a small example of his artistry. I ask my students whom they admire in their life. Well, for me, the most admired man I know is Bob; he is the Renaissance man, the caregiver, the artist, and besides that he saved my life many, many years ago. He generously donated his time to this novel.

The greatest influence in my life is my wife, Pam, who has been there with me going on 25 years. She has watched me struggle with teaching and writing, and through it all she supported me and always made sure that I could follow this passion—even when it meant she had to bear a greater burden because of my attention to this novel or my students. My children Nicholas and Anna have both helped me to understand the secret world of teenagers—even if I was their dad.

Finally, to all those teachers who trudge to their cars with papers, lesson plans, and projects—and you all know who you are—I commend you. You are the people whom students always remember.

Meetings at the Metaphor Café

Editor's Note:

Ms. Anderson's Hand

December 22nd

Four students conceived of this novel, and Tony Buscotti and I are merely character actors making an appearance in their lives. Yes, it is true that this novel's origin came from Maddie's idea to give back to us, metaphorically, all that she and her three friends had learned from us. But, in truth, it is a story about the complicated, dramatic world these sixteen-year-olds try to make sense of, and the compassion that they have nurtured among themselves and their friends; all of which makes me optimistic about this generation.

Maddie and Mickey first came to me at Thanksgiving and told me they were writing about our class and what they were learning about themselves. They told me that Rhia and Pari were part of their "Metaphor Café" group. They were nervous about writing and asked if I would be their "secret editor"—and to keep things from my partner, Mr. Buscotti, whom they often refer to as Mr. B. This story was to be their gift to both of us, but they needed a critical eye—they hoped I would agree.

I was apprehensive, overworked, and flattered.

Then I read Maddie's prologue and a new feeling surged through me. I wanted the next chapter…and the next…and I wanted to find out about their secret world, a world that few parents and certainly teachers have an opportunity to unwrap, gaze into, and try to comprehend.

These are their words; absent the grammatical errors and, interestingly, cursing. Actually, that was *their idea.* Pari put it this way in a letter to me, "I could never say those words to you, Ms. Anderson, so how can I possibly write it to you."

But be forewarned. Cast the stereotypes of this hip-hop, iPod, text message, upgrade, teen rage generation to the wind. To all of those who have been brainwashed into believing that "kids today" can't communicate without falling into the nasty habit of using words that are deemed "Parental Advisory" by record company labels, these four voices will surprise you. To all of you who may actually believe they are simply not capable of articulating profound feelings simply because the pop culture world portrays them as so shallow and selfish, these four writers will remind you of an old adage – from the mouths of babes… Enjoy.

Prologue: Thanksgiving

Madison's Hand

November 20th

Today I am thankful for two things: my Dad is home from Iraq for good, and my three best friends agreed with my crazy idea to write this book.

Not a bad 17th birthday, huh?

Okay, here is the deal. Three months ago I was kinda depressed. My school counselor kept telling me not to worry about getting into college. I wanted to say to her so what if I have good grades, so do a bazillion other juniors. And besides I will probably bomb the math part of the SAT, and even if I don't that won't matter cause how in the heck is my family going to afford college anyhow? I have two younger brothers, a mom who works at a pre-school, and dad dodging bullets and whatever in Iraq, and like I am supposed to be *not* worried? That's hysterical since on top of everything else, I have absolutely no idea what to do with my life.

"Buck up, Maddie." That's what my dad would say to all this. My mom just insists that I not worry because they "will do whatever it takes" to send me to college.

So I do what every "Navy brat" does—I do what I am told. I handle the situation. That means I go to school, deal with all the drama, hope to hold onto my friends, try to make a few new ones and maybe, just maybe, find a guy who actually listens to me and is genuine.

That is why I like Mickey. Hmmm.

So anyway, I remember way back last August when I was having the night-before-school-starts fear; the what-will-I–wear fear; the will-I-measure-up-to-girls-with-their-perfect-hair fear, and it was so crazy. Of course my mom had no clue why I was moody—she thought I was just being ridiculous. Maybe I was. But *ridiculous* is the way I see the world sometimes, you know?

Like for instance, my Dad. I remember that night my Mom told me that—for sure—he was coming home finally, and that he was *retiring* from the Navy. He'd been in Iraq for nine months. Nine months. That's like my whole sophomore year practically. Yeah, he'd send video clips and letters that I'd read at least as many times as my mother, but all that just made it worse. It is hard to explain. So I won't even try.

But every Friday night my mom would watch the news showing that week's dead in Iraq and Afghanistan. My mom thinks I don't know that she'd go to the bathroom and cry. Me? I'd just cry in front of the TV as I stared at the faces of men just like my Dad. I wonder if anybody knows what it's like to have *your* hero fighting in a war that *he doesn't even believe in.* Ridiculous! But he did it because, as he told me the night before he deployed: "I do what I am told, Maddie. I do my duty."

Dang it, I hate when I cry while I'm typing. I always think I'm gonna fry the computer.

So anyway, like I was saying--it was the night before school started, and it was a miserable, hot summer night, yeah, and I was sitting with my bowl of cookie dough ice cream watching some old movie. It was one of those movies that try to make you feel good about school. They show them to inspire the kids and probably the teachers, too.

That is when my story took a seriously crazy turn. The movie was called *To Sir with Love* where this young black teacher is struggling with his students in London. The kids in his class start off as a disaster. They are poor, rude, and they hate their lives—not to mention most teachers, except this new guy. Slowly he changes them from loners and losers, and they become these kids who care for each other and for themselves. They realize how much they appreciate him and what he has done for them. He kinda reminded me of Barack Obama.

Okay, I admit it—I am a hopeless romantic.

So there I was bawling at the end, my ice cream melted, tissues balled up, and a big smile on my face as this girl was singing about her teacher and how she wanted to thank him for all he had done—he changed her life. I was just wishing my school had a *To Sir, with Love.* You know?

Okay, fast forward a couple of days. Mickey and I were both blown away by the first few days in Mr. B's English class, and we texted each other to meet up at the Metaphor Café. That's a little coffee place that's been here in our town forever. Mickey is not my boyfriend or anything—well, he could be—I don't know. Relationships are all so wrapped up in high school drama. It's never simple. Anyway, Mickey and I chilled there with two other friends in our class, Rhia and Pari. We told our parents we were "studying" but really at first we just wanted to get out of the house, drink lattes or mochas, and hang. That first meeting was August 24th.

Yesterday, November 19th, we decided to write this book—to actually call it a book, not a journal. We started out writing this for Mr. B and his partner, Ms. Anderson. But we all know the truth—we are writing it for ourselves, each for the other, because that is what writers do. That is what Mr. B (our very own *To Sir, with Love)* has done for us in just three months.

Just so you have a picture of him, Mr. B is short for Mr. Buscotti—you know, like the cool wafer thing that you can dip into coffee. He told us he is born to battle his weight because he is named after a dessert. He is Italian, and he looks like that Tony Soprano guy on HBO. Rhia made the mistake of telling him that and he just went off. He hates *The Sopranos* because he thinks movies always show Italians as killers and classless. I gotta say, though, *he did* seem a little scary then. But his first name is actually Tony, and he is from New Jersey. He says, "Only people from New Jersey are allowed to call it *Jersey*, just like Vietnam Vets are the only people allowed to call it *'Nam*." Okay, I admit I am stealing some of his lines.

You should know a little something about each of us too. At the Metaphor Café, we like to sit in the corner by the window, at the table with the comfy chairs. Mickey always sails in and plops into a chair, not self-conscious at all. I love the way that Mickey sees through all the crap in high school. He's just different than so many boys. He is an athlete but he is not a jock, you know what I mean? And he likes school, but it isn't some cutthroat competitive thing like with some guys who always act like they are so smart. Mickey is just so cool.

And Rhia is a gentle *and* wild thing, if you can imagine both of those together. Her brown hair is curly and all over the place, and she wears dozens of bracelets that tinkle as she picks up her latte. When she goes clothes shopping at the thrift stores, she call it "treasure hunting." She doesn't seem afraid, but her life has been crazy, and her heart has been broken more times than I can say. Rhia's family couldn't be more opposite from mine. What I love about her is that she is just out there—she says just what she thinks. She stands up for people, like her brother Chris. And she doesn't get intimated by people. I really admire her.

And then there is Pari, who we just met. She is petite, just tiny all over, with these beautiful dark eyes. And she's not flashy. A jeans and t-shirt girl with her black hair in a ponytail. But there's a lot going with her if you take the time to see. Pari is *really* smart, but quiet and seems kinda, hmm, serious, I guess. Maybe, she just is more, what's the right word, more to herself—but she has also changed the most from when I first met her in August. Pari is short for Parivash and her family is Persian. I bet she would be the first to say that sometimes she feels worlds apart.

And you already know something about me. I'm a military kid, and we live in the suburbs just like a lot of other people. Okay so I was "elected" to write this prologue because the whole book started as my idea. During this Thanksgiving break, we figured we could catch you up on what has happened so far. Mr. B's English class is not so much a class as it is an experience. It's like being on a raft in the river. We've been floating down Huck Finn's river as we listen to Bruce Springsteen's "Big Muddy." We've been drifting from love to war to racism, but it seems the current always leads the four of us to our own corner table at the Metaphor Café.

One last thing. I wondered if we really could capture the experience of Mr. B's class and the world he introduced to us. Could we tell each other the truth about our hopes, our fears, and all those dreams we have that seem so impossible? Just as I was starting to have some serious doubts, it happened.

I was in the car, driving back from the grocery store for my mom. She had some oldies station on and I heard it – a song I knew sounded familiar. It was the theme song from *To Sir, with Love.* I just sat in the driveway listening, getting goosebumps.

And I knew. We have to write this. And yes, I know it won't be easy. But we'll try.

SEMESTER ONE

Chapter 1: Jewel's Hands

Mickey's Hand

August 22nd

Look at the date school started—the middle of August! So much for summer vacation. It just sucks. Not that there was much summer anyway with teachers' demanding *summer* assignments for honors and AP classes. It never ends. I guess it's getting us ready for "real life." This way, we experience stress at an early age.

So that's one reason why I decided to take Mr. B's class. My brother had him as a teacher about five years ago. He told me that he connected with kids and that it was the class he loved the most—ever, including college. Everyone I know who has been in his class says that. It doesn't take long to figure out why.

Mr. B does not require any summer assignments although I went by his room anyway last year just to be sure. When I asked him he told me: "Read a good book or two. And while you are at it see a film, maybe even a classic."

"What *you* think is a classic?" I asked. It was amazing, by the way, how he remembered my brother Tommy.

"Oh, something from Hitchcock like *Rear Window*. But if you are anything like your brother, then you should see the film, *Dead Poets Society*."

"What's it about?"

He paused, "It is about finding your voice and swimming against the stream—if need be."

So I watched it. Three times. I saw a little of myself in each of the guys in that movie. My favorite line was something about finding your own verse in life. I guess that is why I am writing this book.

Then I rented *Rear Window* and I asked Maddie to come over and watch it. She was so blown away by the actress in it, Grace Kelly. I remember her saying something about how back then, things seemed so glamorous. I was amazed at how with, like, no special effects at all—just a guy in a wheelchair looking through a window—there could be so much suspense.

Well, like it or not, summer blew by way too fast. I guess it always does.

So school starts. I guess I should explain how Mr. B's class works—it is really two classes. Ms. Anderson is his partner and she teaches U.S. History. We go from his class right to hers, and the kids from hers go to Mr. B's. We are "a village," they say.

Ms. Anderson is younger than Mr. B, very hip, very urban. She is African-American and at least six feet tall, and she looks like she works out. The girls were all checking out her wardrobe, and they seemed to approve. She is very friendly and she has this laugh that is so crazy. She just laughs so hard, like, from the heart—I can't explain. But Mr. B just cracks her up sometimes, and I can tell because her eyes water from laughing so hard.

We met them both that first day in Mr. B's room. All 70 of us in one room, although the room was a bit larger than other classrooms.

"Hi, gang," Mr. B began. "This is one part of the café; it continues next door to Ms. Anderson's room." Ms. Anderson was in the back of the room where she had been checking off our names as we entered.

Mr. B's room can best be described as a rock and roll museum. There are album covers all along the top of the walls. Mostly really old ones from the 60's, I guess. I recognized only one modern one—if you call Run DMC modern. That is when we got the tour. "Check out the albums, gang," Mr. B continued. "Here is Diana Ross, without the Supremes. Billy Joel. Roberta Flack— she was 'killing me softly' with her words. Jackson Browne. Stevie Wonder. There is the *real* Johnny Cash *At Folsom Prison*." That was one I knew since I had seen the movie. Mr. B kept moving around the room, "There is Motown. A little Frank Sinatra. Tina Turner…and of course, there is Bruce. Do I even need to explain who he is?"

He stared at us and I guess we looked dumbfounded.

Mr. B took a big breath. "Springsteen…and the *E Street* Band. That is the cover of *Born to Run*, and that is what a lot of you wanna do, 'Cause tramps like us, baby, we were born to run!'"

He was all fired up. We were still in a state of shock. He was so passionate that I couldn't help but smile. I remember my brother always referring to his class as "The Show." Yeah, now I know what he was talking about.

"Take a look around you because this is 'Our Town.' As you entered you walked under a sign that reads: 'Your 'I Will' is more important than your I.Q.' That is our motto, gang. In the film *Apollo*

13, they explain that 'Failure is not an option.' You know, w... are trying to save the astronauts who could not get to the moc Blank looks. He continued, "It's a long story. But we are traveling about that far and Ms. Anderson and I don't plan on losing anybody."

She was up at the front of the room now: "Not as long as you try. That is your 'I will.' We are less concerned with how smart you are and more concerned with how smart you want to be."

Mr. B then stood in front of the large wall of letters. It was like a mural of photos, newspaper clippings of former students, postcards, letters, even people in military uniforms.

"These letters and the students who wrote them all traveled down the same path as you, and they are there for you to read. Then he pointed to an album and said, "Simon and Garfunkel's *Bridge over Troubled Water.* The album is right above the letters. When you think you are not strong enough to navigate the current in here, just read some of these letters."

"Here's one from Eddie. It's on this funny blue paper because that's what the Army gives you to write letters back home. Here is my favorite part: 'Mr. B, tell those kids back home that I used be just like them, staring at you and Ms. Anderson that first day of class. And now I am writing to you from a café in Italy thanking you…'" Mr. B looked at us. "Eddie went to West Point. I sure hope he's okay. I haven't heard from him in a while."

It was ominous. I looked at Maddie from across the room and our eyes met. Maddie's father has served two tours of duty in Iraq.

Mr. B was moving across the room. "Here is a painting. I call it *The Ghost of Tom Joad.* Anybody know him?"

The first-day-of-class stillness left us paralyzed.

"Well, you will," he smiled, "this was actually painted by art students here at school. Each student painted a square and put them all together and you get this man, Tom Joad."

The painting was of a man in blue overalls, worried face, and pained eyes looking right at us.

"Funny how the work of many can add up to such a powerful product," Ms. Anderson said. "Tom Joad is a figure we study in the Great Depression."

The room was also outfitted with movie posters: *Casablanca, Dead Poets Society, Pleasantville.*

"Most everything you see in here is part of the lesson plan," Ms. Anderson said, and by the way, her room also has lots of history

her students and some real things like a WWII
I. That helmet weighs a ton.

t overwhelming. I could spend hours in the two
at all the letters, art projects from past students,
apers about Mr. B and the class I was now a part of.

m has an ambiance that reflects our other motto," Mr. B con..., "which is simply, 'You don't know where you are going until you know where you've been.' It seems like now we live in a disposable society that asks, 'What have you done for me lately?'"

Ms. Anderson added, "And the wisdom of generations, like Tom Brokaw's *Greatest Generation* of WWII, is being lost as they die off, a thousand a day. Or sadder still, they are just ignored. We are doomed to repeat past mistakes if we don't learn from them. So take a good look around you." Ms. Anderson raised her arms toward the walls. "The past is calling out to you to pay attention…or pay the price."

Then the most unusual thing happened. The bell rang. But we sat stunned because it seemed as if we just sat down.

Rhiannon's Hand

Two days later

Hi. I am Rhiannon (Rhia for short).

Mickey was so right about that first day. It was so awesome that after school I went by Mr. B's room and told him that I felt really connected to him. He looked at me and said, "Thanks. Most kids don't come by after the first day." Then he looked down and said, "But if they do—I guess that means something, huh." And I told him yeah. It was nice. From that moment I knew I could always talk to him. It was weird how he just seemed to get me.

I also loved that I knew lots of people in the class. I know some of them because of my brother Chris. He is so wonderful. I know lots of siblings don't get along. But Chris and I have always been really close. Chris is a year older than I am, and he is in special education. *Sped* is the new term for people in special education.

I hate the word *retarded.* I hate it so much that when I was younger I would get into fights with kids who picked on Chris at school. He was so innocent that sometimes he wouldn't get it. But I did. The funny thing is that if anyone ever tried to hurt me, in any way, he would lose it and beat them up. It could take hours to calm him down.

Last year, a new program started at my school called Best Buddies. It links each special education kid with another student on campus. I am the president of Best Buddies, and it is amazing how the program has grown. Over 100 kids have buddies now, and that is how I came to realize that Mr. B and Ms. Anderson's class had about a dozen kids are in sped. I know that although my brother in particular isn't capable of doing this class, lots of kids in sped *are* able to handle this. Their problems are minor compared to Chris'.

I talked to Ms. Anderson about it yesterday. I told her about my being involved with Best Buddies, and I told her about Chris. She said, "Well, my brothers were not in sped, but they were not gifted either. Mr. B and I think that our village should be open to lots of types of kids. Things can be very elitist in society. Schools, at least, should be open and equal."

I thought about her being black, and I wondered if that had anything to do with her making sure the class was so open. But I didn't know how to ask her. How do you talk to a black person about them being black when you are white? It's like this thing we can't talk about. Weird, huh?

One day during the first week of school, we came into Mr. B's class and discovered on our desks the lyrics to a song by Jewel called "Hands." On the back was an explanation about a project.

I love projects. I love art. Drawing and painting are my favorite classes and I love how Mr. B has art all over his room, but I did not expect what happened next.

Mr. B said: "Keep your eyes on me. Listen carefully. Relax and let the movie play in your head."

Just then the music began, and the music swept me up. I knew Jewel was sort of a pop/folk singer, very pretty, blonde. The music was soft, almost a whisper. I'd heard the song before, I think, but I never paid much attention to the words. Mr. B mouthed the lyrics that he knew by heart. He told us we were all okay and not to worry about the little things in our world.

What? Not worry about all the crazy drama that is high school? Now there's a thought.

Mr. B looked at us, right in our eyes, and echoed the chorus of the song. He showed us his hand and reminded us it was his own unique grip he had on us…and he insisted he would not let go of us.

It was like a motivational speech using a song. He was completely in sync with the music. He knew when Jewel would pause, and right then Mr. B said, "I will lead you through this year with my hands; I will teach you to dance with my hands; I will teach you to write with my hands; and I will not take excuses."

When the song was done, I wanted to applaud, but who applauds their teacher? I mean really? But you know what, *my* hands were in control and I started to applaud, and then so did the rest of the class. We all kinda smiled. It felt like a concert and a sermon rolled into one. I had never seen anything like it.

Then he showed us a drawing of his hand, and he placed his hand right on top of it—it was a perfect fit, right down to the ring on his finger and the wrinkles on the back of his left hand. Now he explained the project.

"I want you to tell me the answers to some very important questions about yourselves. You see, I think Jewel is onto something. Your hand is a symbol of what you are and what you can become. This is what I want you to do: Create your hand. Draw it, paint it, make it, I don't care. The whole point is that it is *your hand*, so make it *you.*"

"Each finger is also symbolic." That's when he told us to turn over the lyrics and look at the questions on the back:

The Fingers:

- The Pinky Finger--What do you worry about?
- The Ring Finger-- What are the obstacles you faced in romance?
- The Biggest Finger-- What was the biggest obstacle you <u>overcame</u>?
- The Pointer Finger--What or who has tried to block your direction; what has hindered your ability to be yourself?

The Hand:

- The Thumb--What important skills have you gained in your life so far?
- The Palm--What is the core of your strength either physically, spiritually, or emotionally? What or who shapes those values? From whom do you gain wisdom?
- The Wrist--What do you stand up for that often has no voice? What are your causes?

These were not questions I was ready for. These were serious questions.

"Now, I have a rule," said Mr. B as he settled into a chair. "You write what you are ready and willing to write. No anonymous people here, and nobody is going to say that people can't read what they wrote about themselves."

That is when Pari asked, "Um, Mr. B, are we going to read these out loud to the class?" Typical of Pari.

"Well, let's say this. People will really want to read *yours*, Miss Pari."

"And when is it due?" one of the twins in the front row asked. I'd never had both the identical twins in the same class before. This was Clare, I think. The other is Shannon, but both are star softball players.

"The Lord made the world in seven days. I think that will be enough time."

Then he told us his answers from when he had done his own hand. The catch was that he did his project as if he was 16, like us. He said he even wrote like he did then.

About his pinky finger he read, "I worry about being smart enough. All my friends are smart—I am the dumbest. I worry about my hair. It is all curly. This happened after I shaved my head for basketball. I got cut from the team anyway. My hair grew in all kinky and frizzy. I look like a dork. I may never have a girlfriend."

We laughed at that.

Then he read his palm, the one that symbolized what he believed back when he was 16: "I go to church. I am afraid of things. I hate smoking and some of the guys I know smoke pot. We call them *stoners*. I am not like them. I never really think about values. My parents have been great. But lately my coach is a big influence. He is cool. Long-hair, hippy. He is against the war. He hates Nixon. I think the war is wrong, too. My cousin Anthony just got killed in Vietnam. So, I guess I am afraid of stuff, like going to Hell. My coach says war is Hell. I just hope Anthony is in Heaven."

I glanced at Maddie. She was hiding her face. It must have been something he said.

When I look back at it all now, it was the whole "hands" project that got us to write each entry in this book as a *hand*. As you read our hands, you'll see that we have plenty of worries and obstacles, but also some skills and things we stand for. As for my palm, my "core"—well, I'm kinda a work in progress on that one.

Pari's Hand

Later that same night

This is how I got to know Maddie, Mickey, and Rhia. I'm know I'm different from the "American" kids. Actually, I *am* American by about two weeks according to my mom who was bursting at the seams with me when she arrived in San Francisco. My father and older brother were already here, and they had sent for us from France where we had lived after leaving Iran. My real name is Parivash, but everyone at school calls me Pari (*par* like in golf, with *ee* on the end).

Our family is Persian—it is a long story when explaining why we say *Persian* rather than *Iranian.* The simple explanation is that we hated the Shah because he was corrupt, but we hated the revolution even more because they were not only corrupt *but also* religious fanatics. So I am Persian—I am *not* an Arab. That is a long story, too.

No, I don't wear a veil, but I do get why some women wear them. And, yes, I am proud to be an American. I can even be elected president someday (as if being a woman and a Persian are not obstacles enough). People are funny. They think I am either Indian or Egyptian. I guess they like me and just don't want to associate me with a nation that President Bush called part of the "Axis of Evil."

Strangely, teachers and other adults always want to remind me of the Iran Hostage Crisis in the 1970's, even though kids my age couldn't care less. Well, my parents were alive then and were mortified by it all. Islamic law deplores all violence and killing. My parents are Muslim, although one would label them reformers or progressive Muslims. Something you should know about Persians—there are Persian Jews, Persian Christians, and Persian Muslims. However, what matters most to Persians is that we are Persian. Religion doesn't define us. I sometimes waver in my faith, but I don't let my parents know because it does mean a great deal to them. I am just not sure it means that much to me.

So when Mickey or Rhia say I am distant, I guess that is because I wear a mask—or at least I did. That is one of the things Mr. B has taught me so far. Remember that first day when he was introducing the albums on his classroom walls? One of them had Billy Joel holding a mask, and I was really drawn to it. I asked Mr. B about it after class and then I downloaded the song, *The Stranger.* Like Billy Joel, sometimes I am a stranger to myself. That was the song playing on my iPod, with its ominous whistling, as I sank down on a soft chair in the Metaphor Café.

I usually go to the Café with my other friends, but I went alone this time because I wanted to think about my hands project, and my other friends were not in Mr. B's class anyway. That is when Mickey came in. He saw me and smiled.

"Hey, Pari, what's up?" he asked as he decided the chair next to mine was now his.

I have to admit, Mickey is so unpretentious that you can't help but like him. I met him last year in Chemistry, and he was one of the few to always talk to me. I was a new kid, and being a new sophomore can be lonely since everyone makes their friends during freshman year.

"Hi, Mick." I liked calling him that, like he was Mick Jagger or something. I've always been a huge Stones fan. Mickey has the cool, longer light brown hair that is so not-trendy now with all the guys shaving their heads. It's a bit wavy and a chunk of it had escaped his backwards baseball cap that night and flopped across his eyes. I explained, "I am trying to figure out what to write about for my hands project."

"Looks like you've already started," he said, staring on the black ink that stained my hand. "Whose phone number is that? Your boyfriend?"

"Yeah, right! I don't even know. And I wrote it in some kind of ink that won't come off very easily…"

He pulled out his cell, "Let's call it."

"Oh Mick, no. I am not going to call some random person."

"Can't be random. It's on your hand."

"Mick, don't call it!" I crossed my arms, hiding my hand.

"Okay, fine. But listen, I'm meeting Maddie here. You know Maddie, don't you?"

"No." Okay, I did. But she is such the leader-type that I was kind of intimidated by her. Everyone knew Maddie.

"Come on, she's in our class. We're meeting here to talk about Mr. B's project, too. You should hang with us."

My independence and stubbornness was showing. "I don't know."

"Look, I know you know Rhia—Rhiannon. I just texted her and she's parking now and wants to ask what we're doing. Let's just chill and talk through this hand thing all together, okay?"

I did not have a chance to answer because before I knew it, Mickey was pulling over another chair and Rhia was heading right for it.

"Hey, Pari, did Mickey text you, too?"

"Ah, no. I was just sitting here and…"

"Cool. I'm glad you're here. I told my mom this was a study group, and she went off on her college days at Berkeley when she met my dad."

Rhia was wearing her typical look: a flowing, poofy skirt and an Obama/ HOPE t-shirt. She always had on big hoop earrings. Rhia has this little purple streak in her brown wild hair, and tonight she had on a brown bandanna too. I thought that was funny because she must have resembled her mother some 30 years ago at Cal.

She bubbled with enthusiasm: "Grab a chair for Maddie, Mickey. She's parking her car."

When Maddie came in, it was apparent that we really *were* a study group. She simply announced, "Hey, guys. Hi, Pari. Cool, we have chairs. Did you guys order anything? I only have about an hour or so."

I was so surprised she knew my name that I completely forgot to try to bail and make some excuse. All I said was that I already had a café latte.

While they ordered, Rhia told everyone her idea. "I'm making my hand out of lots of different fabrics—like a hand quilt, sort of. I want it to be colorful and kinda, um, free and artsy. Do you think a lot of people will do that?"

"That's not the point, Rhia. You should just make it the way you are," Mickey said.

"I think I am going to draw my hand and then text-wrap the lyrics of the song around it," Maddie said. "I downloaded it on my IPod already. I just love the words, yeah. It is like they are way more important than the music." She paused and in her direct way asked, "What about you, Pari?"

I was still stunned. I had not planned on being a part of "a group." But I guess I was now, and I decided to just ride the wave. "I don't know yet. I think I'm going to watercolor something with my hand in the middle."

"Oh, that is so cool—shoot, I should have thought of that," Rhia said to me.

Mickey was next. "You know how our family is a bunch of baseball nuts, right, and how my dad named me after Mickey Mantle, although my mom denies it? So I'm gluing my batting gloves as my hands and writing my answers on them. At least that's my idea so far."

Maddie leaned forward holding her café mocha, "That is such a good idea. But here is my question. Just how much about ourselves should we write? Do you think Mr. B will read them out loud?"

I was pretty sure I would write the facts about me and not go blubbering on with things nobody else would understand or even care about. My mask. But that was not Mickey's take on it: "I'm going to talk about politics and the war and global warming. I am getting so pissed about the way the world is now."

"Yeah, I agree," Rhia sighed, "but I just don't want to sound conceited when I have to say what I'm good at, and I don't want to be too honest about what I suck at. And then there is the stuff that 'blocks us,' like guys. Don't even get me started on that. All that macho-stupid-fighting-WWF-crap, and the entire show-no-emotion guy trip is, like, so incredibly stupid. And if a girl so much as cries, then guys say we are being so 'emo.' And you know they are feeling the same way as us, but won't say so." Just as she finished, Mickey's straw made the empty sucking sound, and we all cracked up.

"I did not mean you, Mickey," Rhia said.

"Tell you what, let's meet here the night before the project is due and bring ours to look at," said Maddie.

"But that means we can't wait until the last minute. *Last minute* is when I do my best work," Rhia pleaded.

"Too bad, Rhia. You've gotta get it done early. Pari, can you give me your cell number? Let's meet here, okay. I love this place. It's so unconventional." Maddie had made up our collective minds. I guess I just surrendered to her will.

On the way home is when it hit me. I was thinking of two flags—the American and Iranian—with my small, olive-skinned hands in the middle, complete with green nail polish and the ring my mother had just given me which used to be her mother's.

And that was *my jewel.*

Madison's Hand

Six Days Later—August 30th

We split two scones between the four of us as we waited for our drinks to cool. The Metaphor Café wasn't packed, but people were scattered here and there, some working on their laptops. Somebody behind the counter was steaming milk making that familiar loud spluttering sound. Rhia gathered her hair over to one shoulder, and said she was so blown away today in class and the rest of us nodded.

Today began with pushing all the desks out of the way against the walls. Then Mr. B had all the girls sit down on the floor in a line. He had the girls lay their hands projects on the floor in front of them. Then he huddled all the guys together and whispered something to them.

"He told us that this would have been a dream for him to be a high school guy who could sit on the floor face-to-face with 15 or so girls and just read about them and look at their faces and ask them questions. He said to check out their ring fingers," Mickey revealed.

When it was the girls' turn, he pretty much told us the same thing, adding: "Guys do have emotions and they are willing to open up—a little—so go out there and check 'em out!"

We had boys in front of us, crawling on the floor reading our hand projects. Each guy was so different. Some said very little. Some said that they totally liked some of the same things we did. When we were looking at their hands, I was surprised that some of them said that they were rejected by a girl and that they were *so* not over it.

Pari agreed, "I was surprised by the shy guys. They actually admitted they were afraid to ask girls out—that was their fear. One guy, Dan I think, was so artistic…"

"I know," I said, "his was the painted hand, remember?"

"Yeah, his hand was connected to an art palette with all the colors," Mickey added.

Pari smiled and said, "And his parents were born in France."

"What about that girl, Maggie, the one whose boyfriend *died?* And of a coke overdose?" Rhia looked mortified.

"Oh my God, did you see Mr. B's face when he read hers?" Pari asked. "He looked up at her and she was just staring at him, dead in the eyes. He whispered something to her. And she just looked at him."

I said that people were much more honest and open than I expected. "They said things I would not say, not yet anyway."

Mickey asked, "Don't you wonder why?" as he popped the last bite of scone in his mouth.

"Why what?"

"Why they said that stuff to us—to Mr. B."

Rhia said without hesitation, "It's because some of them have nobody to tell that stuff to. Did you notice how many kids mentioned how messed up their parents are?" I knew why Rhia said this. Her parents split up when she was 14years old. I think maybe it had to do with the fact that Chris, her brother, was so difficult for them. I'm guessing there's more to it. But Rhia never, ever talks about it. Her father lives in Oregon now, and he's not very involved in her life. I think he's kinda rich. Rhia's mother has never remarried. And Rhia says that her mom refuses to talk to her dad. Yep, there's stuff there.

Pari sat back in her chair, holding her cup in both hands, and said that she thought that they just trusted Mr. B. "Either that, or they are just more open than a lot of us are. Not so worried about what others think of them. I don't want to let people know what I'm really… frightened of."

I was so surprised Pari said that. She had to force out the word *frightened.*

Pari's jet black hair fell like a waterfall over her face as she looked down at the table.

Mickey came to her rescue: "I think that a lot of us want to write about ourselves, but we never do. We are always doing stupid essays or answering questions at the back of chapters. I know I spent serious time on this project."

Rhia frowned, "Do you really think kids were telling the truth—like about having all those boyfriends? I can't really believe all that. It's crazy. I know some of those girls really party all the time, and that's also why they're so messed up. Did you notice that every single person did the project? I think maybe they were trying to impress people."

"Like Mr. B?" I asked.

"Maybe, or maybe they just wanted to impress us—all of us." That was Mickey's conclusion.

We all paused as three people got up and left a table near us. Then slowly it came to me: "Maybe it's not just about impressing other people. I mean, these are our hands. It's about *us* – and someone is finally paying attention. We have something important to say. I think a lot of the time we feel ignored, you know? And that's what feels so terrible. I feel alone a lot. And with my dad in Iraq, it's even worse. So to have others care about you, and listen to you, it helps." Rhia and Pari smiled at me. I put down my cup and looked at my hands and said, "I think it comes down to this. These are our hands. Our hands are who we want to be."

Mickey just stared at me, as if I had just seen me in a totally different light. And I think I blushed.

Okay, I know I did.

Yeah.

Chapter 2: 9.11 and *The Rising*

Rhiannon's Hand

It was September 11th — and it was so crazy. We were up and down and then back up again, like a roller coaster.

See, Mr. Buscotti and Ms. Anderson said that we were having a special class on 9.11 with some guest speakers. All 70 of us would sit in Mr. B's room on beach chairs. They said we do this on special occasions. We were all excited and curious.

I was ten years old when 9.11 happened. My parents were freaking out that day. My brother, Chris, was crying. I didn't know what to think.

But as I look back, we all had different feelings during the two-hour class, and so we decided we would write this one together at the café during our Thanksgiving break. So here goes.

Madison's Hand

Okay. Well, I remember 9.11 a lot more than Rhia since my dad was in the military. And you know last year, he was in Iraq. Before I get too emotional let me just say what I have to say about what happened next in class.

One thing that was cool for me was that when we were together with the other class, my good friend, April, got to sit next to me. We've known each other since kindergarten. Both of our dads were in the Navy, but hers is still active. She's so sweet, but I don't see her much now because of her boyfriend. They are so inseparable. Anyway, April and I joyfully sat next to each other.

The room was packed! There was a slide projector, an LCD projector, and two adult guest speakers. The two guests were dressed casually, and both men were in their 40s, maybe 50s. They knew Mr. B who told us they come to speak to his classes each year on 9.11.

Then Mr. B explained we were together because this is a one-time, one-day event. Ms. Anderson explained that when 9.11 happened, she stumbled through her classes that day. "Kids were asking me why it happened and who was attacking us. I didn't have answers for them. Today is the response to all those questions."

Then Mr. B took over, "It begins with *The Rising.* Bruce Springsteen's entire album and purpose for reuniting the E Street Band was to sort out his feelings on this generation's Pearl Harbor—Pearl Harbor was another surprise attack, but by the Japanese on December 7, 1941." He said, "Bruce wanted to honor and help heal some of the torturous wounds opened on 9.11 in New York City. It was his attempt to stop the bleeding."

Mr. B said that Springsteen had read about the firefighters who had died, and how many of them were huge fans of his. "One day he decided to call some of the widows and he found they were overcome with grief, but they were also soothed by his personal phone call to them."

Then Mr. B pushed the Play button and the room fell into darkness.

Mickey's Hand

The massive speakers boomed out Springsteen's voice on a song called *The Rising.*

And the slides flashed pictures of the New York firefighters racing for the Twin Towers through the smoke and ash.

Then a picture of the firefighters—that famous one of them holding the American flag—with the stubborn face of a firefighter. Pictures of people with candles. President Bush at the scene. People being pulled out of the buildings before they collapsed. Gray smoke and ash. It looked like the buildings were melting. Springsteen's song was echoing in the classroom—the rising, the rising. Mr. B's voice reminding us that that is what firefighters do—they come for the rising of flames, the rising of ladders, the rising tide of panic.

Then the music became soft and somber. Springsteen's voice reminded us of a woman…I think her name was Mary. I wondered who was Mary? Maybe she lost her husband in the fire.

And who was the "I" in the story? Then came the climax of the song. It was about the dark sky and the tears and sorrows of a city devastated…and a hope that we can all rise up from the dust, sort of like the phoenix, I guess.

Mr. B walked into the last slide of a man who had climbed onto the roof of his house where he had painted a huge American flag and without hesitation Mr. B asked, "From whose perspective is this story told?" We were still recovering from the pictures of the attack. "Come on, people. Who 'can't see anything but smoke in front of' him? Who comes to the rescue? Who climbs up the buildings without a thought for their own personal safety?"

A girl named Maggie, the one whose boyfriend had died of a cocaine overdose, simply said, "The firefighters. It is from their point of view."

"Thank you, Maggie. And who is Mary then?"

"She lost her husband. Maybe he was a firefighter. Maybe he was just one of the people who died in the towers," Maggie softly said like she could see it all in her mind.

"Yes, and Springsteen will get back to her later today." We talked a bit about where we were when it happened and how it made us feel. Then Ms. Anderson asked us, "Does this song make you feel patriotic? Does it heal any wounds?"

I remember that Maddie said, "Yes. It makes you proud that they risked their lives for others."

Donald, who was right next to me, told Mr. B, "I don't think it heals, but it feels better after hearing it. I don't know why though."

Mr. B then explained. "Do you know there were men and women standing on the ground floor of the Towers, and do you know what their job was? It was to point people to the exit as they came down the stairs. And do you know when their job ended? It ended when the building collapsed. They waited and waited and waited to get every living soul out of that ticking bomb of a building. They were determined to not leave anyone there. Then most of them got out at the last minute. Three thousand people died that day. And there were some whose job was to keep that number from climbing. How is that for sacrifice?"

We were all quiet. That is when the tissue boxes started being passed around. Rhia was the first to start crying.

Rhiannon's Hand

The music started again and I was trying to keep my mascara from running. Mr. B didn't say anything. He just asked us who the storyteller in this song was. It was sadder and—what's the word?—*crushing*. The song was called, "Into the Fire," I think. The first thing I saw was a slide of all these people's faces looking up horrified, and the next was a slide of the plane hitting the building. I saw pictures of people totally covered in dust and ash. A firefighter was heading up into a heap of twisted steel.

The firefighters were exhausted, sitting down to catch their breath, heads in their hands. A woman, just caked up and down in brown ash, who barely got out alive. That is the one picture I still remember. And everything just sort of all went along with Springsteen's song. It was about having faith and strength and love. It was about goin' into a fire for someone, you know? And the sacrifices people made…still make, every day.

The slides kept coming and I could not pull my eyes away from them: the clouds of dark gray smoke, the flashlights keeping hope alive in the night, the people on stretchers, the towers falling. I figured this song was told by a person whose life was just saved by a firefighter, and I guess she was watching as he left her to climb higher, probably to his death, to save someone else.

But Mr. B surprised us when he asked: "So why did it happen? Were the terrorists crazy? Why do it? *Why?*"

The word seemed to bounce around the room. For a minute, no one could say anything. But then we let loose: "They're terrorists—that's what they do." "They hate the West—they think we're evil." "They're sick." "They think this is some holy cause." "They're brainwashed—like Nazis." "They want America out of the Arab lands." I couldn't keep track of who was saying what.

"They certainly were willing to die to get their way," Mr. B said. "Oh, and what way is the right way according to the terrorists?

"Their way," Mickey told him.

"Ah, but stop for a minute, Mickey. Was American Revolution itself a terrorist plot?" Mr. B continued, "When the freedom fighters rebelled against King George III, they did more than just toss tea into the Boston Harbor. People died."

Mickey didn't back down, "But they were fighting for freedom. The terrorists on 9.11 just aren't the same."

Ms. Anderson asked, "Why, Mickey…anyone?"

I could not contain myself, "Because they murdered innocent people."

"Well, Rhia," she said, "it is that, and something more It is because the 9.11 terrorists do not support a fundamental, universal value we believe in – a value we will die for. Patrick Henry said: 'Give me liberty or give me death!' Liberty. That's the freedom to live your life the way you think is right so long as you don't hurt others. What people forget is that before the American Revolution, they tried everything to avoid war. Here is what Patrick Henry said to the people of Virginia in 1775." Then she opened our own literature book and read:

> *'Sir, we have done everything that could be done to avert the storm which is now coming on. We have petitioned;... Our petitions have been slighted; our remonstrances have produced additional violence and insult; our supplications have been disregarded; and we have been spurned, with contempt, from the foot of the throne!'*

Mr. B paused to let it sink in. "America tried everything to avoid war—but sometimes it is unavoidable when some think there is only one acceptable answer. The Nazis were terrorists because they thought only the Aryan race was fit to dominate the world. What about the KKK? They were terrorists—lynching blacks, burning crosses."

Ms. Anderson then asked us, "What is a pluralistic society?" Real silence hit the room. We had no idea what she was taking about. She explained, "We have a pluralistic society – *plural*, more than one. Pluralistic means freedom of choice. This nation values each person's right to their own beliefs. People here have different religions, or sometimes no religion at all. We have different races with different customs. We embrace uniqueness. We do not force people to have one view, one rule, or one right answer. We embrace 'life, liberty and the pursuit of happiness.'"

"Terrorists don't accept equality of the sexes, and most importantly, the ability to embrace many cultures and beliefs—those things that make us uniquely American."

Mr. B looked at us with a smile. "And that is the best way to fight them. You fight terrorists when you embrace our Constitution that says, 'All men *and women* are created equal.' Terrorists hate that." Mr. B paused, and then asked, "Do you want to know how to fight terrorism?" Everyone was frozen still. "Don't close your mind to the great variety of people and ideas in this world. Don't be afraid. Especially don't be afraid of people who are different than you. Defend everyone's right to live and let live. *That* is how you fight terrorism."

"And it's how you 'form a more perfect union.'" Ms. Anderson slapped the textbook closed.

And again, I wanted to applaud—this time I didn't.

Pari's Hand

I have to admit I felt a bit uncomfortable when the class was discussing Middle Eastern terrorism. I was sure Mr. B was about to call on me and ask me *my feelings*. He looked right at me at one point when he was wondering why terrorists blow themselves up. I was afraid he would make me the spokesperson for *their* ways. But just as he looked at me, he smiled. I felt in that instant that he knew exactly what I was afraid of.

So after school was over that day, I went by his room. I asked him, "Were you going to ask me today why my family left Iran?"

"Well, the thought crossed my mind, but it was a personal curiosity, not a part of a lesson plan."

"Thanks." Then after a pause, "Well, do you want to know?"

"I only want to know what you want to tell me. That is a rule I follow. You are the boss. I am just a friendly ear." He smiled at me like he had said something just like this to countless confused kids like me.

"Well, maybe someday," I said as I opened the door to leave and catch my mom who I am sure was wondering why I was late.

Madison's Hand

So after we finished talking about, "Into the Fire," the lights went out again and the next Springsteen song sounded even sadder than the last. I didn't know if I could take much more. It was called, "Empty Sky." The slides focused on the blackness of the New York skyline and the empty hole there, like some bully had knocked out its front teeth. These were the most grotesque pictures we saw. I wanted to hide my eyes, but my hands would not move, and my eyes could not blink. I realized that my fists were clenched and my jaw was tight. The song seemed to be about a person who just cannot get used to something so horrible as an empty bed, an empty heart, and empty world that used to be filled by a wife or husband who died on 9.11

That is when one of the guests walked up to the front of the room. Mr. B introduced him as Mr. David Rosenberg. He was wearing a black loose shirt and jeans and I thought he was trying hard to look hip to high school kids. As it turned out, I was wrong because he was not trying to be anything else but what he was.

Mr. Rosenberg began, "I am honored to be here, today. You have great teachers and you are listening to great music. I am a *huge* fan of Springsteen. As you can tell by my accent, I am from New York and I grew up on some very tough streets. I am a lawyer today, but when I was your age, I was—and you may not believe this—homeless. My parents were a wreck, and drugs and other vices had taken a toll on our family. And then our house burned down in a fire. I know, it's hard to believe—but it's true. I had no place to go, so my old high school wrestling coach allowed me to sleep in the locker room. That's right. I had a sleeping bag, a shower, a fridge, and I was safe. I owe my life to that high school teacher and coach."

I thought about the things I complained about. Yeah, my father was gone a lot on duty and we moved back and forth from North Carolina to California, but we always had a roof over our heads and my younger sister and knew how much our parents loved us.

Mr. Rosenberg continued: "So I feel a responsibility to help kids today. I have sponsored a home for teenage runaways in the city. I view what I do as payback. Those firefighters ran into burning buildings. I don't do that, but when your home is burning down from the flames caused by others… well, I decided I would do all I could for kids who need to get out of the fire."

We were dead quiet. He had a huge, powerful presence. I'm guessing he must be a great lawyer because he had us in the palm of his hands.

"But that is not the main reason I came to speak to you today. I came here to talk about this song and what it means to me, a New Yorker. See, I worked a lot in New Jersey. And when I came home from work, leaving Jersey, there was always something that grounded me. Something that told me, 'Hey, you're almost home.' You could count on it, like knowing the Yankees were going to be in a race for the pennant every October."

He walked into the center of the room, right among us. "As I was driving, you see, I would look up and every time, there they were—the Twin Towers of the World Trade Center. I knew I was home. I was home. New York City."

"But in 2003, I had to go back East for a trial, and out of habit I took the same route I always took years ago. Only now, there were no Twin Towers. There was nothing. Just an 'Empty Sky,' just like the song says. And I thought of all the souls that departed that day, and all the loved ones whose hearts were buried with them, and all I could see was an 'Empty Sky.'" And then he walked to the back of the room and sat down.

This time we applauded.

Pari's Hand

Mr. B said that for the next week, the city of New York was digging out, hoping and praying to find survivors. And there were amazing stories of people pulled out of the carnage. Ms. Anderson said, "People all over the city were literally, 'Countin' on a Miracle,'" just as that very song began to play.

Slides of heroes were coming across the screen. Abraham Lincoln. Mother Theresa. Gandhi. Martin Luther King, Jr. Helen Keller. Jackie Robinson. All of these people were miracle workers. But I knew even miracle workers have their limitations. And the song, too, had an ironic twist, I thought, because as much as people were counting on some miracle to happen so their loved one could be found—for a lot of people, that was just not going to happen. There wasn't going to be a happily-ever-after.

Mr. B asked about the perspective of the song, about who was "saying" it to us? I surprised myself by putting my hand up. It was as if some puppeteer had pulled a string and raised it. Mr. B seemed equally surprised by my sudden need for the spotlight and shot right to me.

"It is being said by someone who is waiting and waiting for word to come that their loved ones will be found safe." I noticed the other three new friends from the Metaphor Café smiling at me.

On that note, Mr. B introduced the other guest, Mr. Jim Reifeiss. Mr. Reifeiss was an alumnus of our school from a *long* time ago (as he put it). Coincidentally, he too was dressed in black. Mr. Reifeiss was younger than Mr. Rosenberg, although he already had graying hair and a well-trimmed goatee. He mentioned how lucky we were to be here because when he was *our*, age, Mr. B was *his* teacher. "A rookie teacher, mind you," Mr. B carefully added.

Mr. Reifeiss began, "I came to talk about counting on miracles and about 'invisible things' that you cannot always understand when they first happen to you." He seemed very relaxed with us. "When 9.11 occurred, I was angry, very angry. I am still angry. And I don't understand the people who attacked us. And I never, never want that to happen in this country again."

"But that's not really what I came to tell you. You see, this song, 'Countin' on a Miracle,' really happened to me and my friends." He paused and gazed at all of us, then said, "I am sure you remember the big fires of a few summers ago. Did any of you get evacuated? Anybody lose their homes?"

Hands went up and kids said they left their homes for shelters or relatives' houses. No one lost a home, and Mr. Reifeiss smiled, but then said, "I am relieved. But that was not the case for my close friends I work with. They lost everything. I mean everything. The house was gone. They got out with the clothes on their backs, and a couple of family albums. They were in such a hurry that Nancy didn't have time to get her engagement ring and that really left Norman, her husband, feeling empty."

"They stayed at our house that night, and the next day we took my truck and headed up the hill to get to their house to see what could be salvaged. It was devastating. I watched my friends, Nancy and Norm, just looking down at the ashes of all that they had worked for beneath them. Strange, they seemed less bothered than I was. They just kept repeating to each other that they had the children safe and that all the rest were just things…just things. Then they told me about how much my wife and I mattered to them, and it got to me."

"So, here is where things get kind of, well, what is the right word? Spiritual, maybe. They are rummaging in the area that was their bedroom when all of a sudden amid all this debris, Nancy sees a burnt little box. She opens it and there it is—undamaged—her diamond engagement ring. She began to cry as she slipped the ring on her finger. Nancy said she always thought it was too showy and not practical to wear every day, and that's why she didn't have it on, and now she would never, ever take it off again."

Around the room, lots of girls had lost it. I thought about my mom. She was a lot like this Nancy person. She never makes herself the center of attention, never shows off how beautiful she is—and she does not want *me* to be showing off either. It is a cultural thing. We get in fights all the time about what I wear, what make-up I use, what I listen to. All things she calls "western" become issues. And here was a family whose house burned down—much like our family, except in my mother's terms "western" —and they really did not value all that *stuff*. All that mattered was safety and friends and family—and perhaps one symbol of love that could be salvaged.

Mr. Reifeiss then approached the story's climax. "As the two hugged, I left them alone, and I started rummaging. That is when I made an amazing discovery. I think you guys know what a Hummel is. They are beautiful little statuettes. Figurines. There between two charred boards lay a Hummel—in the shape of an Angel. Pure white, not a scratch. As God is my witness, there it was. The angel's hands were in prayer as if this little angel, too, was counting on a miracle."

And again, we burst into applause.

Later that evening I told my mother this story, and to my surprise, my mother's eyes began to water.

Mickey's Hand

The song, "You're Missing," brought us all back to reality. It featured an organ, like you'd hear at a funeral. It was Clair, one of the twins, who thought that maybe this song takes place later, maybe six months later, when it's clear that it's over. No one is coming through the door. No Miracles. Just people who are forever…missing.

We see slides of lots of the pictures that were hung on the fences in New York. There are pictures with words like, "Have you seen my husband?" One picture is of a woman with a tattoo on her upper back and neck that reads, *You will not be forgotten.* Then pictures of bagpipes and the people saluting at funerals. Children crying, wondering if the world would ever be alright again. I was wondering the same thing.

We were emotionally wasted. Mr. B and Ms. Anderson treated us like adults, and everybody was into it. It is quiet and Springsteen's last words were dusted over us as the soft song disappeared like the smoke and ash eventually did.

We needed a break. But we did not expect what Mr. B had in mind.

Rhiannon's Hand

I know what you are thinking. Great class, but how depressing can it get? That is why the next thing that happened took us by surprise and made us so…so…so happy. I know, how in the world can we ever be *happy* after all this? But Mr. B just did his thing.

He began by telling us, "It's time to rise up, people!" So we all stood up and he had us get rid of all the beach chairs and push everything to the walls.

"Girls, over here on my left," he said. His energy was crazy. "Guys, get to my right. Now, face each other. Smile!"

Smile? Was he kidding?

He began playing a song called, "Mary's Place." It became my favorite that day. Super upbeat. He played it really loud. Mr. B shouted to us: "What do you do a year after 9.11? One year later. How do you start over? How do you smile again? What do you do in your life to pick up the pieces?" Just then, we hear the song telling us to rise up and have faith and believe in our futures.

Then Mr. B looked at us and began to spin—I am serious—arms out, spinning around, looking up at the ceiling. He was acting like the sky was full of rain, and he didn't care if he might be getting soaking wet, or that he might be making a fool of himself. And he shouted with Springsteen something about letting the rain just pour down on us. Soak us. "Cleanse us," he said. Then he looked at us, arms still outstretched, and he sang—I am NOT kidding—something about meeting him at Mary's and having a party!

Mr. B turned to us girls and demanded that we sing with him: "Meet me at Mary's place!".

Then he spun around to the boys and motioned for them to shout in a deep voice: "We're gonna have a party!"

And the crazy thing is…we did it. And we all laughed.

Right then, he called for Ms. Anderson and like magic she appeared, and in the center of a circle the two of them start dancing! He turns her, they spin—and we all started smiling at how these two *teachers* were pretending to be on Mary's front porch, really dancing. Then the two suddenly separated and moved into us and pushed us together, telling us to "meet" each other. Mr. B was urging, "Gentlemen, introduce yourselves to these lovely ladies!"

The music was really loud now. Everybody, I mean everybody, was moving and laughing. I caught Mickey's eye, and he looked at me like we had entered another universe. It was like a concert without the band there. And it was so cool that we were *all* into it. We all believed that we were at Mary's house trying to cheer her up. Then Mr. B made us hush up with his finger on his lips. Springsteen seemed to be working up for a big finish or something—just like Mr. B who said to us, "Listen, we're playing our favorite song on the record player, baby! Let's pray this works. Turn up the volume! Turn up the volume! It's almost midnight, baby! The music is poundin'—the band is rockin—the world is shakin—let it rain, baby, right here at Mary's place!"

He got us all to spin around like he had done before, pretending that the rain was falling on us! I was thinking sometimes life just does that. If you can't stop the rain, you might as well just dance in it and get soaking wet.

Then just like when we were kids and would play "Ring around the Rosy"…

…we all fell down.

Madison's Hand

We were all tangled up together, but my friend April was still by my side. Mr. B was sweating. Just then he shouted: "It is time I introduce you to the real Bruce Springsteen and the E Street Band. I am bringing you to New York City's Madison Square *Gaaarden,"* he says. "Because we need to end the day *seeing* The Boss. And grasping Bruce's vision of what America is all about. This is Springsteen's 'Land of Hopes and Dreams!'"

The LCD projector flicked on and we were transported to a Springsteen concert. Bruce (who and also was dressed in black—so now we got the whole wardrobe thing) thundered to the massive crowd and to us sitting on the floor as the guitars slashed and drums pounded, and I totally got the connection to 9.11.

Springsteen sang about this train that we are all on…we are all welcome even if our lives are troubled and our skies are dark. About how the wheels of this train just thunder into every neighborhood and the train is heading to daylight…to the land of opportunity.

I had never seen Bruce Springsteen. Okay, I'd been to a few local concerts like some small bands, and once Rascal Flats 'cause some friends at church got group tickets, but nothing like this. This was a trip. All of us were sharing this experience with Mr. B who was sitting right on the floor with us. Springsteen was singing about a train, but Mr. B pointed out that both trains and paddle-wheel boats on rivers have "Big Wheels" that push them onward. Both trains and rivers roll through the fields of America. He said that we are the new generation of Americans, and this class was part of the "Big Wheel" that would roll down the river – our river. He said, "Don't be afraid, I will not abandon you. There is no going back. These fields are not made of corn or wheat—they are the fields of your coming of age. You are growing up and the roller coaster ride might be dark, scary…but sunny days are coming if you just keep your eyes on your North Star."

I felt it. I knew exactly what he was saying. We could count on him, Ms. Anderson, our families (well, most of us could), and we could count on each other. None of us has to wait all alone for the clouds and the sorrow to part, and for sunny skies to replace the darkness. April and I made eye contact, and I know she had been to the same black place I had been.

I understand darkness. I was in it when my father packed his bags and headed for Iraq. I watched my mother wrap her one arm around herself, and use the other hand to cover her mouth so my father would not see her bottom lip quiver uncontrollably. I saw her eyes brimmed with tears. She wouldn't blink because it would make her eyes burst and the tears would pour down her face. Like mine were. It was the late summer of my freshman year. My parents thought I was still sleeping upstairs. But I was looking from the top of the stairs as they finally embraced at the front door in those last minutes before my dad had to leave.

I was not sure what others were thinking as they heard Bruce that day. But my mind, and I am sure April's, was flashing back to our black mornings. I knew why my dad was going—he had to. My father is my "Big Wheel" and I cannot imagine life without him. Yeah.

As if he read my thoughts Mr. B got up on his knees and explained: "Look, you are about to embark on adulthood, citizenship, the American Dream. You need to know what this nation has stood for, what we believe in, and what our destination is. Your world is so much more complicated than the world we—Ms. Anderson, Mr. Reifeiss, Mr. Rosenberg, myself—knew at seventeen."

Then the song's theme rang out to us like the National Anthem, and then we all raised our hands up as Springsteen urged us to do because we had completely been lifted up—we were 'The Rising!" Our spirits, our hope, our togetherness was peaking to a crescendo just as the song, the concert, and the class came to an end. I was speechless. All I could do was just thank Mr. B and Ms. Anderson. I stood in a line of kids waiting my turn to say something to the guests. Mr. Rosenberg was so happy that we liked Bruce Springsteen. He told kids he has seen Bruce perform at least 100 times. He said we were now a part of the "E Street Nation." His smile was so big that he reminded me of what it is like to have a friend just love something that you have always loved. Mr. Reifeiss fist bumped kids and I overheard him tell Mr. B that speaking to us always makes him feel encouraged about teenagers.

When we met that weekend at the Metaphor Café, we talked until the café closed. Rhia had posted the words to the songs on her Facebook wall. Mickey had downloaded the music to his iPod. Pari said she had never been in any class "remotely like this," and she didn't care if she got in trouble for being out so late.

And me? I handed Mr. B a note as I left class on 9.11 that read simply: *'To Sir, With Love.'*

Chapter 3: The Big Muddy

Mickey's Hand

Two Days Later—September 13th

"Why are Huck and the slave, Jim, going *south* on the Mississippi?" Mr. B asked. He was pointing to the big map of the United States, and his hands were on his hips. We had just read how Huck and Jim somehow missed the town of Cairo, Illinois, which he explained was famous for lynching runaway slaves like Jim. Cairo was where the Ohio River joined the Mississippi. I didn't know that because, somewhere along the line, geography was not a priority in school. I guess I learned about the Mississippi River in 5th grade, maybe. But then again, all I really remember about 5th grade was playing football as soon as we all finished lunch. That was when we didn't seem to have much to worry about.

"Why aren't they heading *north*? North is freedom, isn't it?" Mr. B liked toying with us. That is when he asked Rhia to come up to the front of the classroom and take a long look at the map. Rhia walked up there like she was on her way to the guillotine.

"Don't worry, Rhia, nothing bad is going to happen up here."

"It already has," Rhia looked at us nervously. The class all laughed.

"Seriously, dear, please find the Big Muddy."

"The what?"

"The Big Muddy. Oh I forgot, you don't know that expression, do you? The Big Muddy is simply the Mississippi River—full of mud, you know. Water looks sort of brown. Point to it, kiddo."

Rhia found the state of Mississippi alright, and then the river itself. Her colorful bracelets clinked as her finger traced the river's path up through Louisiana, Arkansas, and eventually Illinois.

"Stop! Look where your finger rests… What does it say?"

"Cairo. So this place really exists?" Rhia looked at Mr. B.

"Yep. Now hang a right at the Ohio."

"The state?"

"No, the river. See it?"

"Yep."

"Keep going. Where are you now?"

"Ohio. And Pennsylvania, I think," said a worried Rhia.

"Now, Miss Rhia, let's backtrack. Go back to the Mississippi River and hang a right."

"Okay."

"Which direction are you going?"

"Right." Laughter burst around me.

Rhia picked up on her mistake, "I mean, north!" She gave some girls a look and quickly stuck her tongue out at them.

"Beautiful. Keep following the river. Where does it end?"

She kept moving her finger up the map and soon she couldn't reach any higher. Mr. B had a stepstool ready and she jumped on it.

"Keep going… Where are you now?"

"Minnesota."

"Isn't that something," Mr. B looked at us, "it splits the country in half, right up and down. Boy, that river goes a long way. Thank you, Miss Rhia." Then as she gratefully started back to her seat, he remembered., "Oh, one last thing…."

Rhia looked back at him as if she would never escape his clutches. "Yes?"

"Which way does the Mississippi flow?"

"Well, I know it's not right or left," she said, and this time Mr. B roared with laughter.

She winced and said hopefully, "Um, north?"

"Ah, that is what so many say. Thanks again, but kids here often don't get the river's flow. The powerful currents all rush *south*, gang. *South.* Jim and Huck are coasting *down* the river, and they are heading right into the face of the Deep South. That's the big contradiction of the novel. Why go south when you are trying to be free?"

"Because that is the only way the river flows?" asked a guy named Donald in the far front seat. Donald is black, plays lacrosse, and has dreadlocks, but he seems different in some other way, too. I've known him for a while. He's kinda more independent than most of the other kids. Like he is more willing to do what *he* wants no matter what other people might think. Donald is in AP Calculus this year, too, and he's just a junior. "The raft is just a raft. It has no power other than the river, right? It goes with the flow," he concluded.

"But the flow is heading straight to the slave states," Mr. B countered.

"That is why it sucks that they missed Cairo," said Donald. Most of the class seemed confused.

"Miss Madison, please explain," Mr. B said as he got his coffee and gathered himself into his favorite chair that sat him up, almost like a conductor working the orchestra.

Maddie took a second to gather herself. "Well, isn't Jim's plan to go up the Ohio River and then get enough money to buy back his family?"

"Exactly! Working in the free states, right? But how is he going to do that… get the family, that is?"

"Uh, that is where I am a little confused, Mr. B," Maddie said.

"Well, if you wanted to find someone, Maddie, what would *you* do?"

"I don't know. Hire a detective, maybe."

"Yep. And that's Jim's plan, too. Only his detective is called an *abolitionist,* someone who is in favor of *abolishing* slavery. Sounds like a good guy, right? But this human bounty hunter, this abolitionist, is not a saint or anything because he always charges people a hefty fee to find and bring back their people."

I spoke up and told him I didn't get it.

"Oh, Jim has it all figured out, Mickey. The bounty hunter would be paid by Jim to find and *buy* his family. The bounty hunter is white, and he would go find Jim's family, and he would make an offer that the owner of Jim's wife and children just can't turn down. Jim would pay the abolitionist, *and* Jim would pay the cost of buying his family. But at least Jim would get his family back. So you see, that ol' Jim is one clever fellow, and a loyal father, too. He has is all figured out – except for what, Donald?"

"Jim didn't know that the waters of the Ohio River would blow him past Cairo." Donald was one step ahead of all of us.

"Yep, and once he is past the mouth of the Ohio, they are just *boomin'* down the river, in Twain's terms. But, you see, forces more powerful than man—particularly a black man in the 1800's—control Jim's fate, and have for the last 350 years in this country. We are one of the last industrial nations to make owning another human being illegal." Mr. B stood up again, looking right into our eyes. "It is the great stain on this nation. The great sin. It took a war to purge ourselves of slavery. And it took a great president, Lincoln, to lead us through it at the cost of his own life. And no matter how hard we try, we still can't wash that stain out of the muddy clothes our society wears."

Mr. B was on a roll now, walking right into the heart of the class and looking back at the map of the United States, which ironically, didn't seem so *united* to me at the moment. "They are heading deeper and deeper into that 1860's South, and with each passing day, Huckleberry admires Jim more and relies on him more. I am surprised that some people in America today still don't seem to get the fact that Jim is the father figure and the hero of this book."

Mr. B looked at me to see if I understood… if I was *reading between the lines* as he called it, finding the deeper meaning. It was one of the first of many times that I felt he had focused on me and I wasn't sure why. And so the sermon came to an end but not before Donald said quietly:

"But Jim was never in control. The current never stops pulling us down."

Pari's Hand

Next Day—September 14th

Mr. B continued the Bruce Springsteen concert. If Mr. B reads this, he will quickly correct me by saying, "Bruce Springsteen *and* the E Street Band." He is a bit over the top on the whole Springsteen Nation thing.

I had heard of Springsteen, but not that I could remember—although when Mr. B pointed to the *Born in the USA* album, I did remember that song being played on the Fourth of July (which we would later find out is ironic when you understand the words).

Lots of songs are like that. A while ago, some of my friends were so into Britney Spears singing, "Toxic." Well, look at her now—*toxic* totally describes her. What were we thinking then?

Anyway, Mr. B's class today began with him explaining that one thing he has in common with us is music. But he told us that we are single-song fanatics, and that the problem with that is that "you guys never really get to know the artists' work." He thinks the whole CD is the real work of art. For me and my café friends, we just like lots of songs - and I mean lots! And our bands are not at all mainstream. Some are just putting out a few tracks and trying to avoid being a sell-out.

So I went into his music lesson a bit skeptical. But I loved that he was going to teach us a song, even if it was old-school.

Mr. B started the day with a really old Springsteen song called, "It's Hard to Be a Saint in the City." He always seemed to be playing a song when we walked in. This one caught my attention because it was about growing up in a tough city—like New York, I guess, and I liked it because I want to go to U.C. Berkeley (very urban) but my parents are not very happy with me. They say I would become too liberal and too wild there. There are times when my parents make me want to scream, but I don't because…well, just because. We don't scream in our house. That kind of drama does not happen, especially not when my father is around (which is not too often—he works all the time). So anyway, when I saw the song's title, it intrigued me—it would be hard to be a saint in Berkeley, I guess.

Mr. B told us he needed to get us in the mood for the trip further down the Mississippi River, so he was playing some song called, "Black Water," by the Doobie Brothers. Mr. B said it had that southern sound he was looking for. We listened to some spooky guitar solo, and then we heard sort of a country, Cajun sounding voice tell us about a raft and floating down the Mississippi. The water was black and the fish were jumping and the wheels of the steamboat were pumping, and I smiled just thinking about Huck and Jim without a worry in the world,

although his lecture was soon to get very dark.

"Yes, it is Dixieland, gang," said Mr. B. "And if all Twain was doing was writing another adventure, like *Tom Sawyer,* then Hemingway would never had said that all American literature begins with *Huckleberry Finn.* Twain sees the darkness in man's soul. And that darkness is rooted in greed. It lurks in the shadows. It obsesses with what one wants, ignoring the consequences."

He paused, dramatically, "It is time to get to the heart of darkness and swim with the sinners in The Big Muddy." Then he played a Springsteen song which begins with a sharp twang and some more spooky sounds, like we are floating down a wild, pitch-black ride. The song told the story of a man named Billy and his secret mistress.

Mr. B suddenly paused the music and asked us, "What is a mistress?"

It was one of those hear-the-desk-creak questions. No one wanted to be wrong on this point since it was basically about sex. But that did not stop Donald.

"He's having sex with some hooker."

The jocks in class, Mitchell and Chase, thought this was the funniest thing ever. These two don't get things very quickly, but if it has sex in it, they think it's funny.

"Maybe, Donald. But why say a *mistress* and not a *hooker?* What is it to be a mistress? And why mention the names of the streets'?" He called on one of the twins, Shannon.

"I have no idea, Mr. B. I don't know," she said, pleading for him to pass the question along.

"None of us does. What do you *think*?"

"I don't know what to think."

He placed a dictionary on her desk. She picked up the clue.

"You can't learn what you don't understand. While she looks *mistress* up, Mitchell, ever been to A Street?"

He was stunned. "Mr. B, I didn't put my hand up."

"Yes, I know. But you laughed. And I just thought we could chat." Mr. B was having a good time.

"About…?"

"Have you ever been on A Street, or E Street, or 5th Street--maybe even 12th Street?"

"Uh, you mean like downtown?"

"Exactly, Mitch. Downtown. Seen those condos built around the new ballpark?"

"Pretty nice, Mr. B," said a now unnecessarily confident Mitch.

"Yep, you could buy one cheaper than a house," he looked up at Shannon, "and put a mistress in one, right? What does the good book say, Shannon?"

"Mistress: One who is taken care of; a woman having an affair with a married man." Shannon did not get it yet.

"Oh, so Billy is having an affair—but he is married—and he is keeping this woman for himself' in a nice little condo downtown so *who* won't find out, Shannon?"

"His wife!" Shannon had her shining moment.

"Yep, his little secret, right?"

Mickey added: "And he went there right after work."

The music was back, even louder: then this man gets in some trouble with her and needs someone else to bail him out. Pretty sketchy what the problem was though, I thought.

"Hmm, what kind of trouble could our friend Billy get into?" asked Mr. B. He added this hint: "Whatever it is it would require a sum of money, a trusted friend, and a little legal maneuver to solve the problem. So back to you, Mickey."

"Why do you always ask me the trick questions?" But Mr. B just smiled at him. Mick was happy to be the center of attention despite his protest. "Okay, okay, okay, I don't know…oh, wait…did he get her pregnant? Or was it AIDS? No wait, he murdered her!" Mick was too much sometimes. He had the class half-astonished and half-hysterical.

Mr. B calmed things down. "Let's eliminate the possibilities, Mickey. Killing her is illegal, right?"

"Okay, he didn't kill her. It's either pregnant or AIDS," Mick conceded.

"It may not be mutually exclusive, Mickey. But let's assume the 'friend' was being paid to solve the 'trouble.' Can he solve the girl's AIDS problem, or the pregnancy problem?"

Maddie came to Mick's rescue, "He was paying off some guy friend to take her to get an abortion."

"Why not take her himself?" Mr. B turned on her.

"Because he needed to keep it a secret. Maybe Billy was like Bill Clinton. I don't know," said Maddie. I was so impressed with her connection to Clinton. She was one step ahead in this cross examination.

"But did she get pregnant accidentally or on purpose, Mr. B?" This was Shannon's voice.

"What do you think, Shannon?"

"I think she planned it. She wants him to leave his wife!"

"Now you're thinking, girl," he smiled. He pushed a remote control and the song's final verses played: Billy's friend told him to remember once you are bitten by a poison snake the poison contaminates you and everything around you. Pretty soon Billy and his mistress are sucked into the lies and it is like quicksand. I guess that is where the title, "The Big Muddy," came from.

"Same poison snake, right, Donald?" Mr. B was tapping Donald's memory.

"You mean how Jim gets bitten by a snake when Huck plays the trick on him?" Donald asked.

"Did Huck learn that it's a bad idea to tempt evil?" Mr. B paused while we all made the connection between the song and the book. "And if you are bitten by the snake that slithers in the Garden of Eden, you become a sinner through and through. The poison runs in your veins. And who do you contaminate?"

"Everyone you touch," Donald said.

Then Mr. B turned to me. "Miss Pari, isn't life beautiful on the raft? Just floating down the river?"

"Um, yeah," I said.

"Mighty pretty—nature is something. Do you like the beach?"

"Um, yeah." He was leading the witness.

"Been there for the clean-up after July 4th, Pari?"

"No—but I saw it on the news. I guess it was bad."

"Yes, but we human beings create such a mess, huh, and we leave this world pretty toxic. We do the same to other people. We are toxic to each other, as the divorce rate demonstrates," said Mr. B. "And sooner or later we are smeared with mud and grime, the symbols of our sins. It is like quicksand. We are waist deep in lies and deceit. And Huck sees all this, and he wants to get away from the world of slavery, of murderers, of liars and cheaters posing as kings and dukes."

On cue, the bell rang. I wondered if and when I, too, would be waist deep in the muddy, black waters.

Maybe I already was.

Chapter 4: Huck's Escape…and Ours

Mickey's Hand

September 24th

The fun and games came to a sudden halt for most. Mr. B announced today that we are preparing to write a paper on Huck Finn. The class cringed—I secretly smiled.

As much as I love Mr. B's sermons as he calls them, I've felt frustrated because I want a part to play in all this. Not like a stage actor. I wanted to write the script. It would be so cool to write the dialogue for Mr. B or Ms. Anderson, to put my words into their mouths and see the reaction of the class.

I have known for a while I want to be a writer. I don't know many kids who have a clue what they see themselves doing. But I must confess—and up until now only Maddie really knows—that I want to be a writer. How this being a writer works with my mom and dad is the subject of a-very-short-one act called "Breakfast with a Black Girl at the Kountry Kafe."

The scene: *An April morning at my house with my folks. A letter for me has just arrived in the mail:*

Mom: You've won what? A contest? What contest? Honey, Mickey won a contest!

Dad: *[looking up from the sports section]* Great. Did you win money?

Me: *[staring at the letter and holding a check]* Um, yeah. I just won $100—First Place.

Mom: *[close to hysterical]* How? What? You never told us anything!

Dad: [sports page definitely collapsing in his lap] A hundred bucks. Hey, that's great!

Me: It was a poem I wrote called, "Breakfast with a Black Girl at the Kountry Kafe." The magazine is publishing it, too.

Dad: A poem? What magazine?

Me: Well, it is a contest for young poets… or writers… in a magazine called American Writers.

Mom: Why didn't you tell us you entered a contest?

Me: I don't know. I figured I didn't have much of a chance.

Dad: You know, if you are going into business, the fact you can write makes you very attractive. And creativity is so important, Mickey. You know, what we were talking about in terms of advertising. You have a great eye for the commercials. This is great, son. Let me read the poem.

Mom: No, read it to us, Mickey. Poems are meant to be read out loud.

Me: Well, okay. *[Clearing my throat and feeling more than a bit self-conscious, still thinking about what my father assumed about my future career in advertising]*…

Breakfast with a Black Girl at the Kountry Kafe

We couldn't find a Starbucks,
So for breakfast we walked down the street
Looking for a place to talk and eat.

And I,
being white,
didn't reflect, measure or inspect.

"I see the Kountry Kafe," I say.
"The one spelled wrong
with the K near that highway?" asks she.

I don't hear the fear. I just take charge. She submits.
And we enter with all eyes upon us,
But I am aloof.

The gum crackin' waitress is short with us…
The 'Good Ol' Boys at the counter look over their shoulders…
The well worn plates are dropped just a bit too loudly in front of us.

And no one says, "Enjoy!"

I look up at her and ask
the obvious have-you-noticed question.
Of course, she has.

For the first time,
Really,

So have I.

--Mickey Sullivan

Mom: Honey, you *wrote* that?
Dad: Mickey, that is really great. Is that a true story? *[Mom's head is nodding vigorously, filled with wonder at whether I really know someone like that… Black, that is.]*
Me: Yeah. I was at that journalism competition the school sent us on, and my friend Zenobia…
Mom: Who?
Me: Zenobia. I called her Zen.
Mom: You never mentioned her before.
Me: Yeah, well, it was last year and she graduated and were just walking to find breakfast…
Dad: *[The sports section begins its reappearance as he says behind it.]* Very nice, Mickey. Nice touch. That award will look good on your college resume at places like USC—if you go there, of course. It's got a great business school.
Mom: That's if he *wants* to go to USC, Tom. What was her name again, Mickey, the African-American girl in the poem? Zenda? You never mentioned her before… *[Heading off to the kitchen to kill a fly that annoys her.]*
Me: No. Zenobia.
Mom: *[Slap of flyswatter.]* Ah, got him!
Me: Yep, you got him alright. *[Blackout]*

Later, Maddie tells me that it's no big deal—all crap your parents expect you to do. "Just let them have their ideas, and then go to a good college, and do what you really want to do. If you are not that interested in business, Mickey, so something else."

Before Rhia and Pari get to the café, we talk a lot. (I know she is going to read this later tonight when we put this selection in with the other pieces of the book.) But the thing is that nobody gets me like Maddie. I try to tell her so but it is easier if I write it. Maybe that is the writer's code. We are bi-polar. Smooth on a laptop, but a bit lame with a person I care about.

Okay, there I wrote it.

So tonight we met to discuss the whole essay-assignment thing. Mr. B was pretty funny discussing essays. He said, "To some kids, a literary analysis is like getting your braces tightened over and over, day after day, until you feel the desire to rip them off and set your bicuspids free!" He explained that it was worse back when he was a kid and the teacher's instructions went something like this:

Old Fart Mean-Spirited Teacher: What is your problem, kid? Just write the body of the essay!

Intimidated Student: Um, how do we organize it, sir?

Old Fart Mean-Spirited Teacher: Well, it's the guts of the essay!

Intimidated Student: Guts, sir?

Old Fart Mean-Spirited Teacher: Yeah, you know, the meat.

Intimidated Student: Meat, sir?

Old Fart Mean-Spirited Teacher: The heart! The crux! Getting down to the brass tacks!

Intimidated Student: Oh. Yes, sir. Thank you for the clichés.

[Old Fart Mean-Spirited Teacher rides off into the sunset, red pen in hand, and bloodied student papers dotting the not-so-happy trail. Blackout.]

Mr. B then proceeded to draw a floor to a house and labeled it *the major thesis*; then he drew three beams that came up from the floor, calling them *the supporting arguments.* He said you need three because if one failed at least the whole house would not come crashing down on you…and with it your grade. Eventually, he explained that facts from the story along with quotes would be the bracing that held up each supporting argument. The finishing touch would be the drywall and paint, which he called the 'impact,' which explained *why* each fact and quote mattered and helped to prove that the major thesis of your paper *is true.* When he was done, he had designed these stick-drawing houses, which made it clear he was *not* to be confused with an art teacher.

As soon as Rhia and Pari sat down at the café with their caramel lattes, Rhia started us off with her take on the Huck essay. "Guys, you know how Mr. B explained the different thesis things? I liked how he built the house where the main thesis is like the floor. But I decided to pick the smallest house." She smiled a little smugly as she tucked her legs under her dark blue dress, one of those loose flowery ones she gets that makes her look like some girl from the 60's or something. And she continued, "I am saying that Twain believes man is inherently evil."

Maddie blew on her coffee and asked, "And the three supporting arguments will be…?"

Rhia tapped her chin with her index finger, thinking out loud, "What did Mr. B call them?"

"The three beams that come up from the floor," answered Pari, her pitch black hair all tied up in a bun with a pencil somehow holding it in place, absorbed in her notes.

"Right, okay, I am going to argue—listen to me, I am starting to talk like Mr. B—I'm going to argue that there are three examples of this…"

"*Character* examples?" I asked.

"Yep!" Rhia counted each one off on her fingers. I noticed for the first time that she has like four rings on her fingers and about six bracelets on one wrist and another bunch on her other wrist. She sat up and recited, "One, Pap's treatment of Huck. Two, the sale of slaves like how the Duke and the King sell Jim in the end. And finally, three, the whole scene at the Grangerfords and Shepardsons when they blow each other away. Whadda ya think? I think it works and I have the quotes to prove it. I know this is so crazy, but I'm kinda having fun… in a sick, intellectual way."

We laughed, and I loved the way Rhia giggled. It *was* fun… in a sick, intellectual way. I guess the whole idea of even liking school at all would be pretty lame to some (okay, most) kids we know. But Mr. B makes us (okay, me at least) feel like I don't care about all that.

I told the girls, "I am going for the *other house* as Mr. B called it. You know the one where we say that Twain believed *nature* was pure, but *civilization* was evil? So my essay is kinda like yours, Rhia, but my last paragraph is going to be about the river and how peaceful it is and stuff, and about how when Huck and Jim get on shore, that is when things suck for them."

"Yeah, great, but I can't find enough quotes about nature and the whole peaceful feeling thing," Maddie said. "I know we read it and it's in my chapter notes somewhere…" Maddie hates when she can't find something.

"It's when Jim and Huck are floating on the raft looking up at the stars. They talk about 'how peaceful it is just lying down with nothing to do,'" Pari said, flipping through several pages looking for the exact quote.

"We could cheat," Rhia told us, "and look on that web site…" Rhea looked at us with raised eyebrows, testing the waters.

"Yeah, or just buy the entire paper off the cheaters' web site," I slammed her down with sarcasm, and her eyes flashed at me, and I knew I'd done it again. My sarcasm slips out like that sometimes before I can think, and I don't really mean to hurt people, so I softened it up saying "Rhia, I know we can find it ourselves. Look, I know kids who copy and buy stuff. I just don't know why they do it."

"Because they're stressed out, Mickey! They freak, and just figure they won't get caught. Whatever!" Rhia looked at me, still angry, and that cute giggle was long gone. "I am NOT saying that's us, okay? But I do get those kids. They don't have a teacher that breaks it down, or even explains it at all. The teacher just says, 'The paper is due next week. Write it on Huck,' or *East of Eden* or whatever they're reading. They're desperate, Mickey. Their grade depends on it, and they don't have a clue how to write it."

"I know, Rhia," I said, "I wasn't saying you were like that. Sorry, really, Rhia. I just think we can handle it—together. "

"I found the quote!" Maddie announced, diverting the tension. Her voice reminded me of Tom Hanks saying, "I've cracked the code!" "It's on page 35, you guys. It says, 'I laid there…looking away into the sky; not a cloud in it. The sky looks ever so deep when you lay down on your back in the moonshine…'" Maddie looked up at us. "I marked a couple of others, too. They're in the chapter notes Mr. B gave in his lecture."

Maddie straightened her shoulders and said, "If you guys are done arguing, can I have my turn?" I smiled and raised up my paper cup in a little toast to Rhia, and she smiled the tilted her head back at me. Peace.

Maddie sat cross-legged wearing shorts and a baseball cap with her brown hat in a ponytail coming out the back of the hat. She was really tanned from the summer and it had not worn off yet. I couldn't help but notice, but I tried to pay attention to what she was about to tell us. She continued, "I'm thinking of writing about the violence, but I am going to use the example of when Colonel Sherborn killed that Boggs guy—you know the drunk in the street—and then the whole town wanted to lynch Sherborn. I like that part because Huck is so blown away by Sherborn's ruthlessness."

The whole time we were talking, Pari had been mostly silent, just looking at her book and her notes. There was something about her. She was scary-smart.

I asked her what she was planning.

"Well, I want to write about religion, believe it or not. I know that Mr. B said that would be one of the harder houses to build and I have to figure out what structure to use. Mr. B's whole house-building thing helped, but I think I need to write it in sort of a problem/effect/solution way. Chronology is just, I don't know, it just doesn't seem to be my style. At least, not for this..." She drifted off, then returned with her face contorted a bit. "It just bugs me."

"What does?" Maddie asked.

"Well, you know, Huck sees all the hypocrites who are supposedly religious and attend Sunday church and read the Bible, but they really are either slave owners or murderers. He knows he can't be like that, and so he figures he must be a sinner since he is such a liar, too."

Pari looked up at us then, right into our eyes, "But then, he begins to realize that in the end it is *freedom* from all that civilized religious crap that makes the most sense. That he and Jim need to be free. And like Mr. B said, 'Freedom is a state of mind.'"

"Maybe *God* really means *good*, and *devil* really means *evil*," Rhia said to her.

"Yeah, maybe." Pari seemed more troubled, "The thing is that what is *really* bothering me is the whole war in Iraq and the whole Middle Eastern thing."

There was an uncomfortable pause. Pari did not continue.

"And that has something to do… with Huck?" Maddie gently asked, trying to make any connection, but we all wondered where Pari was going with this. I think for the first time Pari knew she had a decision to make about us.

We waited Pari out, sipping our lattes. I was really proud of us for waiting,… waiting.

Finally, it came from deep inside her, from a place she must not let most people enter, a secret place.

"I am Muslim. I hate what is going on. It makes me sick. It goes against everything we believe. But it is all done in the name of Allah, God. We have Sunnis, Shiites, the Taliban, Kurds. Saddam Hussein massacred hundreds, thousands, for power. Bin Laden and 9.11. And now the so-called president of Iran says something about wiping Israel off the map! I just want to scream!" We didn't dare say a word.

She looked at me and said, "I understand Huck. I know exactly why he doesn't want to be civilized, why he wants to run off to the wild frontier. But where do I run off to when there is no place to escape? No frontier left?"

Rhia reached out and put her hand over Pari's. We sat together in silence, honoring Pari's words. Honoring her trust in us.

Finally, Maddie said to her quietly, "At least you have us, here, at the Metaphor Café."

Pari faintly smiled.

What we saw that night was really just the tip of the iceberg.

Chapter 5: Three Emily's

Rhiannon's Hand

October 18th

We turned in our Huck Finn papers and hoped for the best. Mr. B said, "The river moves on, past Huck Finn and out to new frontiers." The next stop for us was a play called, *Our Town.*

I love plays. I remember going to the plays downtown back when my parents were still together. I loved *Phantom of the Opera,* especially the gondola scene—the lovers in the fog and all. It was so passionate. My life could use a passion make-over. I mean, like, there are so few guys even worth dating. And they don't even try to ask us to dances; unless of course you are in the very popular crowd—of which I am *so* not. Anyway, I love plays. I just wish they had happier endings. I mean seriously—Romeo and Juliet, Lenny and George—I mean yikes, why does everyone have to die?

So I guess I wish for happy endings, you know. There is just never much of that in school, or in my life. One day, Mr. B asked the romantics to stand up, and the realists to stay seated. I sat. Mickey and Maddie stood up. Pari couldn't make up her mind; she said it was a trick question. Figures, huh?

So yesterday, Mr. B said we would "do" a play in class, and I wondered what he meant.

The answer came today when, before we even got in the room, we saw a cast list posted on the door. For Act 1, I was listed as Emily Webb. For Act 2, Maddie was Emily Webb. We looked at each other and I was excited, but she looked way more nervous about it.

When we walked in, the room was awesome. It was set up like a theater. The windows were covered, and the main lights were off. The desks were in a large circle, and on top of each desk was a script. Inside the circle were two desks face-to-face so that the desktops touched, and there were the scripts for Emily Webb and George Gibbs, and there was a candle in between them. To the left and right were desks for their parents, I supposed, since the scripts were for Dr. Gibbs and Mrs. Webb. The outer circle seemed to have scripts for "townsfolk" as Mr B called them, and there was one area for the choir, so I guessed we were singing, too.

The ceiling had those twinkle-y little white Christmas lights strung out in a circle over our heads. So dramatic. Mr. B had placed three pretty big floodlights on the floor pointing up. It made me feel like I was backstage—or onstage really—and the light reflecting around the room was fantastic.

Talk about setting a mood.

We finally got all settled in our seats and I was right in the center, facing George Gibbs, and Mr B explained that *Our Town* was a play set about 100 years ago. Really though, "Little has changed in terms of human beings," I think that is how he put it.

Donald was playing George, and I was glad because he was smart, cute, and would be fun to act with.

Mr. B said that the play required little explanation, but it did require two things. "Concentration," he said, holding up his right hand, and, "Devotion to the spirit of the play," holding up the other hand. He walked around the circle, looking each person in the eyes. "Simply put—read it with feeling and take it seriously, because it is about your life, your loves, and… your death."

Then the floodlights went out and we saw images projected on a screen of children—with their friends, parents, and grandparents. They were adorable and it was all set to music. It was a song called, "These Are the Days," which I recognized, but at the time I did not know it was sung by Natalie Merchant and 10,000 Maniacs.

Then we saw pictures of kids our age—holding hands, dancing, kissing. We saw pictures of troubled kids, cutters, pregnant girls, some tears. But eventually they became pictures of kids smiling and, I guess, relieved because whatever troubled them had finally passed. Just then the singers repeated a refrain about being touched and blessed because these are the best days of our young lives. Slowly the music faded and we were magically transported.

The floodlights came on and we could see Mr. B wearing those little spectacles and a dark brown vest. He was standing with his script, and he spoke saying our play is called *Our Town*, written by a man named Thornton Wilder. Mr. B had taken on the magical presence of this old fashioned clerk, or maybe a guide would describe it better. He told us we were now in a town called Grover's Corners in the state of New Hampshire. The day was May 7. The year 1901.

And just like that, bang, we were back in time and into *this* play. I was so excited because this really was like a play even though we were in class. *School* seemed to disappear, and the twinkling lights that Mr.

B's character called, "the stars" were criss-crossing above us and they really seemed to shine above our little town.

It was then I realized that Mr. B was really the play's "Stage Manager" and he introduced us to the Webb family and to my character, Emily, who was just about my age—15. And he showed us the Gibbs family with George, who has a crush on me (and I on him—oh, if it were only so easy). He told us this act of the play was called "Daily Life." We had people going to church, the choir singing (and gossiping), mothers cooking meals, fathers working late into the night, children playing sports, and teenagers worrying about all things we still worry about— like being "pretty enough to get a boy to ask you out or something." Hmm.

The Stage Manager peered over his glasses at us and said something like: "It is a really nice town, y'know?" And he winked at me, throwing a gaze over to George. Poor George didn't notice, but some of the girls in the class—I mean in the town— did.

The play's first act was like all typical days in every town, I guess. It was all a race against the clock. Hurry here and there. No one really noticed how quickly time just flew by. As a matter of fact, before I knew it, Act 1 was ending and I felt my time as Emily was over way too soon. I loved it when George was asking me for help on a math problem (when I really knew he just needed an excuse to talk to me) and I was eager to flirt with him from my window to his window that night. We were hanging out our windows staring at the stars and dreaming of tomorrows.

I really loved Emily Webb. She was sweet and kind—and smart. It all seemed so innocent in those days before text messages, non-stop news, and everything seen on YouTube. I don't know. I guess that's progress—but I liked her town and I had a great time…a really great time.

As the Stage Manager told us the act was coming to an end, the lights dimmed and, you're not gonna believe it, but we began to hear Green Day's, "Time of Your Life." And I realize that time really does grab you and pull you, like the song says, and that life is so unpredictable.

One thing I know for sure: during Act 1, I really did have the time of my life.

Madison's Hand

Okay, I like being the center of attention. I admit it. That is not why I was so freaked out when I saw my name next to Emily Webb for Act 2. I wondered if Mr. B knew something about me and Mickey. Well, hey, there's no official "me and Mickey." At least not yet. But I guess Mr. B must have noticed something between us. Act 2 is called, "Love and Marriage." And Mr. B placed Mickey square in from of me as George Gibbs.

Okay, so. Mickey is probably reading this online *right now* (that's how we have been communicating when we are not together). I hope that I am not making a complete fool of myself. He has never told me how he feels about me. Most guys never say anything about anything important. How Mr. B sensed this is crazy. I can't even believe I am writing this!

Mickey's Hand

I *am* reading this right now, Maddie, and it *is* so crazy because the moment I saw my name next to yours I was happy because, I don't know, I just never found the time to…or the courage to…say anything to you about how I was feeling. So go on, Maddie.

Madison's Hand

Okay. Alright. I am trying to compose myself, here. Okay.

So in this play, we get married, and this is our wedding morning, and I am a nervous wreck.

Like I feel right now.

And George is all calm and confident. Hmm.

The parents are all worried about us. In those days, the bride and groom sometimes never set eyes on each other before the wedding. But even back then, when the groom saw his bride walking down the aisle, he knew he would be marrying "the prettiest girl" he'd ever seen. This is what Mr. Webb says to his wife as he reminisces.

Maybe we *know* too much nowadays, and *see* too much, and *say* too much? I don't know really, except that I would not want to get married so in the dark.

Mickey's Hand

Nope. Nobody likes being in the dark. Sorry for interrupting.

Madison's Hand

No. That's fine…okay. Where was I? Oh yeah, my favorite part was the soda shop scene when the Stage Manager takes the play into a flashback, and he ponders how all this romance began—things like a wedding, and planning to spend a lifetime together. This is the soda shop scene where we get to see when George and Emily first knew that they might just be...well, they might just have something special…between them, you know.

Mickey's Hand

Yep. My favorite scene, too. Especially the part when you tell me my faults, and that I am getting conceited, and that I am not noticing you. And all that time, I am trying to walk you home, but you are always with other people and I just can't catch you.

Madison's Hand

Were you?

Mickey's Hand

Was I what?

Madison's Hand

Trying to walk with me and talk to me. And I don't think you are conceited. A little too confident, maybe…

Mickey's Hand

Yes, to the walking and talking part. And, around you, I am not "too" confident because you are… you are *Maddie*, and you have everything "together." Your school stuff, your social world, your whole future.

Madison's Hand

Well, Mickey, you know how Emily says that she's not perfect. Well, I'm not either. I am just as nervous as Emily is….

Mickey's Hand

Well, guys are not perfect either. And I'm pretty nervous too, you know.

Madison's Hand

Isn't it funny, Mickey? How could I have known that you were feeling the same thing I was feeling?

Mickey's Hand

Well, now you know. It's kinda like how George says about finding a person that you like…and finding out that this person likes you, too, and likes you enough to be interested in your "character " Well, I think that is just as important as college is, and even more so. That is what I think.

Madison's Hand

Mickey, I have always been fond of you—and your character.

Mickey's Hand

So this is an important text message we've been having.

Madison's Hand

Yes…yes. And I think we can stop referring to the play now.

Mickey's Hand

Okay. On to Emily and George's wedding.

Madison's Hand

Right, the wedding. Well, the choir hums, "Hear Comes the Bride," and the Stage Manager gives a sermon about couples made to live two-by-two…and the confusion about weddings…and how marriage is a sacrament, although he is not sure what that means. Maybe people were meant to live two-by-two regardless of their sexual orientation? Who knows? Anyway, Emily gets nervous and thinks about backing out. George is also worried, but for him, it's more about all the commitment and responsibility that a man shoulders. Finally, Emily's father steps in and reminds George that he is giving away his only daughter and requests that George take care of Emily. And George says he will and that he loves me…Emily. And I plead with him and say that all I need him to do is to love me… for*ever*. Forever and ever. Until death do us part.

Then we kiss and the ring is placed on my finger (but we didn't really *do* that part). And Mrs. Soames, a neighbor, says that…

Rhiannon's Hand

Don't they make a perfect couple! I love weddings! (Pari and I have been reading this, too, by the way.)

Madison's Hand

Okay…

So Act 2 of the play ended, and the lights went out except for the candlelight of the stars above our heads, and we heard Mr. B (not the Stage Manager) explain softly, "We are all looking for our 'True Companion,' and that is Marc Cohn's theme." Then this singer's voice echoes in the room—singing of finding your true companion. The song was so romantic, dreamy, and wise. It took our class away to some place where lovers meet, fall in love, become so passionate, and no matter what their age, no matter the world does to them, that they never get lost…not as long as they have that true companion.

And right then, the bell rang. The tender mood of the play evaporated in an instant, and we were all highly aware of being in normal school-mode again. I hated for it to end. I looked at Mickey and I didn't know what to say. I'm glad he did. He asked to meet me at the Metaphor Café after school…for a soda.

Pari's Hand

The Very Next Day—October 19th

I am the third Emily. You know, Mr. B does not know we are writing a book about him (and we had not started writing yet at this point). So I have no idea why Mr. B picked me to be the third Emily. My suspicion is that I am a good reader, serious, and that this is the "heavy" part of the play. The Stage Manager explains that nine years have passed. And he takes us to the cemetery. He explains that a lot of sorrow and heartbreak has happened here, but slowly, he says, slowly, all that fades away and things get quiet up here in these New Hampshire hills.

Emily Webb is dead. We find out she died giving birth to her second child. But Emily still has a part in the play as a lost and confused ghost. I feel as lost as she is. I am acting a part I cannot understand. I am 16 years old. I never think about death. I have friends that do. They seem depressed, and I can understand why they are depressed knowing their lives and the pressures they are under. But I never give the end of *my* life a thought.

There are the assemblies at school to remind us not to drink and drive. The names of kids killed when smashing their cars headlong into trees are always flashed before us, and the flowers always litter the ground where they died. I think of it momentarily, remind myself that I did not know these kids, and move on with my busy day. No, death does not enter into my thinking too much.

Not like my parents, who see the headlines in the Middle East and worry about relatives and friends "back home" who are caught in the crossfire between Iraq, Iran, America, and Israel. For them, death is all too real, and they attach names and dates and graveyards to people whom I never met, and now never will meet.

So this is what I was thinking about when the Stage Manager says something about how something is eternal, and a part of us must wait for something to burn off from our souls to be free. There is no telling how long the waiting lasts or what exactly we wait for. That is when I, Emily, appear in Act 3.

A boy named Dan sits across from me playing George Gibbs. I cannot really believe I am dead. I just cannot accept it. I was just at the farm with George.

I think the most powerful part of the play is when I, Emily, realize I can go back and re-live any time of my life, like a flashback. I am warned that for some reason, it is painful to re-live my life. I don't know why seeing the past would be so hard, but it does not take long to figure it out.

When I, Emily, go back to my 13th birthday, I just cannot bear to watch. My parents and I are so oblivious. We are so busy with details and meaningless stuff that finally Emily simply begs her mother to just really stop and see me for a second and pay attention to living in the *now*. But she doesn't.

Do any of us? I begin to wonder if I ever really stop to look at my parents—and do they ever stop to see the real me? What about all the joys and sorrows that pass my way in the course of my day? Do I appreciate any of it? I wonder if I take for granted Rhia, Mickey, and Maddie. I think about how those three have "adopted" me, and helped me fight off my loneliness. I wonder if I have told them how much they really mean to me. I know the answer. I haven't…until now.

Emily realizes all of this stuff is happening around us but we never notice it—or people and all they do for us. And as I say it, I look up into the eyes of a boy, Dan, whom I never noticed and I wonder if he ever noticed me. I hear my voice saying words that my mind is imagining: Do any of us ever realize how wonderful life is while we are living it?

The Stage Manager looks right at me and Dan, and then sweeps around the circle of desks and soberly says shakes his head. No.

That is when I, as Emily, know I am ready to go back to my grave, and the play is about to end. The Stage Manager tells us to get some sleep, and the lights dim one last time as we hear a familiar song we all know called, "100 Years to Live." And we realize we are only 15 for a brief moment—only 21, 35, 46—99—we hope we have 100 years to live. But we know it could be otherwise. It could all vanish in an instant like it did for poor Emily Webb.

That is when Mr. B says to us that in *his* town, this room, we need to remember to make our lives extraordinary. He reminds us to "seize the day," or *carpe diem* as he puts it.

As I walked out of Mr. B's room that day, I felt a new burst of energy and affection for others. I wanted to hug Maddie, and Mickey, and Rhia. And my Mom, and my Dad. And George Gibbs, that boy named Dan, who was staring at me the entire play.

And by the end of the day, I hugged them all.
Except Dan.

Chapter 6: In Love and in War

Pari's Hand

November 6th

Angry. That is how I feel. We met today at lunch and we all agreed that we needed to talk. This is a hard chapter to write because we are all over the place with our feelings. I, for one, cannot separate how my life has gone from what we read and heard that day. That is why I am angry.

We had just read Ernest Hemingway's short story, "Hills Like White Elephants," in which a young man and woman argue over the need for an abortion after "hotel hopping" (in Mr. B's words) when the man presumably goes AWOL (runs away from the military) in Europe during World War I.

So at the café, it all boiled to the surface. Rhia started it: "It was all so sad and so true—the abortion, the drama, the suicide—and then the, 'you can't get over it,' feeling. I know of people… friends… who have seen or done all of that."

In Hemingway's story, the young man just won't accept the responsibility of the baby, won't notice how devastating this is to the woman, and simply won't stop badgering her until she gives in. That is the point where she becomes numb, and surrenders to him, and denies herself.

That is why I am angry. I have been on the receiving end of that type of bullying – many times. I know the pressure that woman is facing, and how hard she's trying to hold on to her own will, her own sense of what's right and wrong. But the assault is relentless. And I *know* how she feels when she starts to crumble. I can tell my friends don't have a clue. As Maddie and Mick and Rhia talked about the story line and whether the woman should fight with the man, or just accept the fact that he is a jerk and that she has gotten herself into serious trouble (and therefore should rid herself of him and the baby)… while all this was flying around the table, I sat there, silent. They had no idea I was boiling inside. Until I exploded:

"Guys, this is a metaphor! Don't you get it? This is about when anyone has felt the forces of others just weigh them down and *suffocate* them! Oh, sure, we are free, or we think we are. But we are not really free at all!"

"How do you mean?" Mickey asked.

"Look, I come from a world you guys just don't get." I tried to figure how best to explain it to them, how to open a window so they could see. "Okay, this is a stereotype, but you know the Asian kids in class? Well, they are from a world where often their parents want them to succeed, go to school, university, and sometimes the pressure on the kids is enormous, right?"

They stared at me with the non-verbal version of *yes…and…*

"Well, it is about expectations—the parents' expectations of the kids." This is when I have to make a huge decision.

Maddie looks at me with eyes I have not seen before—not pity, not surprise. More like someone who, for the first time, really wants to know what is here inside of *me.* And looking into Maddie's eyes, my competitive nature, my insecurity, my walls, my mask, all of it just gently falls away as I decide to trust these friends.

"Last week, you guys, my parents freaked out because my older brother does not want to transfer from junior college to university. His grades suck and he hates school. He wants to go into real estate like my uncle. And my parents were yelling at him, telling him that he is not like my uncle, and that he cannot be dependent on someone else. They resent my uncle because he is pretty successful. There are a lot of Persians and other Arab-Americans here who trust him and use his services, whatever. But he is not 'schooled' as my father says, just 'lucky,' and you can practically hear my father spit when he says that word."

"So they were literally yelling at my brother, ready to kill him, just like so many other times when it comes to an education. And I was just standing there staring at them because they so *don't get* anything!"

As I paused to catch my thoughts, Rhia's chair creaked as she tilted it forward, waiting. The three of them looked at me and I don't think they blinked once. I loved them for that, and so I struggled on.

"And I am like *so angry* because I am the opposite of my brother. I love school. I get great grades. I want nothing more than to get out of my house and go to university and study! My parents always look at me like, 'Fine, Pari, but your needs are not as important as your brother's because he is a man, and he has to make a living and support a family, and do the whole Arab-American dream. You, Pari, need to find a successful, bright Persian man and give us cute grandkids. We can afford university, but you are not the one who needs to go.'"

"And the worst part is, later that night, I heard my parents talking about what if my brother moves out and *doesn't* go to college. They talked about how they could take the money they've saved *for him* and invest it is a local Persian-owned company, or some other stock market deal. And I'm standing there with my insides screaming, 'What about me?' I don't exist, I guess. As a girl, I'm not worth 'an investment in their future.'"

I glanced around the café table. Rhia was looking down at her hands, and Mick was staring at the middle of the table with a grim look on his face. Maddie still looked at me with those completely accepting eyes, and all three, I knew, were listening to me with their whole hearts. I knew my trust in them was well-placed.

"So, I feel *just* like that girl in the story. If I argue, they don't listen. So I just pretend that I feel fine and one day…I don't know…I'll just…"

I don't cry much, at least not when anyone can see. I was determined not to cry now either. Determined.

It did not work.

Mickey's Hand

You know, I can't stand it when girls cry. I want to fix it and make things right. It's a guy thing, I suppose. But they all started crying. I am a Martian according to Mr. B, and at that moment, I really did feel like I was from a different planet. The girls are from Venus. At least that's what we read in an excerpt from a book by John Gray called, *Men are from Mars, Women are from Venus.* The whole thing was about how the sexes handle fighting with each other. Mr. B gave us the excerpt since the Hemingway story we read was about exactly that. According to the book, I guess men tend to either *fight* or *flee.* Makes perfect sense to me. But the women will either *fold and give in,* or even worse, *lie and accept the blame.* This makes little sense to me, but I guess that's how things are on Venus.

It seemed to me like Pari was a mixture of all four right then (she was fleeing, fighting, folding, and accepting the blame all at once). I don't know what planet that makes her. But I get it. I really do. I was just not *crying.*

In an effort to be helpful, I said something like, "Pari, you know your parents love you…"

That did not go over so well. But I am sure her parents do. The girls were wiping their eyes and getting it back together, so I continued.

"My folks, Pari, want me to be a fine Republican, go to business school, be successful, and bring home a…" I stopped short. I was going to say, "a beautiful wife," but I saw Maddie look up at me over her paper napkin, and I don't know why, but I stopped and tried a different tack.

"Pari, those are *their* dreams. They may or may not be *mine*."

Rhia picked up her cup and said, "Mickey, at least they are dreaming *for you*, not ignoring your hopes and feelings."

"I know, but at some point, don't we all have to face them and say, 'This is what I want, and I cannot live *my* life as *your* life'?"

Pari took a deep breath and said, "Yes, Mick. But I think they also need to open the door and help you. Parents, of all people, should not make you feel like a second-class person. Believe me, feeling pressure is better than feeling nothing. It is like…," she frowned, and I started worrying again, but she was more angry than sad now. I could see Pari was choosing her words carefully, tapping her cup, "It is like they are putting a *veil* on me, even though they don't believe in *that*. But I feel it anyway."

Long pause. I could feel the pressure around the table. So I figured it was a good time to get them chocolate. I got one of those major-big brownies and cut it into four pieces. I gave Pari the biggest piece. This is something my father taught me. When all else fails with women, try chocolate. My father is a wise man in many ways.

Finally, Pari smiled.

Rhiannon's Hand

After Mickey's chocolate breather, I really wanted to talk about the song Mr. B played after the Hemingway story. It was called, "The Freshman," by a group I had heard of before, the Verve Pipe (and I have no idea how Mr. Buscotti had heard it because it was so *not* mainstream). I had my iPod with me, and I played the song back to them as loudly as I could without the café people kicking us out.

I was stunned by the song (and it wasn't Bruce Springsteen!). It was simply the best damn song I had ever heard. I said, "Did you guys get the 'baby's breath' stuff and the 'shoe full of rice' line? I thought it was about abortion."

"I thought so too," said Maddie, "but I could not figure out the rice and how that fit."

"And then when Mr. B asked, 'What else is baby's breath?,' I was like, oh, I get it. It's part of the flowers in a wedding bouquet."

"And the rice is thrown on the couple," concluded Pari, now more composed, it seemed.

"So he broke up with her right before the wedding, and he refused to say it was his fault because the whole wedding thing was something she pushed on him," I said.

"I think for more drama, they added the second verse about the guy's friend and what he does to his girlfriend, making her OD on pills and kill herself" Mickey injected, trying to get a word in with three girls ranting about a boy-bashing song.

"Why do you think he never wept after she committed suicide?" I asked.

"Because that would be an admission of his guilt." Mickey was firm on this. "If he gives in, he knows that he was responsible for her death. Or at least partly responsible, 'cause after all, she's still the one who chose to do what she did."

"Do you guys know April?" asked Maddie. "You know, she's in our class, in the other section. I've been friends with her for years."

"She makes killer lumpia," said Mickey, also firm on this point.

I knew that her father was serving in Iraq, and that Maddie's family was close to them, both being military families.

"Well, April did not freak out like this girl in the story. But when April broke up with her boyfriend, it was so awful because so much of *her* was wrapped up in *him*. Her father was gone, and her mom was worried to death. So her boyfriend had become her main support."

I interrupted, "Was this our freshman year?"

"Yep. And he was a junior. April had no clue what was really going on. She told me later that he was just using her to get another girl jealous."

Mickey was lost. "What?"

"The girl he *had* been dating. He was playing games with the old girlfriend, showing her he had a little freshman he could manipulate. He broke up with April just before prom when he got back together with the old girlfriend. Needless to say, April was crushed. She didn't do anything stupid like in this song, but I could see how it could happen. She had a really hard time." Maddie looked at me.

I don't think she knew.
She couldn't.

Mickey's Hand

The last thing in class that day was a song from Jewel. Mr. B said that everything up to then had been from the man's perspective, not the woman's. He said there was no woman's voice in the room, or in that "Freshman" song, that's for sure.

He asked us this question before he began the song: "How long?" That's it. Just that. Then it began… softer, acoustic, melodic, and clearly feminine. Jewel's character, who could be any girl living with a guy for a while who wakes up and gets dumped one day. The guy just says, "It's over." And she is left to pick up the pieces of her life, find a new place to live, and forget about him—I guess. But she can't…she just can't. Everything she sees, everything she touches, everything she did or does or used to do reminds her of him. And there is no one to call; no one to make it better. His voice is what she is desperate for, but desperation is how she feels from morning 'til night.

Boy, is she in denial, I thought. I also thought it was heartbreaking. I also thought that if I said anything like that in class, people would think I am so *emo* that they would think I am a freak or something. But what do you do when you feel you have found the perfect person for you, but you are not that person to someone else?

That is when Mr. B talked about *realism*. He said that in real life, sometimes there is no "happily ever after." There is just "after." I thought about Jewel's line about how hearts are broken and how people can feel so used by others, and I couldn't help but think of the 3,800 or so American soldiers dead in this war in Iraq. And I thought about the 60,000 Iraqi civilians killed. All that heartbreak, and people powerless to do much about it. I wondered if the lovers in this song were equally powerless.

I looked at the girls in the café and asked another question. "Do you *ever* think she will get over him?"

Rhia smiled, "That is why we like you, Mickey. 'Cause you get it."

Maddie seemed pleased.

Pari looked at the floor and said, "Do we ever get over some things, or do we just move on? Sometimes I think we just carry stuff for a long time until we can find a place to stow the baggage—someplace safe."

"That is what we like about you, Pari. You get it, too," Rhia replied.

That is when I unfolded a poem that I wrote after class today and read it to them:

"When Saying 'I'll Call You' Meant That I Would"

Do you remember
when trophies didn't matter
when acne was irrelevant
when saying how you feel was what you said
when humility was so attractive
when cool was being different
when a smile was for real
when "I'll call you" meant you would
when being popular was so unnecessary
when outstanding was standing out
when "getting over it" became something you got over
and when having "so many friends" meant little
compared to the one friend
who meant so much?

They said they loved it. I kept thinking: *What if… I was meant for you, and you were meant for me.* I looked at Maddie.

That is what I liked about her, too. She got it.

Madison's Hand

One week later—November 14th

Mr. B told us to stow away all that realism and cynicism for the rest of the week. Just before Thanksgiving, we were treated to the romantic view of love—love as it *should be*, not love as it necessarily *is*. He said he was, "Talking that 'Perfect Love.'"

So he gathered us up to the front of the room in a tight circle—girls in the center, guys around. "Tighter," he announced, slyly, and we all scrunched up closer, the girls having an easier time of it than the guys. Then the song began. The light drum beat was like a heartbeat. The soft, floating voice of Marc Cohn in a duet, Mr. B said, with James Taylor (who my mother just loves). Mr. B jumped into the heart of the circle and rotated in a circle facing us as we heard about this young couple who met in the 60's and fell in love. They carved their initials in a tree and kissed in the rain; and Mr. B whispered that *it was a perfect love.*

He blew the words at us like someone blowing the tiny pedals of a dandelion. "Perfect. Very innocent, naïve, Camelot kinda perfect," he softly suggested to us. And the guitars strummed and the bongos drummed. "And they got married and saw Bobby Kennedy and faced the Vietnam War, but it didn't matter because what mattered most was they had a 'Perfect Love.'"

Again he blew in our direction. "It was after the assassination of his brother John—JFK and Jackie in Dallas—but Bobby was ready to carry on, to keep moving forward. There was still joy…before the fall…of Saigon, Martin Luther King, Malcolm X, and the fall of Bobby, himself. Before the tears of 1968, before all the sadness that was to come. It was when the world was still a small world, after all. That is when they fell in love. Perfect love."

Mr. B closed his eyes and said, "They danced on the beach, and their dreams were still in reach. But it was not easy. It never is. It took years off their lives and it was the best time of their lives. And time passed—tick tock—until it was the autumn of their lives."

Then there was a sparkle in Mr. B's eye and something unspoken yet became clear to me. He was really talking to us about he and his wife—at least partly. I knew it. I felt it. He had alluded to it before with his, "I married the girl next door…and one up (in the apartment upstairs)," sermon last week. They'd been married for years, and he was obviously still crazy about her.

It was all kind of dreamy, hypnotic. And we were spellbound, as the song slowly slipped to its sunset as the two lovers, aged and bent, but still arm and arm, walked in the rain under the stars and the moon….

And he woke us from the trance. I could not help but smile. He had somehow showed us that cute, old couple in the song—we could all picture them in our minds, clear as day. They were not giving into the pain, or the wind, or the unrelenting power of nature as it ravages them. They know just one thing. They are perfect together.

I thought of my mom and my dad. I thought of the picture of them in my wallet, the one where he has his helmet on with his name, *Davidson,* in bold black letters. His smile. His confidence. Holding my mother by the waist as she looks up at him—her hero. My hero. Their courage.

Just a perfect love…

Mickey's Hand

Maddie was across from me in the circle. I kept looking at her and she seemed far off. Now I know.

But could I ever, ever be that kind of man?

Would any of us measure up that old couple?

Did that kind of love ever really last like the letters carved in an old tree?

Then Mr. B woke me up from my shaken confidence. He pulled out a book and said, "Gang, let's jump ahead a month, to Christmas, with this holiday tale of love and joy." That is when he slowly read to us like we were kids (which come to think of it, we are!). He read the O. Henry story, "The Gift of the Magi."

Now, I know the story. It is one of those you really never completely forget, but you also never remember all the details. And it's from those folds of specific acts and words and smells and laughs that you get the power of the story. The narrator—all knowing—ends by talking directly to us about the real meaning of *giving*, whether it's for Christmas or any special occasion.

"Why are they the Magi?" Mr. B asks us.

Donald is first. "They bring gifts obtained at great sacrifice."

Rhia is next. "They did not care to get anything in return."

Maggie follows. "They did not care about the cost."

"Why not?" he asked.

I found myself in the moment. "Because the gift is not *the thing* they give but what they *do* to acquire the thing."

Maddie continues the explanation, "The watch he sells is all he has of value, and he sells it to surprise his wife with the combs she longs for to put in her beautiful hair. He would give anything to make her happy."

Pari made a rare appearance without being called on, "And her hair that she also sells is what so many girls, women that is, value as a part of… well, it is everything to them."

Rhia said, "It reminds me of Locks of Love where people donate hair to make wigs for people who've lost their own hair because of chemo treatments for cancer. You have to have like 10-inches of hair you're willing to cut off." Rhia quickly looked at Pari, putting two and two together. “Pari, didn’t you do that when you were a freshman?”

“Yes.”

“Wow,” somebody said quietly. There was a respectful pause.

Of course, O. Henry’s short story concludes that the combs for the woman are now useless because she has cut off and sold her hair to buy her husband the watch chain, just as the watch chain is now useless because the husband sold the watch to buy the hair combs.

“If that is what real, mature love is, then what standard does that set for you and the loves or infatuations you hold?” Mr. B asked, rhetorically.

As I walked out of class, I caught up to Pari and asked her about the hair she cut off. “How did you feel afterwards?”

“I cried. Twice.”

“Why twice?”

“Once for me,” she said, “and once for the girl whose picture is in my wallet.”

Then she pulled out her wallet and showed me. The stranger in the photo looked beautiful… wearing the gift of her Magi.

Rhiannon’s Hand

Two days later—November 16th (the Friday before the Thanksgiving vacation, just four days before the prologue)

“There was this TV show,” Mr. B reminisced, “called *M*A*S*H* in which doctors, during the Korean War, tried desperately to keep boys alive in mobile surgical centers. It was a losing battle and a bloody one, too. In one poignant moment, one older doctor turned to a younger doctor and said something like, ‘There are two rules in war. Rule One: Young men die in war. And Rule Two: Doctors cannot change Rule One.’” Mr. B stared at us.

“Let’s add the numbers. As of today, roughly 3,800 U.S. soldiers are dead in the battles of Iraq; 60,000 are wounded; and former President Jimmy Carter reports that the casualties among Iraqi civilians are equally staggering—50,000. So what was true in the 1940’s is still true today.”

I heard the numbers. I guess I knew them. At least I knew of them, but I did not *know any of them.* That makes all the difference, huh? They are just numbers. Just faces that flash at the end of the news each

Friday. When it happens, my mom looks so discouraged. She stares at the TV and just shakes her head back and forth, back and forth.

I know what she's worried about. I know. It's my brother. He knows he's in sped. He knows what special education is. He will not go to college. He wants to enlist. He wants to serve his country. He buys into all the military commercials with the "adventure" of it all. And I don't want to be negative—too negative—because I know Maddie's father is an officer in the reserves and all that.

But it frightens me so much. I know he wants to go. He wants to have a purpose, to be trained, to be somebody. He is so desperate to show others that he is normal. Chris knows now when he's being laughed at. He hates it. You know, it doesn't matter if you're in sped or not – every person knows that they deserve dignity.

And I also know Rule Three: Sisters can't talk brothers out of going to war. My mom shakes her head at the screen because those faces, those faces, haunt her. Lots of things do. Like the face of that person she counted on for better or worse, in sickness and in health, 'til death do us part. That face that left us a couple of years ago, right about now, at "Thanksgiving."

And my mother loves *M*A*S*H*. Do you know the theme song of the show? It's called, "Suicide is painless." She told me that once. I just now remembered it, although I never quite put it all together before.

My friends don't know.

Not yet anyway.

Sometimes you can keep a secret inside your soul only so long, and then something happens and it just jumps up out of your heart, through your fingertips, and right out onto the keys of your laptop, and your brain just cannot stop it (and maybe you don't want to stop it).

But first, I'll tell you this. It is Mr. B, reading to us the tearjerker of a short story called, "50 Missions," about this soldier who can't believe he actually survived the impossible—50 missions in a bomber plane. Nobody comes back from 50 missions. It's basically suicide. But somebody has to fly those missions. Somebody gets elected, and somebody goes.

The trouble is that he did not die. He survived because his girlfriend made a deal with God. It went something like this: "God please save him, and for that I will serve you all the days of my life."

And God came through. Now the soldier is back in the States and is fulfilling his promise—to see her, once more, in the Catholic convent where she will stay forever having traded her life for his.

They loved each other with that love that stings the heart. When they meet, I can barely stand it. I want him to just grab her in his arms. I want her to kiss him and tear off the clothes of chastity. I want them to sob and sob and thank the Lord for their good fortune. I want him to do what he so desperately wants—to never let her go.

But he cannot. She cannot. "A deal is a deal is a deal," Mr. B told us quietly.

"Do you remember *Forrest Gump*?" Mr. B asked. Everybody has seen that movie. "Well, gang, Forrest makes three promises in that film. Tell me about Jenny."

Dan, normally quite, said, "She says, 'Run Forrest, run.'" The class laughed. Dan continued, "And he says something like, 'Jenny, I will always love you.'"

"Yep. And he did, didn't he? Why? Because a promise is a promise is a promise. Tell me about Bubba." Mr. B looked at Mickey.

"The shrimp guy, right, Mr. B?"

"Yep. What does Forrest say to Bubba when Bubba is dying in Vietnam?"

Mickey looked around at the class, "I'm not sure here. But I have a feeling that it has to do with the restaurant called Bubba Gump, right?"

"Yep. Forrest doesn't know anything about the shrimping business, but he promises he will look after Bubba's business if and when he gets home. And so he does," said Mr. B.

"And I ate there!" Mickey retorted. We laughed, again, but nervously.

"Tell me about Lieutenant Dan. He's the one who gets his legs shot off, remember? Anybody?"

Maggie quietly said, "Mr. B, Forrest goes back to save him, and that Dan guy is pissed about it because he wanted to die and he doesn't want to be a cripple."

"Yes, and Forrest saves Lieutenant Dan because he promised them if they listened to him they would all come out alive. And Forrest was making sure that happened. It is all about the promises we make…and the promises we keep." Mr. B simply stopped right there.

That is when I lost it. Only Maddie saw.

"And so you want the woman to leave with the soldier." Mr. B looked at us. "You want a happy ending where we all get just what we want. Me, too. And that is what happened."

One of the twins said to him, "But Mr. B, she does not leave with him. He doesn't even ask her too."

"She can't leave. It would be like a sin or something, like she would get hit by a car the moment she left the convent," said Donald.

"He lived. That is the happy ending. She was the person who fell on the grenade for him," Maggie seemed angry.

"Well, just because she is a nun doesn't mean she is blown to bits," Pari spoke up, to my surprise.

"No, but she does not want…to finish the deal, but sometimes we just have to…" Mickey trailed off. The whole argument trailed off for me, as if it was out there echoing in my head, but all I could focus on was not crying, and one simple word… Promise.

Two years ago. He walked out. Got on a plane. Left for Oregon. Flew away to a new love, a new life. Adios, baby.

My mom had no real idea it was coming, but she suspected. She had that uneasy feeling that something was up.

I got shot right between the eyes. It was like that Springsteen song Mr. B played last week that went something like—you got shot right between the eyes and the little lies…you got shot point blank.

Bang. Dead. Just like that.

My mom tried to cope. She was so brave. It wasn't until a year later that I found out the "flu" she had was her half-hearted attempt to overdose on sleeping pills. I guess she figured suicide was painless, and she had a moment where she couldn't take the pain anymore. But in the end, she could not do it. She vomited it out. She could not leave us – me and Chris. She would not. She promised. And a promise is a promise ***is*** a promise.

I found out the same way you found out about my father. My mom's soul just spit it out to me one night when she was sitting in the dark with a candle lit, listening to an old John Denver album. This song was "Leavin' on a Jet Plane." It must have been my mom's secret wish—that he would come back someday—that he really didn't want to go.

I made a promise that night. I promised I would care for her, care for my brother, care for my friends. I don't know for sure if there is a God (who does?), but I do pray every day *for us*.

You know, he did not leave us a nickel. Nothing. We were (and still are) just scraping by. So I pray for my mom whose heart may never heal. I pray for my brother whose anger may send him into harm's way. I pray for me because I don't want to hate my dad. I don't want to hate anyone.

But I do.

Do prayers get answered?
Do people come back from their 50 missions alive?
Can a doctor put together a broken heart?
I don't know.

All I can hear is John Denver's warm voice pleading to hold me and never, never let me go.

Chapter 7: Jay and Daisy Faye

Mickey's Hand

December 3rd

Mr. B had us drink this slowly, carefully. We sipped down a masterpiece of storytelling. I have to tell you—I loved *The Great Gatsby!*

I loved how Fitzgerald describes the stars like they are silver pepper on a black sky.

I loved how all Gatsby lived for was the romantic idea that Daisy could be his.

I even loved how Fitzgerald described how Gatsby had been destroyed like he was a fancy wineglass that gets shattered maliciously by Tom Buchanan.

I loved it despite Daisy's pathetic words that rich girls never marry boys who are poor like James Gatz.

So after we finished reading the book, heard Mr. B's lectures, and even watched the new version of the movie, we decided to do something different. We met at the café with a camcorder. We figured we would video ourselves "live" (in a YouTube sorta way) just so it could all be spontaneous. When I watched the vid later, I typed it up just as it happened. This way you get to see (well, read) all of us together.

December 14th

Pari: I hate Daisy almost as much as I hate Tom. Like the book said, they were careless people. They just trashed everything and everyone.

Rhia: But Daisy had good inside her…

Pari: That makes her worse! She knew better. She had a choice. She had Gatsby."

Maddie: But Gatsby wasn't real. He wasn't even "Gatsby." He made the name up and everything. He was a bootlegger—a thug, or the manager of thugs.

Rhia: He had to do that to earn enough money to get her!

Pari: He was a fool to not realize what Daisy was—a spoiled, pathetic woman. She knows she's a fool, but she doesn't care because she has her money to numb her.

Rhia: I know. I know. But that's the way she was raised, coming from "old money" and all…

Mickey: And we can't rise above that? Are we doomed to be like our parents? Am I locked into a Republican existence because my parents voted for Bush—both of them?

Rhia: It does shape your life.

Maddie: Yes—but, well, remember when Daisy was going to run away with Gatsby in 1918, and her parents discovered her plan and they would have cut her off. She would have had nothing.

Rhia: So she was caught in a world she couldn't possibly escape.

Pari: You can say that about anyone. At what point do you just say, "This sucks. I'm not going to live like this!" Her husband had an affair with the chambermaid!...while they were on their honeymoon!...and she knew it!

Mickey: She knows everything about his affairs. So why doesn't she leave him?

Pari: Because what she *has* is all that really matters to her. She wants the security. The money. She will just drink her way into some state of oblivion.

Mickey: But isn't that what lots of marriages are about? Just going through the motions 'for the kids.' Or how about the people who are so dependent on each other's money that they can't do anything else?

Rhia: Not my parents! My dad didn't give a shit about us. He followed his "dream girl" to Oregon like we didn't exist.

Maddie: And you are the people he shattered. You and your brother and your mother. The careless people don't care about those they leave behind.

Rhia: He can't care, because if he did…

(Long pause here…very long)

Rhia: If he did, how could he live with himself? So he tries to buy us off with gifts and crap like that.

Pari: It is all about the "green light." My parents are so materialistic.

Maddie: Are *we* any different? Look, we all want to go to a good college, get great jobs. We want all that *stuff*, too.

Pari: I don't. I just want to be *(pause)* what *I want to be…*

Rhia: Meaning…

Pari: I want to be great. I want to be really good at something—and I don't know what yet. But I am not second class. I am not less that my brother or my male cousins who are all deemed deserving while I am reduced to "girl" status. I just want a fair chance. That's all. To be whatever I want to be. And I will work hard…harder.

(Another long pause in the tape)

Rhia: Well, I like Gatsby anyway. I imagine he's cute, *really* cute.

Maddie: But Nick is the honest one…

Rhia: and boring…

Pari: and cynical…in the end.

Maddie: Who wouldn't be after reading this novel?

Mickey: I'm not. Really! Fitzgerald saw America as a land of hopes and dreams—like the Springsteen song Mr. B played for us. And I really do believe everyone can make it. Even a "nobody" from North Dakota.

Maddie: But he wasn't "great."

Mickey: Yes, he was. He was like Mr. B. said—Don Quixote.

Maddie: Yeah, I saw that play, too, and lots of people thought Don Quixote was a crazy old man who thought windmills were—I don't know—dragons or something.

Mickey: He fought for the honor of a woman.

Pari: This woman doesn't deserve the honor. Daisy Faye is a fake.

Mickey: Now who's cynical? I agree with you, Pari, but look at it this way. Don't we all sometimes go after things because we think they will be great? Then in the end, sometimes they let us down? Well, Gatsby doesn't hesitate to chase the dream—to get Daisy Faye back. And he knows she is fool's gold—or at least he learns it in the end. But he did make something of his life, and he did get his dream! That is a lot more than most people ever get close to.

Maddie: I don't know, Mickey. It was only temporary. And do the ends justify the means? Remember Mr. B said Gatsby was a 1920's version of Tony Soprano! He probably did "kill a man"…or two… or…

Rhia: He is no different than a drug dealer today—okay, a lot cuter. Maybe he just ordered the "hits." Doesn't that change your opinion?

Mickey: No. I agree with Nick Carraway in the end when he says that Gatsby was better than all of them: Daisy, Tom, Jordan…even himself. The thing about Gatsby is that he believed in you and that you could do anything you set your mind to. I mean, don't you wish you knew someone like that? Someone who believed in you like that? That's why Nick thinks he is "the Great Gatsby."

Mickey's Hand

December 21st

So about then, the battery ran out (conveniently, right at my big moment). The Metaphor Café was closing anyway. I decided to take the tape home with me and I watched it. It was pretty jumpy, especially the parts when Maddie and Rhia kept passing the camera around. But there we were, talking about Gatsby, talking about us, talking about life. So I typed it up.

And I put it in a box with a red bow and a note that read:

Merry Christmas,
Mr. Buscotti

From your fans
Who meet
At the Metaphor Café

I left it on his desk today.

Chapter 8: The Other Ghosts of Tom Joad

Rhiannon's Hand

December 20th

Well, Mickey spilled the beans with our video, I guess. Mr. Buscotti never said anything this week. Nothing. Not even a look. I wondered if he'd watched the video, and what did he think? It was killing me to know, but I just pretended that nothing had changed even if we were no longer undercover.

This week, I felt I understood what Mr. B and Ms. Anderson were getting at. Not that the others didn't, particularly Pari. However, for me the grapes of wrath are pretty sour sometimes.

During our history class, Ms. Anderson went over the grim details of the Great Depression: the Crash of '29—the Stock Market plummeting to 46 total points— Hoovervilles—FDR's New Deal—the Dustbowl—the Route 66 travels of the Okies as pictured by Dorothea Lange. Ms. Anderson even played us some of the music of the era. She set the stage well for both classes of us coming together to see the film version of *The Grapes of Wrath.*

Mr. B warned us it was like a documentary. We wouldn't see any fancy visual effects, although the movie was "state of the art" in its day, which was sometime around 1940, a year after Steinbeck wrote the book, *The Grapes of Wrath.* Mr. B went on to read us a letter written by Woody Guthrie, a folk singer of the time. Ms. Anderson had played us some of his songs. Woody Guthrie said, "Seen the pitcher last night, Grapes of Wrath. Best cussed pitcher I ever seen."

Well, although I don't think it was the "best cussed pitcher I ever seen," I have to admit it did hold my attention, and I'm not the only one. It was funny how this old black and white movie that seemed to have nothing to do with life in our suburbs or our cities today did touch a nerve with all of us.

The grandparents were cute…but their death was sad. They did not want to change or to leave their farm, but they traveled with the family anyway so they could all stay together. The old folks weren't placed in some nursing home. Every other month, I see my one remaining grandparent who lives in exactly one of those places about an hour from here. She's my mom's mom, and it's depressing as hell to go see her.

Grandma does know us, but she is losing it quickly. She thinks we just saw her, or she asks us the same questions she just asked. She insists she just moved into the "home" when my mom put her there four years ago. My Grandpa took out some insurance plan so the bills are taken care of, I guess. Then my mom mentions something about Medicaid, but I get lost about that. We all feel guilty we don't see her more often. Guilt. It's like the shadow Peter Pan can't ever shake. It just attaches itself to me and my family. Everyone except my dad, that is. I guess he is in Neverland.

And then there is the guilt in the film. Nobody can eat around those starving children the Joads see in those Hoovervilles. Ms. Anderson told us, "You've seen the children in Africa with their bellies sticking out from starvation. They were like that in the Great Depression, too."

Maggie asked what they died of.

"Heart failure," said Ms. Anderson. "Ironic, isn't it? When the body is starved, eventually the heart just gives out. And it is happening in Afghanistan and Iraq, too."

Then there is Tom Joad, played by a handsome actor named Henry Fonda. I have heard of his daughter, Jane Fonda. She did some workout video or something. Apparently, she is a big-time actress, and her dad was a big actor, too. But I'd never heard of him before. Generation Gap, I figured.

Tom Joad was great. He was the conscience of the movie, and maybe of the times themselves. Mr. B said he was the champion for the people and their needs. President Roosevelt said there was "nothing to fear but fear itself." Well, I'm guessing he had never been on the roads that the Joads traveled because Americans sure had much to fear. It's like any panic where people stampede for safety. "Dog eat dog," as Mr. B remarked. And the times made people mighty mean.

Homelessness can do that to you. Hopelessness, too.

I know. It was the holiday season of my freshman year.

My mom kept it from me. The details, not the tears. The tears just kept coming, like the bills. All the stuff my dad used to handle. He sent some money. And he sent some more eventually. I guess the courts or his conscience got the best of him. But for a while there, it was just terrible.

Some family helped us out. Grandma wasn't any help, of course. My uncle was 3,000 miles away. Friends chipped it. People were kind, but I felt like we were the receiving area for Salvation Army donations.

We moved from the house I'd grown up in into an apartment. We tried to keep it quiet because we didn't want pity. We told people we didn't want to talk about it, or think about it, and certainly not worry about it. But my mom bit her nails 'til they bled.

I lied to everyone. I lied to myself the most. *He's coming back. She will take him back, forgive him, and we will move back home and get our stuff out of that stupid little storage unit. Any day.*

The phone became a double-edged sword. Was it him? Was it bill collectors? Or was it my friends? And even when it was my friends, I lied to Maddie about why I didn't have a cell phone anymore. I made up this huge story about getting in trouble and my mom taking it away to punish me. Anything to keep seeming normal.

That was the first time I ever dreaded Christmas.

And the last time, too.

Something out of *It's a Wonderful Life*, the Christmas movie, happened that year. Chris and I were both in classes that raised money for what the teachers called, "families in need." Our school's student service program was organizing it. His class and mine were "adopting" families anonymously. We only knew the ages of the kids, parents, or grandparents. In my freshman Spanish class, we passed the teacher's "Santa mug" and collected bills and change. Needless to say, this was not something I could afford to do. But we had a coin jar at home and I was determined to drop *something* in that mug, and make sure nobody suspected that my family was struggling. Everything was going okay up until the day the teacher told us we were expected to buy actual gifts for the little kids we'd adopted.

I knew Maddie pretty well then (and Mickey too, but only a little). Maddie and I went to a toy store together. I'd raided the coin jar again, and I got so lucky. I saw a gift I knew an 8-year-old boy would love. Remember Woody from the movie, *Toy Story*? Well I got him a small Woody action figure – on clearance! I knew any boy's face would just beam when he opened it, and I had enough money to buy it.

So the big day came when we walked to the gym with all the gifts and met the teacher who organized the program. Our class was as bubbly as freshman can be with our bundle of gifts. We felt so great seeing so many other classes pouring in with their gifts. The gym was filled with different "family zones," where gifts were placed. We all wandered around and saw how generous the kids at school (and their families) were.

The more I looked the more emotional I became. Maddie was there and we walked together. Her dad was in Iraq back then, so Christmas was a tense time for them too. I was starting to lose it completely, but I pulled myself back together when I looked at the grim set of Maddie's chin. I realized that although I was down about money, at least I did not have to worry about my father dying.

On the other hand, my father was as good as dead to me.

So to distract myself, I asked a teacher when the families would get the gifts, and she told me they would be called today, and they would come by tonight to pick them up. Sometimes just the parents would come because of the whole Santa thing.

At home, we had a tree slightly better than the Charlie Brown tree, but there wasn't anything under it yet. I worried my mom would feel guilty and maybe buy stuff we couldn't afford. I figured my dad would send us some money or something equally impersonal. Chris was having a harder time of it than I was. He was pretty angry back then, angry about everything from dad, to school, to girls, to just being a kid in sped.

So when my mom came home and told me something was wrong at school, I thought it might be Chris getting into a fight. Mom had gotten a phone call from the principal asking her to either come to school or call back right away. And Mom just freaked. She waited to ask me what might have happened at school before she called the school back so she could be prepared. She asked about my brother, and I didn't know anything, but told her that didn't mean something hadn't happened. Chris was very angry then. Anything could set him off.

There's this line in the *Great Gatsby* book where Gatsby meets Daisy again after five years and he goes through all these stages of emotions. He feels something like *embarrassed,* then *astonished,* and then he stares *in wonder.* Well that is exactly how my mom reacted on the phone when the principal told her that our family had been "adopted" by the school. The principal said my mom could come by to accept the gifts that had been given to make our Christmas "a little bit merrier," as she put it.

I was in shock. Chris went with her to pick up the stuff. I stayed home. Frankly, I did not want anyone to know that I was one of "those" families. I guess it was my pride, stubbornness, immaturity…whatever. I just stayed home and waited. It seemed like an eternity.

You know those scenes where the middle-aged mother has been crying so much that her mascara makes her look like a ghoul in some weird gothic music video? Well, that was mom when she got back home. She told me that the families at the school were so grateful. She was so grateful. And Chris was beaming. There was so much stuff: wrapped boxes; gift cards to cool stores; CD's; even grocery store gift cards—one for $150 dollars! I can't tell you what that food card meant to me then. I held that card and the tears just came. I can't tell you. You can't know unless you've been there... Whoever you are reading this, I hope you never have to go there. It makes me cry again just remembering it. And all we knew was that one of the senior classes had adopted us. And I have to tell you that I love every one of those anonymous people.

In the *Grapes of Wrath,* the Joads are beaten down and about to give up. Then they finally get help from the "government." A government guy (who looks like FDR) is so nice to them, and he treats them with dignity. They'd faced so much meanness that they were beginning to believe there wasn't anyone out there who cared. Then someone comes along who treats them right, and their hope is restored.

Well, that is how I felt that night. Someone cared about the three of us. Someone gave us back our hope. Boy, did we need it that year. But I was puzzled about how anyone had known.

As we were putting the gifts under the tree, my mom said there was one I was supposed to open myself. The principal herself had made a point of showing her this one small box she had been holding. She told my mom that I had to open this evening.

It explained it all.

It was a cell phone with 200 pre-paid minutes. And it was my favorite color, too. Purple. There was a note:

Merry Christmas
Please call me tonight
I love you
Woody

So I immediately called Maddie.

We screamed.

I cried.

It was the most important Christmas I've ever known.

Madison's Hand

December 22nd (the last day before winter break)

Mr. B looked at us like he was about to spring a trap. "So that was a nice movie, huh? Time for us to just go out and gorge ourselves on holiday mirth, right?"

We just stared at him.

"Well, gang, I did not show you *The Grapes of Wrath* because I just love watching old black and white movies…although I do. Here is the deal. A whole lot of this country is hurtin' right now. Some are legal citizens, some are migrant workers, legal or illegal, some are unemployed and some are underemployed. Do you know what underemployed translates into?"

No one said a thing. I think it was a rhetorical question.

"I got picked up recently by this company that takes you home from the airport—a shuttle service. It was about midnight. Nicest guy driving. He was in his late 50's I thought. We struck up a conversation. I found out this was the job he had to take since his software company "downsized." He told me, 'It pays the bills.'"

Then Mr. B unfolded a laminated front page of the local newspaper. The big banner headline read, *The New Grapes of Wrath.* "Here they are folks. These are migrant workers today. Not Okies. No. These folks are from Mexico or Central America or even South America. Some of these folks are legal, some are not. They pick your fruit, particularly your grapes. They pull the wheelbarrows full of grapes for the wine industry in northern California. And they too are losing their jobs."

That perked Mickey's interest. "I thought that manual labor like fruit picking was always in demand."

"Yeah, well so did they. But remember the 'Cats' in the movie—the Caterpillar tractors? This article explains that some clever industrialist has figured out how to pick grapes with a machine. So now they need fewer workers. Many of these guys are being 'downsized' too."

That's when he passed out these lyrics and told us to listen carefully to a song called "The Ghost of Tom Joad."

"Yep, I know… Bruce Springsteen, again," said Mr B. "Thing is, he read Steinbeck's book. He looked around this country and wondered what was going on. Was history repeating itself? Do you know how many folks in this nation are homeless? Sleeping in their cars? Building a cardboard hut out in our own Southern Californian canyons?" Mr. B was walking up and down the aisles looking at us, talking right to us.

"Did you know that people go down there where the illegal folks make a camp in the canyon and ransack those places?" Mr. B paused as he strolled back up to the front of the room. I was imagining being in those cardboard huts when the angry, violent men came through. I hadn't realized.

"Have you served food at a homeless shelter, like for instance at St. Vincent de Paul, downtown? I am sure you see these people on street corners." We all had. "Do you assume they are all druggies, losers, criminals, or just bums?" Nobody was dumb enough to nod, but of course that's exactly what we thought.

Mr. B continued, "Did you know that the largest percentages of homeless people are woman and children? Do you wonder how they got into such a mess? Did you know that the men on the streets are disproportionately combat veterans who served in Vietnam?"

The music resumed: Springsteen actually quoted a line from the film (and the book) that talked about how Tom Joad was going be looking for people who are so beaten down that they need his help. Tom Joad vowed he would always be there. I couldn't help but feel that Springsteen was also talking about himself.

Mr. B stopped the music. "There are an awful lot of people struggling to make ends meet. Some have control of their destinies. Some, not so much. I wonder what your generation's legacy will be. I guess before you can tell how you feel about homelessness, neglect, and the indignity it brings, you have to first witness it."

He then played a video from of this man being interviewed by a news reporter. The man was living in his truck.

The Reporter: So you lost your leg in Iraq?
The Man: Yep, an RPG blew up right under our Humvee. Killed my two buddies instantly. Mangled my leg so bad it was just hanging there.
The Reporter: You were the driver?
The Man: Yes, sir. That is what saved my life.
The Reporter: Tell me what happened then.
The Man: Well, I would be damned if I was gonna leave them dead in the road. No f-ing way. So I

put them in the Humvee. I had to get their body parts…

The Reporter: I'm sorry…their body parts.

The Man: Yes, sir. I wasn't gonna leave any part of them back there. Look I got nothing against these Iraqi people—shoot they are getting blown to bits, too. But I just was not gonna leave 'em. Just wasn't.

The Reporter: (after a pause) Then you got to the hospital and they amputated your leg?

The Man: Yes, sir.

The Reporter: And they fitted you with a prosthetic leg?

The Man: Well, not exactly. They did start the whole process. They sent me home. That was four months ago. They discharged me—honorably, of course.

The Reporter: But you still don't have the leg?

The Man: No, sir. They say it takes a while. And I can't work without it. There is still a lot of pain and the medicine is expensive. I cannot afford much else…so I am just living in my truck. Waiting.

Mr. B shut off the video and looked at us. "I guess he is just 'waitin' for the Ghost of Tom Joad.'"

We just stared at him.

When my father got home that night from working at the Naval Hospital, I just ran to him and hugged him as hard as I have ever hugged him.

"Daddy, I'm so…"

"Sweetheart, what wrong?" He looked at me with tears falling down my cheeks. I told him how my heart went out to the man in the truck—how it could have been him.

"Maddie, I don't know about that man. I am just a radiologist. I see X-rays and broken bones. And you know, darlin', that you can't tell on an X-ray when a heart has been broken." I looked at him and raised my eyebrows. He could tell that I wasn't a little kid anymore, and I needed to hear more. "Sometimes the army or the government just gets so bogged down in red tape and crap that people slip through the cracks."

And he hugged me hard, looked me in the eye, and made sure I was okay. Then he walked to the kitchen to do the same for my mom.

He is my Tom Joad.
And thank the Good Lord he is not a ghost.

Chapter 9: Dance Through the Decades

Rhiannon's Hand

January 6th (the rehearsals)

Oh my God—I have died and gone to heaven! For our final exam, I get to dance! Not once, mind you—but with 20 different guys. We are learning six different ballroom dances. And we get to practice for a week with different partners. Tango! Swing! Charleston! Cha-Cha! Fox Trot (whatever that is)!

And that is not all. No. We get to pick a famous person to be for the dance. It has to be someone from the 20's through the 40's. Can you believe it? No, neither can I. I get to be Grace Kelly or Audrey Hepburn or Rita Hayworth or Billie Holiday or even Judy Garland.

Okay, yeah, I have to write a "Press Pass" where I write as that person would about who I am and what made me famous and stuff. Yeah, I have to "cite" my sources and work in some images. But who cares? This is so much fun. And this is school. I get a grade for it!

Ms. Anderson emphasized that we also have to add a part about who we are most comparable to today. That is a nice twist. I am leaning toward Grace Kelly or... Oh I know, Scarlet O'Hara—what was her name? Vivian Leigh. God, she was gorgeous. There was just something about these women. I look at Audrey Hepburn in the movie, *Breakfast at Tiffany's,* and she is stunning. Elegant. Do we even have women like that today? Okay, Princess Di was like that, maybe. But really, our "famous women" today are so out there. There is no mystery to them. Britney Spears, Paris Hilton, Beyonce. (What is her last name? Does she rate Madonna status?) And oh my God, Anna Nicole Smith (sorry to pick on dead people). But these "celebs" are just cheap. What does Ms. Anderson say? *Tawdry.*

So I have to learn the dances, find a person to "become," and get swept off my feet.

I can do this.

Okay, I have two words for you: Mae West.

Madison's Hand

Rhia is right. It is the big event of our class. But not all of us are *eager* to dance. I mean we are, but some of us, okay, me, Maddie, I am scared.

I have two left feet. I just don't hear the beat. I watch the dancers at school in Air Bands or Hip Hop dance competitions and I think to myself, "I am a boring, stiff, white girl with absolutely no rhythm." That is my reality. Ask me to write a paper, and I get A's. Tests, no problem. Speeches, cake. Dance?!? Oh, I don't think so.

But I *want* to dance. I do. I want to be like those cool couples you see in those old movies. Fred Astaire and Ginger Rogers. Debbie Reynolds and Gene Kelly. I watch those old movies sometimes with my mom. I envy those girls who seem to just twirl and float. I guess this is the secret that lots of girls like me keep tucked away. We want to be those long-legged girls in A *Chorus Line.* Somewhere in my heart of hearts, I want to be a Rockette.

Boy, am I a big chicken! You know what this is all about? One thing—control. And I want to know that I am not only in control, but I also want to know for a fact that I will succeed. Type A's like me, we pride ourselves on that 4.00 GPA. We never want to look bad because, well, because, then we become the kids we look down on. If I'm absolutely, brutally honest with myself, I do look down on kids I think don't try, or act dumb, or just don't know very much. I hate the idea of looking like I don't know what I'm doing. Gee, I guess the shoe is on the other foot, now. My left foot…

Both of them.

Pari's Hand

I have a confession to make.

I am a dancer. I really didn't think it mattered in the whole we-are-writing-a-book-thing, so I just never included it. I have taken dance classes since I was little. I've studied jazz, modern, some ballet (when I was in middle school), and even tap. I have no idea how to do most of the dances Mr. B and Ms. Anderson are teaching, except swing. I have done some swing in recitals. It is so much fun! But I've always danced it girls-with-girls. The bigger girl just plays the "guy," and we have a great time. But this is different. These are real guys, and they have to learn it, and they have to lead it. Hmm. This could be a disaster.

I am in a dilemma. I don't want to lead the guys here at school and intimidate them. But I don't want to get my feet crushed either by some of these very large, awkward (being nice) boys. I look around and see maybe three or four guys that look like they can move. Mickey can. The boys that are sports guys have coordination.

I don't know about this. Some of them are so dorky.

But all in all, it is going to be fun.

And then there is Dan. I think I am going to find myself standing right next to him for the tango.

Mickey's Hand

Okay, now that all the girls have weighed in on the Dance Through the Decades, I guess it is my turn.

Mr. B is so funny. He says stuff like, "This is your great dream, guys—to have girls just standing there, swaying to the music, looking at you, and their eyes say, 'Dance with me!' There are guys who would kill to be you!" And you know what? He is so right. I am just smiling away, laughing at my laptop as I write this.

Okay, yeah, we are so totally nervous, especially with all this talk of us guys leading and being in control and stuff. But it is so amazing. Rhia is right—what a final exam. You talk about a big finish to the first semester. Wow.

Madison's Hand

January 7th

Today began typically for Mr. B by referring to Bruce Springsteen.

Mr. B. told us, "All this sitting in desks has got to go. It is time for a little of that human touch....time to get skin to skin. Push those desks back out of the way!"

We began with the fox trot, and with our hands instead of our feet. We moved our hands to a slow-slow / quick-quick beat. He told us (me, in particular) that we weren't hearing the rhythm of the music. He said we needed to sway, rock, slide, glide to the song. Then he grabbed Ms. Anderson, and they modeled how the fox trot should look. There, they were, dancing away right in the middle of the classroom. Mr. B told us we were turning back the clock to Cole Porter's, "Begin the Beguine." They moved back, sideways, hesitated in embrace as we heard the orchestra play a song that I could only describe as "My Grandparents' Sound." It had swaying, and stars, and tenderness, and tropical palms and all the romance that makes those old black and white movies so special.

The two moved so effortlessly—he in control, she floating with him. The room was filled with the sound of the "beguine," which Ms. Anderson said, "came out in 1935." As I looked around the room, all of our 70 faces were glued to them, even the boys who seemed either shy or in a state of denial that this was their fate.

I was watching their feet, trying to move mine to the rhythm. I started to figure out which foot goes back, how to do the "quick-quick" tap, how the shoulders needed to softly sway. I was focused, so much so that I did not have a moment to think when all of a sudden—whoosh! Mr. B had me in his arms and said, "Look guys, hold her like this. No, the hand does not go lower than the middle of her back. The front arm points direction. Stand up straight. Maddie, get your left hand on my shoulder. Good. Now, listen for the beat. Slow-slow / quick-quick." And we were off!

I was trying to look down at my feet to see if I was doing it right. But he moved in such a way that he helped me to feel the song's rhythm. I was a klutz a couple of times, but he smiled and his confidence in me was in his eyes. It was like I was in one of those tractor beams in a Star Trek movie—I just could not mess up too much.

All the girls were watching me. That is when I realized how much my hands were sweating, and how warm my whole body was and just then—whoosh! I was back in the circle of kids, and Mr. B was shouting that we needed to pair up, and that the first twelve couples were to "Hit the floor." Mickey grabbed me before I could think…and I had begun to begin the beguine!

I was dancing! Mickey was trying hard to lead. We fought each other a bit. I pulled back, he wanted to go sideways. I bumped into the couple behind me. We got off beat, laughed, concentrated, and found the rhythm again. And after what seemed like only seconds, we were swooshed off the floor as the next twelve couples had their crack at it. We all watched intently. There was nervous laughter from the group still waiting to hit the floor. And then they were on. Everyone was electrified to some degree as they left the floor, wondering if they did it right, who would dance with them next, could they remember the moves?

It went on like that for several rotations. Ms. Anderson was coaching the girls, Mr. B was encouraging the guys. We were all looking at our feet a lot, and Mr. B said, "Look into their eyes, guys. It's love. It's magic."

That's when he changed the song.

Pari's Hand

Michael Buble was the singer. I knew his voice and his music, but the song was really old. It was called "Fever." And it was hot—the song and the room. We were all getting sweaty. Even though the song was slow, the temperatures were rising. I danced with three different guys, but Dan was not in my group. Some of the guys were pretty good, some nearly paralyzed with fear. Mr. B was funny, too, telling them, "Look, you're not Frankenstein. Relax. Don't take such big steps. Little steps, small girls. Smooth. Think James Bond."

I caught Dan's eyes, hoping he would just somehow cut in. I heard the singer moan something about how Romeo loved Juliet and how they kisseth and they were on fire. But just as I was starting encourage Dan to dance with me, Mr. B (of all people) caught my hand and said, "Girls, look! This little Parivash can dance. Watch how she floats with me." And as we moved, he whispered to me, "You are a dancer, girl. I can tell." Then projecting to all of the class, Ms. Anderson piped in, "She is light on her feet—on the balls of her feet. She does not try to lead like some of you girls are doing. It is about trust. Remember, dance was about men giving direction and woman looking fabulous with their beautiful dresses. I know girls, times have changed. But that was then, and this definitely is now."

Mr. B then grabbed Dan's arm and pulled him over to me just as we heard Buble croon something about how chicks were always giving boys a fever and it was a lovely way to burn.

I looked at Dan, and he seemed a little intimidated. I didn't say anything. I just kind of nudged him in the right directions—just a little. He smiled with relief that I was helping him, but not judging him. His sandy, blond hair was in front of his blue eyes a bit. He smiled, not at me, but at us.

Do you know what I mean?

Yeah. What a lovely way to burn.

Rhiannon's Hand

January 8th

"It's the swing, baby," is how Mr. B got us to "cut the rug" today. "It's the #1 hit single of 1940! Glenn Miller and his Orchestra with, 'In the Mood.'" I hear this song when I go to weddings. The song begins with a famous saxophone anthem, then the trumpets and trombones blast away. And we were swinging! More than anything, most of us wanted to learn how to swing.

"It's all about the rock-back, and the arms taut so you get that bounce and speed on the turns, gang," Mr. B demonstrated. When I saw him (and I don't mean to say he is that old), he so reminded me of my grandparents when I saw them dancing at my cousin's wedding. That effortless bounce back and the cute turns with each other. It made me beam just to watch them—seeing how the music made the years just seem to peel back, revealing a youth that could only last for part of the song. But for a few minutes, my grandpa was so smooth and my grandma was laughing, and all the younger girls hoped, like me, that one day we could find that swing boy.

Donald was that boy for me. I think he had done some swing before. I don't know where, and I don't care, because he could rip it up. I so wanted him to teach me the more complicated turns and moves that he knew. Ms. Anderson showed us girls the basics, with the barrel role and the cuddle being fun. But Donald, with his dreadlocks swinging in time, and his smile revealing big dimples that sort of made him seem boyish (even though he's a strong, sturdy athlete)… Wow.

I asked Donald if he would meet me at lunch today in Mr. B's room. Some kids were going because they were absent for the first day, and others were going because they just needed help, and some, like me, just wanted to learn more. And truth is, some were going just to flirt. Lots of that was going on.

When I walked in, there was no music playing. People were just working on footwork. Donald saw me and showed me this move I think he called the octopus, where we just wrapped ourselves up together. It was fast and tight.

"You have to be really close to me or we'll lose hold," Donald said. "When I pull you in, you are right here." *Here* meant I was back to him and we were pressed tightly together. Then he showed me how to get out, and the absolute coolest thing of all was when he said he would literally pick me up and wrap me around him.

"You gotta hold on tight." He looked at me and I said something like, "Don't let me go, because if you do, I will go flying."

"I won't let go. Don't worry about that, Rhiannon."

I liked that he called me Rhiannon.

We tried it a couple of times (and it worked!), and then we asked Mr. B, who was talking to another teacher, if there was a song we could practice it with. That is when I first heard, "Zoot Suit Riot":

And it was a riot! Donald whipped me around like a rag doll and I loved it! I was so out of breath that that I could not laugh, or breathe, or think. I finally stopped spinning, and the words few out of my mouth just like I flew into the air.

"Donald, tell me you don't already have a date to the Winter Formal!"

The look on his face scared me for a split second. Then I realized what I had said, and I scared myself. I must be crazy. He probably has a girlfriend. Oh, my God. I am an idiot.

"No." He said with a sincerity I did not understand.

"No," I said, "of course. I totally understand. You have plans, I…"

"No, Rhiannon, I am *not* going. Do you want to go…with me? I mean, if you can't, I understand because…"

"No… Yes! Yes, I want to go. Yes."

"I don't know if we can do anything fancy for dinner but…"

"I don't even care. I just wanna dance with you, Donald."

"Yeah?"

"Yeah."

"Cool."

"It will be fun. It's not for a month or so. I think probably Maddie and Mickey are going, and other people we know. Maybe we could join up with them…"

And the rest was a blur.

We danced some more, and the music changed. It was a fox trot. Some people needed to review it.

All I remember was the voice of Frank Sinatra singing that he's got me under his skin.

Pari's Hand

Wednesday, January 9th

"Guys, I want you to think you are Antonio Banderas. Girls, you'll have to use your imagination!" We burst with laughter. It was Latin Wednesday.

"Gentleman, move your hips. They were meant to rotate. It drives girls wild. Mine, not so much. But you are young. Ricky Ricardo, the band leader of *I Love Lucy* fame, brought the Latin face to TV, and with it the rhythm. He was no great dancer, but to the wonder-bread white world of television, he was breaking ground." Mr. B was, at that very moment, demonstrating the cha-cha with Ms. Anderson.

I loved the feel of it. The passion. I have danced my whole life, and I think there is just some music that is so filled with joy and romance and energy and sadness and grace and power.

I can barely stand still, waiting my turn to dance. I realized today that my role in class has changed. Gone is the demure, mysterious Persian girl who speaks only when asked. Instead, I'm the girl who all the girls look at and go to for advice. "Pari, how do I turn…which foot…does his hand switch…?" The questions swirl around me. I am answering as fast as I can, stepping into couples and showing girls which foot to swing back on. I have gone from the corner of the room into the spotlight.

Then the music changed, and the moment I'd been waiting for finally came.

Tango.

I looked around and saw Dan. Here I was tracking down a guy. Me. I tried to slip and slide through people as Mr. B was explaining that the tango is a five-count: T-A-N-G-O. Mr. B and Ms. Anderson were demonstrating the dip, and Mr. B was joking that the last time they did the tango, "Ms. Anderson had a carnation in her teeth." We all laughed, camouflaging me as I slipped through to Dan's side, but I overestimated my speed and bumped into him.

"Sorry."

"Hey, can you be my partner on this one, Pari? 'Cause it looks complicated."

"Sure." I smiled. I held his gaze—for a second longer than he expected. He did not look away. I know my eyes were giving me away.

I know we all don't spend a lot of time describing ourselves, but a dancer's eyes are trained to be expressive. My round, dark eyes are sometimes my best asset on stage—I am told.

My black hair was pulled back, as was the case for a lot of us girls. We had dressed in layers since it was cold out and as the room got warmer we stripped down. So by this point, I had on my tight black shirt, jeans, and flats.

"Tango really hit America in the 1920's coming out of Buenos Aires, Argentina," Ms. Anderson said, ever mindful of being historically accurate.

Then the music began. Mr. B encouraged, "'Ole Guapa'—it's got the great tango beat! You can't screw it up, guys. Lead her. Get cheek to cheek!"

And we did get closer. Well, closer than usual. Actually he got his cheek to the top of my head, touching my hair. Our arms pointed direction. We were just getting the feel of it when we slammed into another Antonio Banderas impersonator. It was funny looking at the whole class because every couple looked like sword fighters all going off in zany directions. The song was *so* dramatic that it was borderline corny. But that made it all the more fun.

Dan tried to dip me. His arms were tense and like hard wire as he overcompensated for what he assumed would be my fall to the floor. He did not realize how light I was.

"Whoa, you are like a feather, Pari. I didn't mean to whip you up like that."

"No, that's fine" I told him. I wanted him to actually dip me lower, but for now it was fine.

He was fine.

Just fine.

Rhiannon's Hand

I have to interject something here. I am jealous. Pari and Dan looked great right from the beginning. I swear. I looked at them. Straight backed. Her arm up high on his shoulders. She whipped around on the pivot so fast and flashy, with her beautiful, full ponytail wrapping around her, brushing against him.

Okay. That is all I have to say. Some people just have it.

Pari, you go girl.

Mickey's Hand

January 10th

What a week! We have learned so much so fast. Today we learned the waltz, which was easy compared to all the other stuff we've been doing. One-two-three, one-two-three, yadda-yadda-yadda. It was fun dancing to the Christmas song, "Silver Bells." Who would have known that was a waltz?

That is one of the amazing things this has taught me—maybe all of us. The idea that there is a way to dance, a formality to it. This is a kind of like a "mating ritual." Okay, that sound really geeky, but it is true. We all pair up. We stand close—but not too close. We laugh. We are all pretty much on equal footing. And we listen.

I am the first to admit that I am bad at listening—to music and to people. I want to talk. I think sometimes that I catch a breath just so I can rear up and roar some more into someone's ear.

Now I get the whole "play it by ear" expression. I have to make myself feel the beat. Sometimes I have to count the 1, 2, 3, 4's in my head. I envy how Mr. B can just close his eyes and flow with the rhythm. I guess it's all the practice he's had.

I think this whole dancing through the decades thing is also about us realizing that what was *then* was so *cool*. But if Mr. B just stood up there and lectured to us about the Big Band Era, and maybe showed a few videos, we would have nodded off thinking, "Yeah, right. Another teacher telling us about how great it would have been to have lived back when they lived." This is usually followed swiftly by the teacher saying that everything about today's music sucks.

But cool isn't cool because it is popular. It is cool because it lives within us. It is cool because we love it, thirst for it, and want it so badly that we dream about it. Mr. B is fond of saying he is "so un-cool that he has become cool." Yeah. I get it. Kids at the school are jealous because they wish they could dance like we are. They might not be thrilled with the essay/press-pass we have to do. But all the same, this dance isn't merely about nostalgia for us. This dance is happening in one week, next Wednesday. And we have tomorrow to learn the Charleston.

So I am twirling one of the twins (dang, I can never tell the difference, Clair or Shannon), dancing to the song, "Silver Bells," and we are just so…

Cool.

Madison's Hand

January 11th

Yes! Finally something I can memorize! I did the Electric Slide at my 8th grade party—and I think the Hustle, too. Okay, disco was pretty cheesy, but all that Saturday Night Fever stuff was fun (in a 70's-retro-big hair-kind of way).

Today is the Charleston. This one I know, sort of. Ms. Anderson is in charge of this one because Mr. B said: (1) his knees are shot, and (2) he can't remember the pattern. He is still out there, though. I love the kick and the spin—it reminds me of the Hustle, and just when I said that, Mr. B was saying the same thing: "Patterns come and go, gang. Line dancin'. Janet Jackson. Hip hop routines. You name it."

One of the good girl dancers, Vanessa, asked him, "Can we do, 'Soldier Boy'?"

"Well, I don't know. Is it 'appropriate for school'?" Mr. B got a laugh from that. Lots of kids said sure, it was okay. Soldier Boy is this hip hop dance and from what I knew it was fine, but what do I know?

The best parts were the jumps at the end of the pattern—but I admit they're tough on the knees. Jump twice to the left, twice to the right—then hop back and forth. We all laughed when we tried it. It showed off the athletes for sure. Mickey was great at it.

Ms. Anderson explained that the Charleston originated in African-American jazz clubs, and then it became a popular (even international) dance craze in the 20's. Funny how so many things are rooted in the South and from Black culture. And yet what we associate with the Charleston are white flappers and the speakeasy—and Gatsby, of course.

So eventually we got in a long guy-girl-guy-girl line, and another line faced us. It was a relief, I think, for everyone to dance to a song that required no connection to someone. You could screw up and it was okay. We all felt comfortable with a dance that is just "doing your own thing." After all, that's what we are more familiar with. Yet still, we were all a team moving to the same beat, with the knee-knocks, and the snaps and claps. And the arms! How the arms swing in the Charleston.

For a minute there, I thought to myself that even though we are in a modern-day classroom in jeans and converse and baggy pants and spaghetti straps, we are all morphing back in time. Just watching the lines start to get it, and repeat the whole routine, all together just like people our age used to do—yep, we are definitely in a time warp.

And that is exactly what Mr. B and Ms. Anderson had in mind.

Now all we have to do is remember all this because the big dance is next Wednesday—during our two-hour final.

Oh, and I need to decide what Ginger Rogers should wear because Mickey already borrowed a tux from the choir teacher.

And then there is my hair.

Oh, to be a girl getting ready for a dance.

Rhiannon's Hand

January 16th (the introductions)

Five, six, seven, eight….

Wow. What a day. We all had a blast. The Dance through the Decades was so much fun. Where do I begin? After two days of more typical tests and quizzes (some basic review of the history we have studied for Ms. Anderson and a writing sample for Mr. B), we just *could not wait* for today.

The way the school was organized for finals, we had two blocks of time—two hours for History, and then two hours for English. So for the first two hours, we met in the theater—in full costume with our press passes—and we introduced ourselves to the class.

I had the red flowery boa, the slinky red dress, and my hair was all curled for that Mae West look. I told the class (but secretly to myself I was talking to Donald), "Come up and see me sometime." You know, Mae West was no dummy. She was a blonde bombshell but with a brain and quite the business woman. Ms. Anderson asked me whom I was most like today and I told her Madonna. Yep, Madonna.

Pari's Hand

"Anna Pavlova is my name and I am the most celebrated dancer in history. My mission is to carry the art of dance to the four corners of the world." I was dressed in a ballet tutu—white and black—because her death came in 1931, before color television or movies, and she would be best remembered in those stark colors.

My hair was up in a tight bun, and I hoped I did not look too weird. Of course, when I saw all the Al Capones, Rita Hayworths, and Judy Garlands in Dorothy outfits, I figured I fit in just fine. I liked the fact that Dan had come in a full Naval uniform. He was Admiral Nimitz. He even had the white hat to go with the black uniform. I have no idea where he got it, but I thought we would match perfectly.

Madison's and Mickey's Hands

"Bang, you're dead. Right, baby?"

"Yeah, Clyde. Girls, doesn't my guy *kill* ya?"

That's how we introduced ourselves. Mickey had dark pants, suspenders, a wide red tie, and a hat borrowed from his dad—the 30's look. And I had a beret, because I saw Bonnie had one in a picture—a tight skirt and a silk top—also red. Red was our color.

"Bonnie and me was notorious outlaws, and we traveled the Midwest during the Great Depression."

"We got known nationwide, though. Huh, Clyde? We captured the attention of the American press."

"In the 'public enemy era,' between 1931 and 1935, we was Public Enemy Number One for awhile. Mostly we was famous for bank robberies. 'The Barrow Gang,' we was called. Bonnie, she never fired a gun, ya know."

"Ya, they called us the Robin Hoods of the time because we always robbed from the rich, and we never hurt the poor."

"And when we got killed, me and Bonnie, we went down in a hail a bullets. But we went down together. Blood on blood, baby."

"Yeah, like he said. Blood on blood."

Mickey's Hand

Same day (the dance)

Cameras flashed. Videos whirred. It was crazy. Mr. B had invited parents and they showed up in full force. We were in the big dance room—wooden floors, big sound system. Parents passed out the dance cards to the guys along with a small pencil. Guys had to write the names of at least 20 different girls on their dance card. Yep, our assignment was to dance with 20 different girls during these two hours. And I did!

I loved it all. It's hard to put it into words. Of course, I danced with Maddie. We looked for each other on the slow fox trot where Mr. B played "Unforgettable" by Nat King Cole. And I found her again for the cha-cha to a version of "Smooth" by Carlos Santana. For that one, we were all laughing as Mr. B told us we all had the "Latin rhythm coursing through our blood!" Sí, señor!

But I have to say that he kept the dance moving so fast, and we changed partners so often, that he forced us to break out from just dancing with people we knew. And I was glad. I danced with girls I rarely talked to, barely knew their names, and yet I felt their nervousness recede. There is something to that "human touch" thing Mr. B was pushing our way. We applauded after each song, and we thanked each other. It was old school. And it was… magic!

Pari's Hand

You know those old-fashioned movies where you see a couple dancing in some ballroom? It is always romantic and soft lens, fuzzy in glamorous black and white. Well, I watch those old movies. And that is exactly how I felt during the Dance Through the Decades at times—especially with Dan in his uniform.

During the tango, Mr. B kept telling others to, "Check out couple #1, Pari and Dan, as they tango the night away!" My mother was there, of course, taking a picture. But I did not care. I did not care at all.

Mickey is right, though. I danced with so many guys—good ones and not so good. And they were all fun, really. I think before this, some of the guys thought I was a little stuck up because I am quiet and a good student. So it was really fun when one of the big football guys, Chase, and I did the swing to "Boy from New York City." My hair bun came flying down, and when we went into the cuddle, my long hair whipped him in the face so hard it made his eyes water. It was a riot.

What it did—the dance—is something hard to say in words. But for me, it bonded me to the guys and to all the girls, too. Between the introductions and the dance, all the girls went to Ms. Anderson's room where we re-did our hair, make-up, and—everything. The excitement was measurable. You could feel it. All the drama about who would dance with whom, and girls glamorizing themselves… It was just a flurry of hair spray and laughter!

By the middle of the dance, we were all sweating, and all that glamour had twirled away and left us as we really are—kids, just happy to be with each other. Since Mr. B made the rules for the dance, and we all had to dance with 20 different people to pass this final, we didn't have time to think about anything. He just threw us together and off we went.

At one point, Mr. B cut in and danced with me. It was a cha-cha. He told me I was a wonderful dancer. And then said that he loved that video we had sent him at Christmas. He had never mentioned the video once, to any of us, so I was so surprised. Mr. B said that the video was the nicest compliment we could give to him—that we cared that much about his class.

That is when I told him he was cool…and the song playing was "Cool Operator."

That was Mr. B alright.

Rhiannon's Hand

Okay, highlight reel. Best moment. First, we danced the Charleston—a blast. But later it was even better. Ms. Anderson got us back into two lines again facing each other—guy, girl. Then she said that it was time to update the music—that the Charleston was then, but this is now! She told us to simply follow the same pattern and the beat would work. That's when Mr. B hit the music, and we heard the Bee Gees singing something we knew was disco from *Saturday Night Fever*!

The room exploded as we realized we were doing a version of the Hustle. It was so crazy. Mr. B was slipping down the center of the line doing the John Travolta thing, and he got us to all sing in high voices, "Night fever, night fever—we know how to show it."

But the best, best part was when he played, "At the Hop." And he played it twice!

That is when Donald and I really, really ripped it up. We were so good, so fast, people started looking at us. Donald had taught me some new moves, and other kids were trying to pick them up from watching us. Even Mr. B and Ms. Anderson were watching. I had kicked off my shoes by this time, and my red boa was long gone. The slinky dress was stuck to me, and all I can say is I did not care at all.

It was all feel—all faith in each other, all timing and foot tapping and speed and bounce. Boy meets girl. Boy whips girl off her feet. Boy, oh boy.

So later, when I got a chance to dance with him on a slow song, "Beyond the Sea,"…I kissed him—quickly.

On the cheek. Cheek to cheek.

Madison's Hand

Grand Finale. Yes, of course I had a fantastic time. I felt so good because I really went in nervous and worried that I was not going to be good enough. I came out amazed. Boys who struggled at academics were awesome on the dance floor. Boys who were shy were suddenly smiling.

And I loved dancing with Mickey. He was confident and calm. I had him under my skin. But I want to tell you about what Mr. B said at the end of the dance. After we played the last song, "Jump Jive," and the place was hot and we were exhausted, he gathered us together for a final "sermon."

Mr. B said: "I want you to know how proud I am to be your teacher. I know Ms. Anderson feels exactly as I do. You know, this is the 10th year of the dance. And you guys all got so into it! As you head home with the first semester under your belt, I want to tell you about that first dance and about a boy named Ben.

"Ten years ago, Ms. Anderson and I really did not know how a dance like this would go over. It's a big gamble having kids dancing—egos, drama, shyness, too cool to dance—the whole nine yards of problems. But it turned out great. And as we were cleaning up afterwards, a big guy named Ben was the last one helping us.

"Now, Ben had a jaw problem. He knew someday his jaw would need to be broken, and reset, and because of all this, he was terribly self-conscious. And he had glasses, not contacts. You know how it is. He was at that awkward age. A lot of you can relate to that, right? Anyway, that kid was so focused during the week of dance practice. That's because, above all else, Ben wanted those girls to know *he could dance*. And he had to work at it. Not much, except math and science, came easy to him.

"So at the dance, he ripped it up. Every girl he danced with had a great time. And he was never, never without a partner. So after the dance, when it was just Ms. Anderson and me cleaning up, he comes up to us and says, 'I just want you two to know that this was the best day I have ever had in high school. I never in my life thought I would *ever* get to dance with all those pretty girls. I've never danced with *any* girl before.' And then Ben looks both of us right in the eyes, and he says, 'Thank you.'"

Mr. B paused, and some girls gushed out, "Oh." The guys were quiet, but their hearts were right there with Mr. B. We waited. It was absolutely still.

"Ben knocked us out. He went on to the University of Colorado, and he had that operation on his jaw. And looking back, who can say how much confidence he gained in that one day at the dance. But I wonder sometimes how much that experience shaped how he faced his future. In getting ready for the dance, we literally saw him reach down and find strength inside himself he didn't know he had. So when he looked at us that day and said, 'Thank you,' that is when Ms. Anderson and I knew in our bones we were on to something."

We burst into the biggest round of applause I have ever heard a bunch of students give a teacher.

And that was just the first semester.

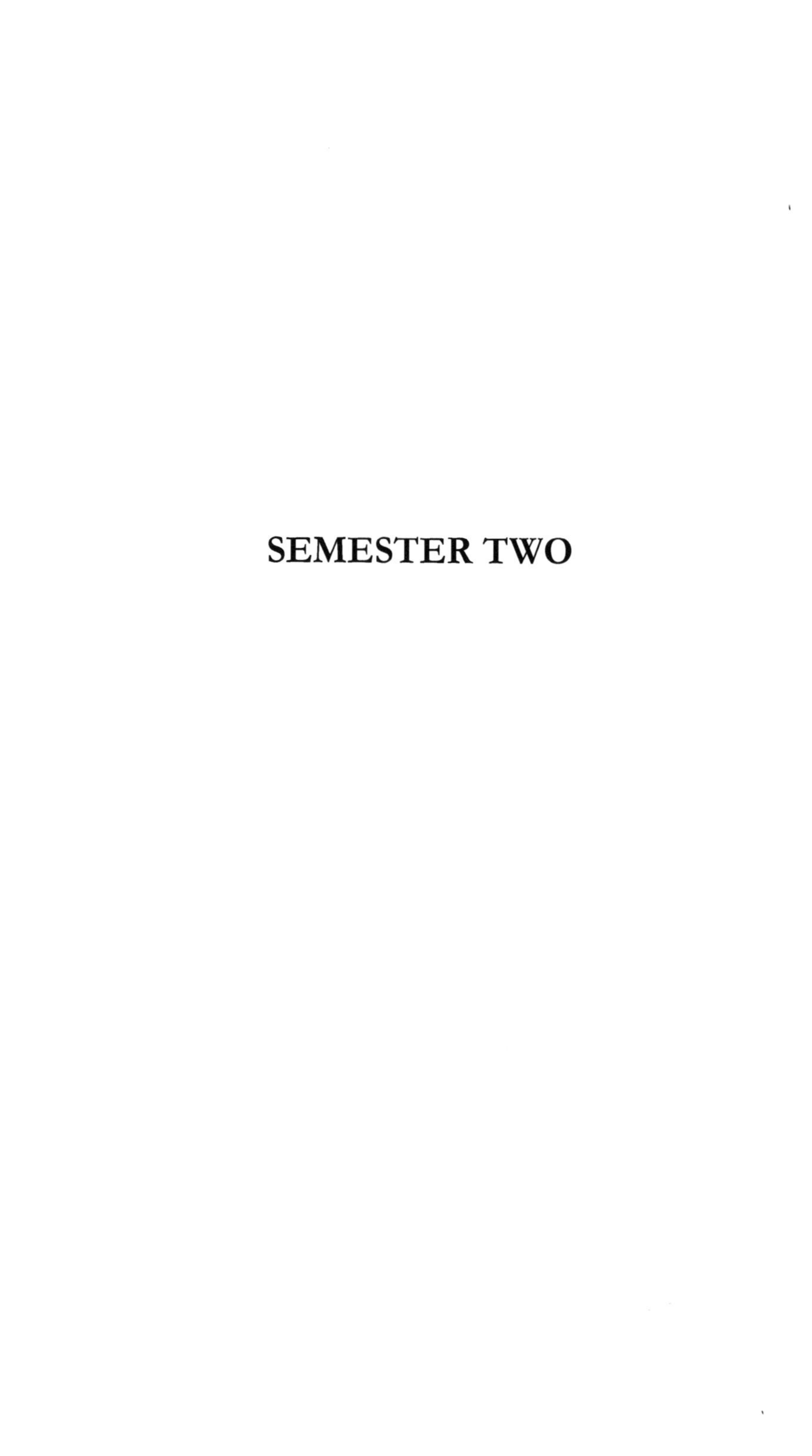

SEMESTER TWO

Chapter 10: Everybody Comes to Rick's

Mickey's Hand

January 10th

Happy New Year!

It was a great break for all of us. After the stress of classes, teachers cramming things in before the holidays, and the whole get-ready-for-Christmas rush that parents have going on, we teenagers just wanted to sleep.

Ah, sleep. I didn't wake up until 11:00 a.m. that first day of break. The simple joy of lounging on the couch watching ESPN's *SportsCenter* was to be savored. Once Christmas was over, the four of us met at the café. We talked about what we got for Christmas, how we would finish up the latest chapter, and what Mr. B said about the video. He is being very mysterious with us. We talked about putting our video on YouTube, but thought better of it.

Maddie and I watched a bunch of movies during break. Sometimes it was just the two of us, and sometimes we were with Rhia or Pari or our other friends. Rhia thought that *Juno* was very cool, and all of us agreed. Maddie liked *Atonement* more than I did. Pari loved the Denzel Washington movie, *The Great Debaters* (I did, too). But my favorite break movie was *Charlie Wilson's War* about the secret war that some congressman (played by Tom Hanks) funded to support the Afgans in their battle against the Russians for control of Afghanistan. The irony did not slip by us. I mean here we are today fighting against these same forces that *we* armed and trained. And of course they see us as the invading "occupiers." I know it is not that simple. I know we are in Afghanistan to rid that country of the Taliban and Osama Bin Laden. I also know (from my mom mostly when she read *The Kite Runner)* that the Taliban destroyed Afghanistan, and that the different factions of power in Afghanistan have driven the nation and its people into chaos.

People don't give teenagers enough credit sometimes. I like knowing about things that are happening in the world. I know things because of films, or the media, or my parents. And lately I've been learning things from teachers like Mr. B and Ms. Anderson. I know that while it may be a Happy New Year in America, it is anything but happy in the Middle East and Africa.

And one thing I know for sure is that we in America are privileged.

But getting back to break, the time flew by as it always does. Visiting relatives said their goodbyes, and school loomed ahead, filled with pressure. But there was one thing we all looked forward to—*Casablanca.*

We had all heard about this movie. It seems to be on every film critic's top ten all-time-greatest list. We'd all seen clips of famous scenes. But only Maddie had seen the whole thing. Back in class, we watched it together, all 70 of us in the theater. We had various questions to answer, and Mr. B and Ms. Anderson stopped the movie and held a "press conference" every so often to help us understand what was happening. This was helpful because the dialogue is so fast and the movie assumes that you know the politics and history of the time. For instance, we had no idea that the movie is set in early December of 1941, just days before Pearl Harbor. Rick says something about how it's December 1941 and America is asleep."

And I suppose we were. Ms. Anderson explained that President Roosevelt's "Fireside Chats" on the radio were somewhat planned to wake America up to what was going on. Americans just didn't want to think about concentration camps, Hitler's march through Paris, the bombing of Churchill's England, and the refugees who were pouring out of Europe in every direction. People wanted to go on dreaming that these things didn't have anything to do with us.

The film captured so much that we decided to write our reactions to it. Then Rhia had a surprise for us, one that proved to the four of us that we were not alone.

Pari's Hand

Refugees.

Casablanca begins with refugees trying to escape Hitler and the concentration camps in WWII.

Well, my own parents ended up as refugees. They were both well-educated. They met at the University in Tehran and they were married in 1977. My father was 21 years old, and my mother was a year younger. My parents decided to leave Iran when they saw the fierce and growing power of the conservative Islamic rebellion against the Shah of Iran. My parents wanted children and they knew that this movement was a step backwards. My mother was fearful, my father angry.

My parents knew the Shah of Iran was corrupt. Everybody knew. No one cared much because as my father said, that is the price tag that comes with power. And after all, Iran under the Shah was prosperous, and an ally to America. However, Iran's wealth was not shared fairly—and certainly America and the West got all the oil they needed at a cheap price. So as my parents began planning their future, they could see the inevitable. The Shah would fall from power, and the radical Islamists would take complete control. My parents did not want to raise a family in this new Iran even though it meant leaving everything they knew and all who loved them. It was a bold move, but they felt there really was no choice.

But where to go? My father hated the Communists, but he says that at least the Communists believed in education (for women as well as for men). Nevertheless, my father says the Communists had it all wrong because there was no profit motive in the Soviet Union. "Look at the Yugo," he said. "It is like so many products made in Communist countries…of no quality. Nobody cares, no personal integrity. Not like in America." So going to the Soviet Union was out. It was the United States that they both admired. America was their goal.

So my parents said tearful goodbyes to friends, sisters, brothers, and their own parents, knowing they would likely never see them again, and they left Iran in 1978. With heavy hearts, they went to Paris for a belated honeymoon. Paris was all the romance they imagined. As I watched Rick and Ilsa in the movie at the Eiffel Tower or on the Seine River, I thought of what it must have been for my own parents, two young lovers sipping French champagne and toasting, "To America!"

My father eventually found work in California, and my two brothers were born in 1984 and 1988. Financially, my father's engineering degree and knowledge of computers put him in the right place at the right time. They were living the American Dream.

But my parents wanted a girl.

Pari.

Just add an *s*.

Mickey's Hand

Politics

Rick tells the Germans he doesn't care about politics. He is just a saloon keeper. I don't buy a word of it.

Barack Obama just won the Presidential election.

Politics is a strange subject in my home. My parents are lifelong Republicans who supported John McCain. They say he is a maverick, a war hero, and experienced. He better be experienced—he's 71 years old! I admit that McCain has my respect. Anyone who has been in concentration camps as a POW in Vietnam has to be respected. He was tortured. Brutally. In fact, he reminds me of Victor Laslow in the film. During the war, both men had a cause. But McCain is just not my hero. He's my parents' generation's hero. I have to admit that even my folks think us being in Iraq for another 100 years is like way extreme!

Obama has me. It's his words: "There are no blue states or red states. There is just the *United* States of America." When I discuss Obama at home, my parents turn into cynics. They say things like: "Politicians are corrupt. Obama is naïve. He has big dreams, but what has he done? And don't even get me started on Hillary." And it goes on and on.

As for Obama, I ask them, "What hasn't he done?" He comes from the lower middle class, he's black, he went to Harvard, and he's done public interest work on the south side of Chicago. He's a lawyer, he's married, he's a father, a senator, and now a president, and *he even writes his own books*. Obama admits he used drugs, unlike Clinton's lame, "I didn't inhale," crap. Yes, he could be assassinated. Reagan, whom my parents love, was shot, too. I watched Obama's wife, Michelle, explain her feelings about this. She said, "He is a black man and he could get shot anytime, just filling up for gas. Does he just hide away?" I tell you, my parents remind me of what Rick says in the film: "*I* am the only cause I am fighting for." Is that what Americans like my folks have become?

"Look," I told my dad, "I get that we have problems in other nations, and we have problems here, too. New Orleans is still a mess. The world is a crazy place. But do we make it better by blowing up a country like Iraq and killing 60,000 civilians all in the name of freedom? What if we put the money we spend, the billions we're still spending in Iraq, into putting the world back together instead of blowing it apart?"

After I say this, he says what he always says.

"Fine, save the world. Just don't raise my taxes. When you get older and you pay taxes, then you will understand."

And I am left to wonder—were they always this way?

Madison's Hand

Heroes

Rick tells Victor Laszlo he is a hero to the free world. Laszlo merely replies that he tries his best.

April's father is back from Iraq. In one piece, thankfully. We had dinner with her family and he told us about the latest events. Cities in Iraq are still in ruin. Broken glass, broken dreams. Rubble. The people are digging out. They know the troop surge has kept the violence down. He says, "The thing is that the last seven years has been one surge of violence after another."

The evening's words were a tornado of images: lost highways leading to nowhere; fear of suicide bombers at any corner; body parts found; children lost; orphanages; beggars; businesses trying to rebuild; shoppers fearful; electricity off and on and off again; people torn between the land they love and the prospect of a better life if they leave; tribal leaders ruling; religious intolerance; jihad.

In the kitchen, my mother said, "We push our values on these people and we don't understand their culture. Do they even want our Western ideas of freedom?"

April's mother said, "Do we want to be 'occupiers?' I want my husband back. This next tour coming up in April is his last tour, I swear, Linda."

Occupiers. I thought of *Casablanca.* It was officially "Occupied France." Do we want the Iraqi people to see us that way? Is there such a thing as a good occupier? We started out heroes in Iraq, didn't we? Are we still the liberators, or are we the enemy? In *Casablanca,* it was all black or white—heroes and villains. Rick reminds Ilsa that the Germans gray uniforms, but she was always in blue. Is it all shades of gray, now?

April's father talked to my dad later that night about an investigation he did. I sat near enough to hear him. The investigation was about the suicide of a young American in the infantry. The boy killed himself—shot himself right under the throat, up through the head. April's father put his fingertip under his chin. Evidently, something had happened between the boy and his commanding officer (his C.O.). April's dad said that he read the soldier's dairy as part of the investigation. He said, "It was obvious from reading that this kid was cracking up. Getting bawled out by the C.O. was just the last straw."

My dad said that the media here recently reported that there have been 2,000 suicide attempts by Americans serving in Iraq, and that some 150 had actually happened.

April's dad said he understood. "You don't know who to trust over there. We send kids into this with a degree of training in Middle Eastern values, but it is far too little and often too late. Sometimes these kids are just praying they come out alive." April's dad said at the funeral for the soldier—after learning what made this kid take his life—well, for the first time in a while, it got to him. He broke down.

He and my dad looked at each other in a way that required no words.

I couldn't help thinking that a hero is someone who puts a cause—the needs of others—before their own. But what is the cause in Iraq?

Ilsa Lund was right. She looks at Rick and tells him that the world is a crazy place and anything can happen.

Right before she leaves Rick in Paris, she pleads with Rick to kiss her—kiss her like it might be the last time they will ever be together.

I wonder if my mom said that to my dad at the front door when he left on his last tour.

How could they be so brave?

Rhiannon's Hand

Play it again, Sam

In Casablanca, the owner of the Blue Parrot asks Rick if he would sell Sam, the piano player. Rick explains that he doesn't sell human beings."

Sam, of course, is black.

Today I told my mom that I am going to the Winter Formal Dance.

"No, Mom, it is not the Prom. The dance is at school—but it's more dress-y than other school dances."

I watched my mom carefully when I told her I was going with Donald…and that Donald is black.

"Black…you mean African-American…?"

"Yeah, Mom. Dreadlocks, too."

That is when I got the, "Is this something serious?" talk. I wonder if this would have happened if Donald was white. Maybe so. My mom not racist. I mean, I think we're all a little twisted about race in this culture. All of us, black, white, brown, everybody. My mom says it's our history, our legacy. And she says we all have to work to get beyond it. You see someone, and right away you notice their race.

I remember an experiment my mom and I saw on *Oprah* where these black guys asked people for the time or for directions, and then the same guys were made up to look white and went to the same places and asked the same questions. It was amazing—appalling, really—to see how differently people reacted to them when they were "white" as opposed to when they were "black." A lot of people wouldn't talk to the "black" men, and if they did talk to them, they wouldn't smile or anything. During a commercial, my mom asked me if I thought the experiment would turn out the same in London, or Tokyo, or Cairo. That's when I "got it" about race here. Sure there's racism in other parts of the world. But if you grow up here, you learn our particular brand of it.

So when I say my mom is not racist, I mean she's not any more racist than any of us who's grown up here, and at least she's working to move beyond it. No, her worried look about Donald was maybe partly about race, but mostly about something else. She said her problem is that she is too trusting. She said this is her fatal flaw with men.

"Mom, it's not contagious, you know. Your fatal flaw isn't genetic or anything," I said sarcastically.

"But don't be naïve, Rhiannon." She paused and then asked softly, "Does he like you?"

"I guess. I don't know, Mom."

Then came the barrage of questions:

What do his parents do?

What do you mean, "You asked him"?

You say he is a good dancer?

"No, Mom, I don't need a new dress. I will wear what I wore to the wedding."

"Yes, Mom, he is cute. Tall. Dimples. Nice smile. Round, dark brown eyes. And he's strong." She still had that worried look. Oh, why does it have to be so complicated?

When Ilsa and Rick are in Paris, he wants to know about her background, where she came from, and who she was before they met. Ilsa just reminds him that their deal was "no questions." I think Ilsa just wants to stay in the here-and-now, and not worry about the past. I get that, completely.

My brother, Chris, came into the kitchen as we were talking about Donald, and in between scoops of ice cream right out of the carton muffled, "He's cool, Ma."

"Yeah, Mom, you can meet him before the dance. As a matter of fact, this Saturday I am thinking of inviting my friends over for a movie. How about we spring for the drinks and they chip in for the pizza, Mom?"

"Okay. How many kids?" My mom started to lose the worried look.

"About ten."

My Mom loves it when I invite people over. She loves being everybody's mom. Maybe I should open a café myself. After all, "Everybody comes to Rhia's."

Mickey's Hand

Saturday—January 12th

The cast of characters going over to Rhia's was set: the four of us, plus Dan and Donald, Rhia's brother Chris, the twins Shannon and Clair, Maggie, and April with her boyfriend, Nick, who is not in Mr. B's class but wishes he was.

Seeing *Casablanca* again was great because there was so much I missed the first time. For instance, Rick is so interesting because he comes across as heartless, but he is not. He is heart*broken*. He seems jaded and bored. He plays chess with himself because he trusts no one. He is the anti-hero. You know, he reminds me of Han Solo in the *Star Wars* movies. And if you notice, Han Solo (the anti-hero) is the one who saves Luke Skywalker.

I guess Rick has the force.

Pari's Hand

Ingrid Bergman, the actress who plays Ilsa, is so beautiful. I read that she refused to do what Hollywood wanted, like plucking her eyebrows and smoking. Her character in this movie is so complicated. Of course, I can understand why she fell in love with Victor. He was her hero, so wise, and such an adult. He opened her eyes to the world. But I also understand her obsession and passion for Rick. He is not only romantic and strong, but he's also her age and her equal. Victor is more like a father figure. Oh, why does love always have to be so sad?

I guess they will always have Paris

.

Madison's Hand

Rick's Café Américain is so symbolic. It's carefree, a blend of nations, filled with music and song, a perfect escape from the hardships of the rest of the world. It's like the country it's named for, and maybe it is "sleeping," or maybe just playing.

And this got me thinking about what the Metaphor Café is to us. That's where we come together to talk about the stories in Mr. B's class, and to share the stories of our own lives and our loves. Sometimes those stories play out in films, books, art, or music. But if each of us was sitting home alone, without the others, it wouldn't be the same. It would be just another lonely bar stool.

I guess this is the beginning of a beautiful friendship.

Rhiannon's Hand

Louie is such a player! Beautiful woman can only get visas to leave Casablanca if they agree to sleep with him. He closes down Rick's Café because he's *so shocked* to find that there is gambling going on at Rick's…just as his winnings are deposited into his hands. He pretends not to care about politics and says he has no convictions and just follows the political winds, and yet he steals the film's climax by having Rick's back. At the moment of truth, with the dead Nazi leader laying at their feet and the smoking gun in Rick's pocket, Louie tells his police offices to simply…find the usual suspects.

I guess even a corrupt player like Louie can be a hero.

Mickey's Hand

It comes down to this. The fog. The plane. Victor Laszlo. He is so important. As the former editor of the Prague newspaper in Czechoslovakia, Laszlo must get to America to confirm the Nazi genocide. He knows the truth about the Nazi concentration camps because he escaped from one. Yet Laszlo is powerless without Rick's help. He lectures Rick that people have a destiny—a purpose that is either for good or evil. And Rick says he gets the point, but Laszlo wonders if Rick really knows that no one can ever escape their destiny. Laszlo knows that if you do run, your conscience will haunt you forever.

So now it all makes sense, Rick's speech to Ilsa, sending her away. She had asked him to think for the both of them, for all people, really, who have to make sacrifices bigger than their own needs. And he did. He tells her in the fog, with the raincoat, the hat, the propellers of the plane, the soft lens, the tear falling from her cheek, that she has go to with Victor. She is a part of his soul and she keeps his hope alive. Rick knows if that plane leaves Casablanca and she does not go with him, she'll regret it for the rest of her days.

Damn, I did not want it to end like that. But I guess it had to.

Madison's Hand

Conscience.
Sacrifice.
Romance.
Patriotism.

The fundamental things do really apply… as time goes by.

Chapter 11: We Were Warriors

Mickey's Hand

February 4th

"World War II is over. One war ends and new kind of war, a Cold War, begins," Ms. Anderson announced. Today all seventy of us were together in the library—soon to be our home away from home. In front of us was a display of books. We were curious and nervous all at once.

"This semester is about you understanding one important concept," Ms. Anderson continued, "and it is this: You don't know where you are *going* unless you know where you have *been*."

From the back of the library, Mr. Buscotti boomed, "It is our North Star!" Both of them looked like two Cheshire cats who had just set the mouse trap for us, the mice. "Look," Ms. Anderson said, "someone has to teach you that history is not just a memorization exercise for Final Jeopardy. You need to understand that *our* past affects *your* present."

Ms. Anderson pointed to the display of books, "So we selected these books for you—fiction and non-fiction. And believe it or not, *you get to choose* what you want to read this semester." Mr. B piped up from the back, "We want you to think of this as a book club where you read, talk, plan, and research together. Your book club will do all of this with the goal of writing your first major research paper."

I noticed immediately that the books seemed pretty new, like I had actually heard of them outside of school. All of the school history textbooks seemed to be written centuries ago by dead white men. In contrast, I had a hunch that what was lying before us was a panorama of pretty interesting issues.

Mr. B had walked up to the front of the room, and he picked up one of the books. "First, this book is Tim O'Brien's story of the articles and memories that the soldiers of Vietnam carried with them—sometimes to their death—appropriately called, *The Things They Carried.* This book will give you some real insights about what it's like to be a soldier in Vietnam."

He picked up another book, "Next is a memoir of the Little Rock Nine, the black teenagers who broke the color barrier in the Deep South in 1957. It is called, *Warriors Don't Cry,* by Melba Beals, and she was one of the nine black kids who attended the previously all-white

Central High School in Little Rock, Arkansas. Read this book and see if you don't agree that those kids were indeed warriors."

Ms. Anderson picked up a couple of books and took over. "We also have two different John Grisham books, one fiction and one non-fiction." She raised the book in her right hand, "Let's start with *The Street Lawyer* which deals with the homeless crisis in America. This one is fiction, and it's a terrific story that will keep you turning the pages." As she raised the book in her other hand, she said, "Grisham's other book is a true story called, *The Innocent Man,* dealing with how a small town in American rushed to judgment and put a man with a mental disorder on Death Row. Imagine that—sentencing someone to death for something he can't even understand."

They mentioned a few other books like *In Country* by Bobbie Ann Mason, and Sue Monk Kidd's *The Secret Life of Bees.* But the last book they talked about was one I knew would be a popular choice. "*Reviving Ophelia* is more like a therapy session than a novel," Ms. Anderson explained. She thumbed through the book while she talked about it, "Mary Pipher is a psychiatrist who tells the true stories of 'her girls,' the patients who come to her for help. The girls feel like they are drowning in a culture of pressure and popularity in America. They tell Dr. Pipher about the events that, 'blow them off their feet,' like the need to look perfect and the tragedies this leads to. They talk about depression, sexual confusion, and even the self-mutilation and suicidal thoughts that follow."

"Remember," chimed in Mr. B, "they just reported that one of every four teenage girls has an STD. One out of every four." Throughout all of this, Mr. B seemed intent on watching us and how we reacted to each book. And needless to say, that statistic got a lot of girls' attention. It did seem hard to believe.

I could not tell if it was shock or fear or just the surprise of being talked to as if we were intelligent, responsible beings. But I knew one thing—we were all listening.

"Pick the book you want to read, but remember," Ms. Anderson warned, "it will also be the topic you will research and write about." What followed was a practiced routine between the two of them, back and forth, beginning with Mr. B:

"Have we learned the military lessons of the Vietnam War?"

"Has racism diminished significantly since the Civil Rights Movement?"

"What creates homelessness in America and is it being ignored?"

"Are the mentally challenged and the poor victims of a criminal justice system that uses the death penalty as the ultimate consequence?"

"Are today's American teenage girls still struggling emotionally and physically even with all that has been accomplished through feminism?"

Then they looked at us and Ms. Anderson simply said, "Think about it. You decide."

What we did not realize was that for the next two months we would think of little else—at least in their classes.

It was time to meet at the Metaphor Café.

Pari's Hand

February 7th

Lattes in hand, the four of us writing this decided right away that we didn't all need to read the same book. It was better to follow our own instincts, each of us free to pick the book that seemed right. So for for me, the choice was clear: *Warriors Don't Cry*. My book club included Donald, Shannon, and a Vietnamese boy named Long who was so quiet that I was not sure I had ever heard him speak. He seemed scared. Shannon told me he was in the English as a Second Language program and still struggling with his English. I think this was his first "real" English class. His nature seemed gentle, calm. But something in his eyes told me that he had seen things that were bound to make you grow up fast. I would bet the need for kindness and patience had not been lost on him.

Typically, Shannon was super-organized because her soccer schedule demanded her to measure out her minutes with a dieter's keen eye. She had this much time for this activity on any given day, and that was it. Donald (I understand he's Rhia's new dance partner!) was so into the novel that he gobbled it up all at once, and we had to remind him that the rest of us are on a pace. It was hard for Donald to slow down. And poor Long was struggling to keep up.

We were swamped by history. There was Rosa Parks and the Montgomery Bus Boycott, which I never knew lasted over a year until finally Greyhound Buses backed down. There were Martin Luther King's non-violent civil rights protests. There was Linda Brown in a Kansas school being defended by Thurgood Marshall, who would later claim that his replacement on the Supreme Court (Clarence Thomas) was just what the government wanted, "A good nigger." There was the concept that "separate is never equal," and President Eisenhower's decision to protect the nine students we were reading about in Little Rock. We were appalled by the vicious, stunning attacks on the nine students each day as they tried to go to school. It was so bad that President Eisenhower decided to place around them the protective blanket of the 101st Airborne Division.

It was all like a scab that starts to heal over a bloody gash, and then it is ripped off again and again, and the blood runs down one's arm or leg, and no matter what we do, it just never seems to heal.

It made me think of Barack Obama. It was just 50 years ago that Melba Beals and Earnest Green could not attend a white public school in the South. And here we are now and Obama was winning presidential primaries in those same states.

So I bought an Obama t-shirt—and wore it proudly to school.

February 14th

When Shannon, Long, Donald, and I met in the library during school for our book group, we discussed the fact that we represented four different races and different cultures, which is very lucky because we will bring more perspectives to our project. We also agreed that although we saw the discrimination of the past, we felt *we* were colorblind.

But later, when we met outside the classroom, I was not so sure. I asked them to meet me at the Metaphor Café, and it was a little strange meeting my book group instead of Maddie, Rhia, and Mick. I even chose a different part of the café for us to sit, a wooden booth with high sides over by the wall. There was a big colored glass light hanging over the table. I hopped down from the booth to get some extra napkins, and when I came back Shannon was showing Long how to dunk a biscotti, and his eyes lit up as he bit into it. We found out Long likes strong coffee with lots of milk, and now he likes biscotti too. Donald and I split one of the big cookies. Shannon pulled out her notebook signaling that we'd better get started, and I was feeling quite hesitant to bring this up because we were all feeling so good about being colorblind. But I felt had to.

"Don't you see the looks that the Middle-Easterns get at school?" I asked the group. *Middle-Easterns* was a new word going around, like *gi-normous,* which I assumed was even bigger than *enormous.*

"I know, said Shannon, "they seem to just hang with each other—and talk Farsi."

"I understand some Farsi, and I hang with you," I said.

"But you're different."

"Really? How so?"

"Well, you're more… American, I guess," said Shannon.

"What does that mean?" Donald asked.

"Well, you want to be American. You aren't putting down our country."

"So is it not American to question or wonder about what America does in Iraq?" I asked.

Shannon was defensive. "Look, I am not a racist, and I don't have anything against Middle-Easterns. I just think that if people live here they should accept what we are and be more…" she flipped her hand around searching for the right word, "…you know, American."

"When do you become American?" Donald asked. "Look, Shannon, I am black. In 1957 in Arkansas, I wouldn't have been allowed to go to school with you. Those people in Arkansas didn't think people like me were even citizens. We had to fight and prove ourselves, that we deserved the same things as white Americans. And we are still doing that."

There was an awkward silence.

"Am I American?" Donald asked. There was no way Shannon was going to say a word.

Long just looked at us. "I am not. I was born in Vietnam. People are nice to me, but many people call me Asian, as if that is one big country. We ran from Vietnam because of Communists. I like America, but we have to start with nothing here."

"Why is it that outside of class, all the Asian kids hang together?" I asked.

"Because we are the same." Long smiled at us, shyly. "I don't know." I wondered if we all look for friends among people who we think are like us, who feel familiar, at least on the surface. Long took a sip of his drink, and said, "But I like being with you. You three don't look at me like some students do."

"And how is that?" asked Donald.

"Like I am a foreigner." *Foreigner* came out of his mouth like it was something distasteful—like stepping in something. We all nodded. We'd seen it, and we knew exactly what he was talking about.

Shannon took a deep breath and seemed to rally. "You know, we all get stereotyped," she said. Then she leaned forward and whispered, "Just because my sister and I play sports and we are, you know, bigger and jock-like, people think, 'Oh, they are probably gay or something.' That is such crap. Anybody who even thinks that—I don't even want to be near them." I don't think Shannon or her sister went to the Winter Formal Dance.

It was then that I saw the tears well up in her eyes and I realized not all warriors can avoid crying.

February 26th

"The Throwaway People" was the topic of conversation in class. It was a documentary from the TV show *Frontline.* Mr. B showed it to us yesterday. "The Throwaway People" are poor, black people—specifically, in Washington D.C.—that have been disconnected from America and have lost the American Dream. The author was a professor named Roger Wilkens who is also African-American. He interviewed many black people including a man named Pete Peterson, who lived in D.C. and ran a business there. Pete Peterson was clearly the hero of the documentary. One thing he said struck me and I wrote it down:

> *Middle class dreams are lost on my community. And when you are beaten down day after day, you give up. And the norms that society conforms to don't apply to you because as far as you care society has stuck you, so you say to hell with those norms…and you develop a fatalistic attitude. And once you develop a fatalistic attitude, then you cross the line between living and dying and neither one really matters.*

I always wondered what gangs were about and why people would be so desperate that they would join one. I wondered why gangs even existed if Dr. King and the Civil Right Movement had made such an impact. I always thought there was a happy ending to the whole race issue. I'm starting to see that it's not so simple. This documentary and Mr. B's lecture revealed the facts that were not provided in our nice "politically correct" textbooks.

Mr. B told us about what happened to him one night. He was leaving the film, *The Great Debaters,* with Denzel Washington, and behind him he heard an older white man who must have been 70 years old talking to his wife about how the movie reminded him of James

Meredith. So Mr. B stopped to introduce himself and the man told him this:

> *I guarded Meredith in '63 when he was going to Ole Miss—the university—and breaking that color barrier. It was pretty scary times. But I tell you something, I am damn proud of what I did and what he did. Hell, I even remember getting in trouble for standin' in the colored line to get an ice cream cone and the lady told me she would not serve me until I got in the white line. Crazy times.*

Then Mr. B made sure we understood the theme of the documentary. He said, "Look, Martin Luther King got his first wish—integration. We got integration in schools and housing as well as voting rights. But ironically, he never would have imagined that the Second Great Migration. That's when 250,000 people left the cities like Harlem or Shaw, which was the African-American suburb of Washington, DC. That migration left the poor, the weak, the old, and the uneducated in these inner-city ghettoes. Those throwaway people were abandoned by whites and even successful blacks."

Donald asked him, "But the successful blacks must have cared about the people they were leaving behind, didn't they?"

"Sure, they came back to visit," Mr. B answered, "but the money and the security and the stability that middle class folks brought to the community when they lived there was gone. And besides, successful black people wanted to escape the cities that had the memories of racial segregation and slavery. They were 'movin' on up' to the suburbs, just like their white counterparts."

"But Dr. King's second wish—economic equal rights—never came true," Mr. B continued, "because he was assassinated in 1968. Programs like poverty assistance and job training disappeared as the money was diverted to the Vietnam War. And if that wasn't enough, the 1970's brought with it three recessions that affected the poor the most. Manufacturing jobs were slipping overseas, like in the auto industry with the growth of Toyota and Honda. And in cities like Detroit, wages for poor black men dropped by half."

"Meanwhile," Mr. B was on a roll now, "in the suburbs, we began to see a new phenomenon—*white flight.* If there was a house for sale in a white area, and a black family bought it, you'd hear the phrase, 'There goes the neighborhood.' White families who didn't want black families in their neighborhoods would immediately put their houses up for sale. As white people panicked, the prices of the houses would drop with every sale. The white people who resisted white flight, and also those first black families who moved in, watched as less and less affluent people moved in. As the neighborhood became poorer, the schools went downhill."

Mickey said, "Wait a second. So successful blacks who wanted good schools for their kids left the city and moved to the suburbs where the nice schools were. But the whites moved out, and poorer people moved in, and the schools went downhill, so they were screwed. But just because you're black or poor doesn't mean your school should suck. That's not fair."

Mr. B pointed at Mickey and said, "Right you are! And the Supreme Court made matters worse in a decision called Milliken versus Bradley, in which the Court said that children could not cross district lines to go to a suburban school—they had to stay in the inner city boundary."

Maddie asked, "Why does that matter, Mr. B?"

"Good question. In the book *Savage Inequalities* by Jonathan Kozol," of course Mr. B had the book right there, and he held it up as he talked, "Kozol explains all this would be okay if all schools were funded equally. But they are not. Since the people who lived in the nice suburbs made more money and paid more in taxes, they insisted that their schools get more funding. So in many states, the 'savage inequality' is that upper-class and middle-class neighborhoods get sometimes two to three times more money per student than the inner-city schools."

"Two or three times more money? And that is legal?" Maddie asked.

"Not here in California and some other states," Mr. B said. "But in many states in this nation, yes, it is perfectly legal to fund school unequally. Kozol argues that the impact is that America's schools are once again separate and unequal. He says that now it's not race that divides us, but money."

We were quiet.

"Didn't the Supreme Court know what would happen when they decided the case you mentioned…Milliken?" Maddie pressed on.

"Yep, one Supreme Court justice did. He even said they were essentially reversing the impact of the famous 1954 Brown versus Board of Education case, which said that separate is never equal." Mr. B paused, but we knew there was more coming. "Oh, his name was Thurgood Marshall. Yes, the same man who argued the Brown versus

Board of Education case in 1954 was explaining in 1978 how the United States was going backwards."

I thought it was all shameful. To my surprise, Mr. B then said, "Kozol's newest book, *The Shame of America,* continues to document how this was still going on now."

I made a note to find that book, and I decided then that my theme for my research paper was as obvious as black and white.

March 4th

So my research began. Is America a less racist nation since the 1968 Civil Rights Act and Affirmative Action in the 1970's? Ms. Anderson explained those policies to us—and tested us, too! But I still asked myself about "The Throwaway People." Why do so many poor, young, black men find their way to prison? My research shows as many as 40% of poor black inner-city men under the age of 30 have been incarcerated. I wrote down what author Roger Wilkens implied that drugs for some poor blacks have become an escape…or the only way to make lots of money—but he concluded that drugs are a death trap.

The violence and the murder spill out not just from the inner-city streets, but also into the mainstream music that is wired into our ears through our iPods. Gangsta rap, with all its parental advisory labels, often dominates music sales. It is usually demeaning to women, and it also glorifies the drug scene and the criminal lifestyle. After all, "You gotta get rich or die tryin'," proclaims Curtis "50 Cent" Jackson, who brags that he has been shot nine times. He said this was necessary for him to achieve "street cred." His movie, *Get Rich or Die Tryin',* was a huge box office hit. I wonder why it is so appealing to white kids. The appeal really crosses all teenage worlds. Is this man, and others like him, the new media "hero?"

The music is dangerous. Rebellious. It is in-your-face anger.

This is the best I can understand their world. These people feel so powerless that the only way out is selling drugs, pimping, arming themselves, and having a gang. The vast majority of poor black inner-city households are female-headed. Where are the fathers? Gone. Where are the stable families? Where are the jobs? Gone. And is there anything that the inner-city schools can do to end this cycle of poverty? Oh yes, I forgot… the schools don't have any money.

My book club compared our research. Donald is arguing that while overt racism in America is not politically correct, the Jena 6 case shows that racism itself is still alive and well. On September 20, 2007, between 10,000 and 20,000 protesters marched on Jena in what was described as the "largest civil rights demonstration in years." This clearly shows that many people are against racism. The case itself is about the black students in Jena who had beat up a white student who allegedly was involved in putting nooses in a tree. The white students had picked that particular tree because the black boys would often sit under it. So nooses, the ugly symbol of the lynching of black people in the Jim Crow South, have returned.

Shannon has statistics on American neighborhoods where whites and blacks live in segregation. Sometimes this segregation is for economic reasons. But often, the segregation is because the two communities still want it that way.

Long learned that Affirmative Action has been dismantled, and that the violence in inner-city America is sometimes so bad that the police refuse to go in. Long was really surprised that sometimes the police fear that they will be "out-gunned" by the gangs themselves.

I am not sure if I believe that this is all any one race's fault. It all seems so complicated. I know that to really pull someone out of poverty requires effort and education. And I am not sure the government is making an equal effort for all kids in all schools. I'm not convinced that poverty and racism are really on the decline. It seems as if the rich or the middle class, regardless of the color of their skin, is saying to the poor, "We are not helping you. You need to help yourselves. Unless of course, it is Thanksgiving or Christmas, and our conscience gets the better of us."

Yes, there is Oprah and all the good she does, and the good she encourages others to do. And yes, many care and give and try. But as I was researching for my paper I came across a headline from the *Washington Post* regarding the Hurricane Katrina disaster saying that some critics of President Bush believe he undercut flood-control funding for New Orleans. This just kept bothering me. Reporters Jim VandeHei and Peter Bake wrote that President Bush kept asking for *less* money to fight against floods from huge storms that hit New Orleans. Less! Mr. B would remind me to site my sources so here it is. (*Washington Post,* Friday, September 2, 2005; Page A16) You can look it up.

Anderson Cooper, a CNN reporter, has this expression: "Keeping them Honest." As I wrote my paper, I promised myself I would make that phrase, "Keeping them Honest," my North Star. And I promised myself that no matter what racism and callousness I saw—from black people or white people or any color in between—I would remember that my generation has to rise above this. We have to understand the words that would begin my paper: "It is not the color of your skin, but the content of your character that matters."

If the people of my generation ignore these words of Dr. King—well, then there will be reason for warriors to cry.

Chapter 12: The Things We All Carry

Madison's Hand

February 7th

Mickey and I decided to break up—into different groups, I mean. All of us decided to spread out and grab as much as we could from the books, the history, and from the others in class. While I chose the book *The Things They Carried,* Mickey is reading a different book on Vietnam called *In Country,* and I know he wants to write about it here when I'm done. However, he heard about something Mr. B does with the song, "American Pie," and he is cooking up a special project for later. He won't even tell me what it is, but we are all intrigued.

Anyway, my book club is very different than the others. Other than my friend April (who transferred in this semester from the other class), there is Dan (who I really like), Mitchell (who I usually cannot stand), and Po. I've known Po since we were freshman together on Academic Team, which is a school club where we competed against other schools in a game sort of like *Jeopardy.* Po is very witty and probably smarter than all of us put together, but what I really like about him is he never, never makes that a big deal. Dan is quiet and thoughtful, which makes it really easy for me to get along with him. Mitchell, on the other hand, has a big mouth to go with his big ego. He thinks there are huge athletic scholarships out there waiting for him in football or lacrosse. Yeah well, good luck with that. It will be interesting to see how we all get along. April and I are like sisters. I mentioned earlier that we are both from military families and her dad is—as I write this—in Iraq. He is a communications officer and deals with the media a lot. It is his third time over there.

Yeah.

So we started reading the book, and I liked it and hated it all at the same time. Being in that jungle, those rice paddies, swamping through the murky water, the leeches, the sweat and the anxiety pounding on the nerves, the drugs, the depression, the smell of fear… It is so powerful that it makes me just lean forward into the book, and I feel like Harry Potter being sucked through the pensieve and dropped into the war walking right beside those guys.

But I hated this book. What really repulsed me was the fact that real men, boys actually (just a couple of years older than us), got drafted and were there for years and years dying for a cause they often either did not fully understand or they disagreed with. And people back home hated them for doing what they did. It's different today. The military is an All Volunteer Force (AVF) and has the support from the American public. At least for the soldiers, I don't hear or read anything but positive thanks and appreciation coming from everyone.

This book club discussion is pretty typical of how we get along, and how we see the book and the war in Vietnam. At least this is how we try to see Vietnam, even though we keep arguing about Iraq.

Mitchell: So what the hell were we there for? It was stupid.

Po: We were there to stop Communism.

Me: And because they requested our assistance because they were being invaded by the Viet Cong.

Mitchell: Yeah, well, that was stupid because we couldn't tell the difference between anybody anyway.

Po: Uh, what are you saying? That all the Asians look the same?

Mitchell: You tell me that you can tell the difference between the North and South Vietnamese. Besides, it was a guerilla war, and those guys just hung on the trees and sent their kids into the American troops with bombs and stuff. It was crazy. I sure as hell would not have gone, dude. I would be headin' to Canada.

Po: Okay, would you have fought Hitler?

Mitchell: Yeah, but that's *way* different.

April: He was taking over the world, and so were the Russians.

Dan: The Communists.

April: Whatever.

Me: Remember how Ms. Anderson explained that we believed in the Domino Theory. That was the idea that if we don't stop them somewhere, they would keep taking over more and more nations. They invaded Poland, Hungary, the Balkans, Czechoslovakia, and eventually Afghanistan…

Mitchell: Yeah, well, who cares? Let those nations defend themselves. Besides, that is not what I call, "taking over the world." I am not stupid. Those were nations that the Soviets thought belonged to them anyway…

Po: But that is exactly the point. Saddam Hussein thought the oil belonged to him, and that is why he invaded Kuwait during the first Bush administration. At what point do we say that international borders are legit, and you're not allowed to invade someone else?

Mitchell: Well that's all nice and everything if it could work. But, like, look at the news. We just invaded Iraq…

Dan: Several years ago.

Me: That is true, I agree, but we had reasons. I know, I know, we were not going to find WMDs, Weapons of Mass Destruction. But there were other reasons…

Dan: Now we're there to spread democracy—that is what President Bush said.

Po: Whether they want it or not.

Mitchell: Yeah, well, and judging from the friggin' suicide bombers, we're not exactly wanted…

April: But Saddam murdered his own people. He gassed them, and he probably still had chemicals of mass destruction—maybe not nuclear stuff. My father knew guys in the first desert war who were affected by the gas they used on them.

Mitchell: Okay, that was different, and then we kicked Saddam's ass.

Po: Bush tried to tell us Iraq was supporting the 9/11 terrorists even though we all know now there was no connection at all.

Mitchell: They're all terrorists to me.

Po: What does that mean?

And that is how it usually goes. We argue about everything that's going on today, and we lose track of what we're supposed to be talking about—Vietnam.

So tonight, I went home and Googled, "Vietnam war-protest songs," and I found a Wikipedia entry that was intriguing. Eventually I saw a link for a YouTube video by Bob Dylan called, "The Masters of War." I clicked on it and…bang, I was staring at Hitler, and American presidents like Nixon, and battlefields and guns and ships, and napalm in Vietnam, and all those images I have seen before in *Time* magazines from the 60's. Dylan's voice seemed timeless: he hated the men who dropped the bombs; he hated the men who sat behind the desks and approved of it; he hated the men who built the bombs; he hated the men who built the planes that dropped the bombs; he hated the leaders who toyed with people's loves; and he hated the leaders who hid behind masks and ran when the blood started to pour out from the young people's bodies.

I was blown away by his passion and his anger. I had heard about Dylan, but I never really listened to him. Like a lot of people, I thought his voice was weird (okay, bad). But tonight, I realized that this was the voice of a poet, not a pop star. I could not help but think, "Wow, he wrote this in 1963. He was so ahead of his time." I listened to his words from 1963, knowing that 58,000 American soldiers would eventually die in Vietnam. And 300,000 would be severely wounded. Those are the numbers they found as they tallied up the lost souls in 1970 (just American souls, of course).

And here's the part that makes me crazy. How many wars since then? How many presidents or congressmen or senators led people like my own dad into wars? How many good people fight for reasons none of them really understand? How many people never ask why? I think it's because we're afraid to ask. If we knew the real reasons for war, we'd have to make some big changes.

I am sure some people in 1963 thought Dylan was some punk—some long-haired, hippie, Communist who was too afraid to go and fight. It was the end of the song that really cut like a knife. It made me think of WMDs, pre-emptive strikes against terrorists, protecting our resources—our oil. I made me think of ethnic cleansing, a tyrant who must be stopped, and all those words that men use to justify the orders they give to attack. Yeah, Hitler was a master of war—but he wasn't the only one.

As the Dylan song echoed in my head I thought about the worst fear of them all—worse than guns and bombs—the fear that parents have when sending their children off to war. And I thought about the fear to even bring children into this world in the first place.

February 14th

Well, if I wasn't angry after "The Masters of War," then I certainly was after Mr. B came to our book group today to answer the questions we had. We asked him how we got into the Vietnam War because we were arguing, again, about whether it really was a *war* that

Congress had voted to support. Mr. B said that this was something the whole class needed to hear, so he called for everyone's attention and explained it this way:

"I need to fill you in on a disturbing set of facts that often get ignored in textbooks. Let's begin with an American ship—the *USS Maddox*. On August 2nd, 1964, the *USS Maddox* crossed into North Vietnamese coastal territory and was attacked by North Vietnamese patrol boats. On August 4th, both the *Maddox* and the *USS Turner Joy* claimed to have sonar detection of incoming torpedoes. However, this second attack was never confirmed. President Johnson supposedly hid the telegram from the *Maddox* indicating there were no torpedoes fired in the first place, but that will not come to light until much later in a famous case called the Pentagon Papers—more on that in a second."

"So in response to our ships being attacked, President Johnson ordered the first bombing raids against North Vietnamese military targets. Then on August 5th, he asked Congress to approve what he had already done, and Congress overwhelmingly approved what was called the Gulf of Tonkin Resolution. This was a big deal because the Gulf of Tonkin Resolution allowed the president to take 'all necessary measures' to protect U.S. forces. This included actions 'to prevent further aggression' which widened the battle to a full-on undeclared war."

"However, when the Pentagon Papers were leaked to *New York Times* by a man named Daniel Ellsberg, those papers revealed that the Gulf of Tonkin Resolution had been drafted months before the incident on August 4th. The President had the Resolution ready to go before any attack ever happened. The Pentagon Papers proved that President Johnson had even been committing infantry to Vietnam while telling the nation that he had no long-range plans for war. In other words, he lied."

Hmm. I was leaning forward in my chair, amazed at what the Masters of War would stoop to in order to have things go their way.

Mr. B had reached his crescendo: "And so the clincher came 4 years later, in 1968, when Congressional hearings revealed that President Johnson and the U.S. Department of Defense had 'misstated the facts' in order to gain public support for expanding the U.S. war in Vietnam. This is American history, folks, not opinion. This is how we got involved in a 'conflict' that never was a declared war. Needless to say, Congress and the American people were pretty unhappy—feeling lied to." Mr. B paused and looked around the room at all of us. "Sound familiar?"

Three letters kept hammering at me.
WMD.

February 26th

My God, 1968 had to be the most tragic year in American history. In Ms. Anderson's class we watched a documentary called *1968* and it made me cry. To think that Dr. King and Bobby Kennedy were both assassinated that year and that two dreams were snuffed out within months while war was raging out of control is just amazing.

We saw footage of the riots that followed King's shooting in Memphis—almost 40 years ago. Ms. Anderson also showed us a clip from the film *Bobby* where he spoke about the need to solve poverty in America. She explained he was opposed to the war in Vietnam and it seemed so similar to Obama's stance.

One thing Bobby Kennedy said in his last speech to the Senate about Vietnam struck me:

> *Are we like the God of the Old Testament, that we in Washington can decide which cities, towns, and hamlets in Vietnam will be destroyed? Do we have to accept that? I don't think we do. I think we can do something about it.*

Try replacing the name *Vietnam* with *Iraq* in that speech. And then ask yourself how different is this world, really, 40 years later?

In our book club today, we continued our discussions and arguments. But now there was a difference. It was becoming evident that we were, in the words of the Beatles, starting to "Come Together:"

Po: So President Nixon escalated the war after President Johnson left office, and therefore more and more troops were sent over with less and less training.
Me: And the anti-war movement was really getting going.
Mitchell: Yeah, but some of the hippies were just into the drugs, though.
Po: Wouldn't you want to get stoned then? It sucked.
April: I dunno. I always thought it was so cool. The 60's—people were always talking about it like it was this great time…
Mitchell: For drugs and sex…

Dan: Well, not for Tim O'Brien's soldiers in this book.

Me: And we're not even talking about the Agent Orange stuff that was sprayed on them, like Ms. Anderson told us about today.

Mitchell: That was so stupid. How could anybody think that some chemical that burns the crap out of the jungle and wipes out the trees would not hurt someone's skin! I mean that is so freakin' stupid! No wonder people got cancer…

Dan: Leukemia.

Mitchell: Whatever. I'm glad they got their asses sued off for that Agent Orange crap.

Me: You guys, I want to talk about that Kent State thing, where the students were shot…

Mitchell: Another stupid thing.

Po: I read an article about that. The girl was like four football fields away and was, like, not even protesting.

Dan: Yeah. She was working with some deaf kids or something.

Me: I think it was the beginning of the end of the war. I have an article in here somewhere that says the Kent State shootings turned public opinion against the war. It was the first time in U.S. history that unarmed civilians were fired upon and killed by armed U. S. servicemen. How horrible is that? I'll bet after it was all over, those servicemen never forgave themselves. It probably all happened so fast.

Po: But those four college students were dead, and nothing could bring them back.

April: So when did we finally get out of Vietnam?

Dan: Around 1973.

Po: We slowly pulled out.

Mitchell: What a waste. I don't know. We do all that and then bail out—it just sucked for everybody.

April: The book is really sad. The whole thing is sad.

Dan: And we did it all for rubber.

Me: What?

Dan: For rubber. That's what my dad was telling me. We wanted the rubber that we could get from Vietnam—

Mitchell: Are you serious?

Po: I believe it. There is always a money angle. What is in it for us?

Dan: I don't really know if my dad is right, but he sure seems convinced.

Rubber then. Oil now. Yep. It was all coming together.

March 2nd

It's been two weeks of heavy-duty research. The librarian is my new best friend. I have learned that books are better than websites, and that procrastination is a bad thing. Both Mr. B and Ms. Anderson have shown us how to break down a complicated assignment into little bits. On any given day, I can handle doing one little bit of the project. That's OK. Writing anything takes time and commitment.

The other day, the four of us at the Metaphor Café were wondering just how much we had written here. We just write (mostly at home on our own) and then email it. We don't even count the pages. I guess I've become the editor because I try to blend all the writing together before we go over it at the Café. So before I go into the whole Vietnam versus Iraq comparison, I have to tell you what happened today at lunch.

We kept wondering why Mr. B had said so little about the video—the one we made about his class. He'd never said anything apart from mentioning it during the dance in January. But today, he asked the four of us if we could eat lunch with him in his classroom and talk about the journaling we had been doing on his class. He said he was curious.

Well at lunch, we booted up our four flash drives and showed him what we had done. Some of it was still not blended together since I've been busy with research. Nevertheless, he was blown away. He asked what motivated us to do all this work.

Rhia said something like, "You did. We did. I don't know exactly. It's fun. It is like we are these underground artists writing a book, and meeting at a café to discuss it, and we have all this stuff going on in our lives." Rhia picked up a chip, and absentmindedly waved it while she continued, "It is weird, but when I write about my mom or Donald or my brother, it just makes me feel something, like I am just seeing things clearer."

Mickey agreed, saying, "Mr. B, the music helps, too, because I think that's the common language between us. I am sure you don't watch some things we do. And you always say you don't get us and all the video, rap, iPod stuff we are into. But the music—that is the thing that binds us. Even though all the Springsteen stuff is old school, we want to understand it. And we want to let you know we get it, and that we like music that's important, too, ya know?"

Mr. B was as intent as I have ever seen him, like he was absorbing us. Then he said, "I have always had students who talked to me about their lives, their problems, whatever. But I have never, never had students work so hard to chronicle my class. And what you all seem to do, too, is to open yourselves up to each other—on paper and in person. I am so flattered and so impressed."

We were all silent for a moment. Then Mr. B said, "I haven't said anything because I didn't know the extent of your efforts. Actually, it was April who told me how much work you guys had put into this. I feel like I need to contribute."

That blew us away.

I asked how, and he said any way he could.

Then I got up the courage to say two things: "First, would you read what we have written and let us know what you think? And second, we had this dream that we would try to publish this. Okay, we know this is crazy. But we also know a lot of kids wish that they could have a class like this. There are kids that want friends who really care, or who have problems just like us. And we think that maybe, just maybe we have a voice that others might want to hear. Is that stupid?"

Mr. B said, "No, of course not. It's not stupid at all. I think that there are moments, opportunities that come our way every so often. Sometimes things happen for a reason." And then he stopped, and closed his eyes and kind of laughed to himself. He looked behind him at the whiteboard and said, "Check out what I just wrote on the board."

> *There are those that look at things the way they are, and ask why?*
> *I dream of things that never were, and ask why not?*
>
> *-Bobby Kennedy*

We looked at each other—then at him. I said, "Then can you help us?"

He simply said, "Why not?" And we agreed to send him the chapters we had written and then meet soon at the Metaphor Café.

As we stood up to leave, Pari, who had been quietly taking all this in, turned to Mr. B and said to him: "I want you to know that I really like *how* you talk to us. You talk *to* us, not *at* us. You talk about what we think and how we act as if it's just as important as what you think and how you act. You have no idea how much that matters."

Then Pari really surprised me, because she said something that I have felt. I know Rhia has felt this, too. "You don't know how many times I went home and cried about things. Good tears, I mean." Pari looked down as if it was just too much to hold eye contact with him.

We all nodded.

March 4th

Watergate, Iran hostages, the Berlin Wall, Operation Desert Storm, Bosnia, 9/11, Operation Iraqi Freedom. We had to struggle to understand most of this—if it is understandable at all. I came to this conclusion:

Shakespeare got it right 400 years ago.

The Capulets. The Montagues. The unending battles between tribes, families, cities, and nations that *Romeo and Juliet* portrays will remain with us *until* we figure out that we need to have tolerance and compassion for each other. Without those, we are lost.

Are there similarities between the Vietnam and Iraq conflicts? Sure. But one major difference is that we support the troops today. We don't blame them. We honor their commitment. They are doing their duty—and doing it well.

I am not talking about Abu Ghraib and the military personnel who were dishonorably discharged because of their misconduct there. I am not saying that atrocities haven't occurred. What I am saying is that we are trying now to bring peace and order for the Iraqi people. I know that our "shock and awe" blew their nation to bits. But what is done is done, and we cannot ignore our part in it. I believe we have learned lessons from Vietnam, but we have also ignored the reasons America got involved in the first place.

Mickey's book, *In Country,* deals with what happens to the troops when they return from both Vietnam and Iraq. In both cases, the troops pay the price, not the Masters of War. The troops are the ones who face the horrors of war, losing limbs, losing friends, and sometimes losing faith that the USA will really support them.

Mickey's Hand

PTSD: Post-Traumatic Stress Disorder. Walter Reed Hospital. Hummers with no armor. Donald Rumsfeld. IEDs. Prosthetics. We had to struggle to understand most of these. Maddie is right that we have supported the troops, but we also have left too many without the treatment that America owes them.

Walter Reed Hospital, for example, is where a great number of troops end up as they leave the war. In my paper, I quoted the *Washington Post* writers Dana Priest and Anne Hull who reported the pathetic situation for one such soldier. His name was Jeremy Duncan, a wounded soldier staying in Building 18 of the Walter Reed Army Medical Center. He was recovering from a broken neck and a left ear that was half ripped off in Iraq. The article said that parts of the wall in Building 18 were missing and black mold was all over the rest of it. In his shower Duncan could look up through the rotted hole in the ceiling and see the bathtub of the room above his. The list went on: mouse droppings, cockroaches, worn out mattresses—disgusting. And the thing that pissed me off the most is that it is five miles from the White House. Hundreds of injured soldiers have suffered in these conditions in the wars of Iraq and Afghanistan, and the article concludes that another 700 soldiers are still waiting for treatment, wading through the bureaucratic red tape. (*Washington Post*, Sunday, February 18, 2007; Page A01)

It is appalling that we can send them in harm's way and then not give them the best care in the world. That is shameful. Just as shameful as when Secretary Rumsfeld was asked why the Hummers did not have armor underneath to stop the IEDs from causing such damage and he responded that we could not always do everything needed, saying, "As you know, you go to war with the army you have, not the army you might want or wish to have at a later time."

I just wish we had thought of all this before we went to war.

Madison's Hand

April 8th

Just before I turned in my paper, I saw a book at Barnes and Noble called *The Three Trillion Dollar War* by an economist named

Joseph Stiglitz who won the Noble Prize in 2001. He concludes that cost of the Iraq war already exceeds the 12-year Vietnam War…and that is not counting the long-term care for the wounded. I cannot even fathom what three trillion dollars means. I am not sure anyone can.

And so when I finished researching, I knew that the things soldiers carry, that innocent civilians carry, that presidents carry, that Americans carry is so heavy a load that it must be shared, or else the weight of it all will make us crumble.

Chapter 13: Drowning with Ophelia

Rhiannon's Hand

February 5th

I have the coolest book group and this is the book I really wanted to read—*Reviving Ophelia.* My mom recognized the book when I asked her about it. I think it was on Oprah or something. It's about teenage girls today and how hard it is to deal with things like weight, depression, boys, and sex. You know, the usual high school drama. I guess we will write a paper on whether things are really all that bad for girls today compared to, like, my mom's generation. I think it's a true story because Mary Pipher is a doctor or therapist or something and girls come and see her. I haven't even started reading it yet.

My book group is great. Maggie is in it. She is kinda tough, kinda hard core. Like she told the class way back in the hands project that her old boyfriend died of a cocaine overdose or something. Maggie is a little gothic—just a little. She wears lots of black clothes, but she's got dark brown hair, really curly and wild, but not dyed jet black or anything. Maggie wears lots of eye liner (but I've noticed that she is toning it down lately). She is very opinionated and smart. I knew right off that she'd be pretty interesting to get to know.

Then there is a girl named Elisa. She is very pretty, petite. I heard she is a bit of a party girl, you know, with a "flavor of the month" boyfriend. She *is* very flirty with the guys. Can't miss it. In class discussions, she didn't say too much during the first semester, but I noticed that she was quite the dancer. I sort of knew Elisa in middle school when she was less status-oriented, and even then we didn't talk much. She is talking more in class these days—seemed very interested in the love stories we did. Come to think of it, I saw her crying in the quad last week—I mean really crying, but mad crying, if you know what I mean. I wanted to say something, but I just didn't. I had to make one of those instant decisions, you know? Stop or don't stop? I just kept walking to maybe give her some privacy, but I felt weird about it just the same.

Now, Grace is very cool. During the first semester, Grace was in the other class with Ms. Anderson, and now she's switched into our class. Her real name is not Grace—Mr. B read her real name aloud during roll on the first day (I can't remember it). She is Chinese and changed her name to *Grace* to be more "American." But I think *Grace* suits her because she seems way more mature than a lot of girls. Not like mature sexually or anything (although I have my suspicions). It's more just the way she dresses and talks to me. It just seems that she is older. I know that she was born in China, and moved here in seventh grade. Grace has a sort of chic-Asian-fashion thing going on. She is always dressed casual but you can tell there is nothing casual about how she puts her outfits together. She is intentional about how she looks, and how she talks, and how she does everything. I like her.

And finally there is Tiffany—very much the surfer girl. Blonde in that oh-so-California way. I used to play soccer with her when we were little, and she also used to play softball. Now she is big into surfing. I imagine she is really good. She is a little on the quiet side. Tiffany is not the greatest student—you can kind of tell—but I do know she really likes Mr. B's class. She was a really good dancer in the Dance through the Decades, and she dressed up as Jean Harlow, the sexy actress of the 1920's. The boys were lined up for her. She sometimes hangs with the surfer crowd—which can be good and bad. Good because some of them are fun and very cool about people and laid back. Bad because a couple of guys and one of the girls are major partiers. Some are hardcore into drugs and others just smoke pot… a lot of pot. So I don't know where Tiffany fits into all that.

I decided to tell you a lot about these girls because *Reviving Ophelia* is really about us girls. I wanted you to know at least what I know going into it all.

One last thing: Mr. B made us promise tonight to see the YouTube video on Pipher's book. He said it was like the trailer to a movie…a very scary movie.

February 7th

Holy crap! The video is about six minutes long and it's just crazy. One of the most amazing things Mary Pipher explained in the clip was that after about three minutes, 70% of women who look at fashion magazines get totally depressed or feel ashamed because they don't look like those women.

Boy, did that hit home. Look, I haven't described myself physically, but I am kinda short and I could drop ten pounds. My clothes are just a little too tight and if I wear some things, I don't know, it would look way better if I was thinner. So when I see these magazines, I totally feel fat. And very short. And very much like I could *never* be like those models. Not that I want to be like them *exactly*, because I know about all the stupid things they do to look like that, and all the Photoshop touch-ups that are used. But it just makes me feel jealous—or like Pipher said, guilty—that I am not "better" than I am.

I know it is stupid. But as I discovered talking with the girls today, I was not alone.

First though, I wondered about the title of the book. I heard it had to do with the play *Hamlet* which is by Shakespeare, and which I have never seen. So I Googled the book, and I found that Mary Pipher was listed in an interview, and when somebody asked why she named her book *Reviving Ophelia*, she said that her book's title comes a tragedy where Ophelia is a totally happy girl until she falls in love with Hamlet. But she tries to please her father and Hamlet and she gets totally messed up, depressed, and eventually kills herself. So Ophelia's death is sort of a metaphor for what happens to many girls who are completely confused about what is expected of them. They lose themselves to what boys and others want of them…or from them. They become someone else. Who they *really* are just dies.

So I did a little more reading and discovered that some people say Ophelia kills herself by drowning in a brook, but others say that she falls from a branch of a tree that broke from the wind or something, and so her death was accidental. Either way, this book is Dr. Pipher's attempt to revive poor, dead Ophelia—and us.

When our book group began talking with each other, we all had a lot to say. Grace said her family is conservative and out of it, as Chinese parents tend to be. "I feel like my Chinese friends and I have had to figure out growing up in America by ourselves. My parents demand good grades, and want me to be a doctor or lawyer. But they think I am too opinionated for a 'Chinese girl.'"

"Well, you are!" I said, and we all laughed.

"But talking about sex or boys or anything like that with my parents is just not happening, believe me," Grace declared.

Maggie told a different tale. Her dad was into drugs, and so her mom divorced him when Maggie was a little kid. Maggie never sees him. Her mom is close to her, but she is so paranoid that Maggie will screw up that she makes herself and Maggie both crazy.

"It's like my mom is afraid I have too much of my father's genes or something, and that I am going to be a druggie just like him. She sees some people I know, and she assumes I am like them. And of course my old boyfriend—my mom just about went insane when I was seeing him. I tell her I am not into drugs no matter what anyone around me is doing, and she needs to trust me. She wants me to be all goody-goody, but I'm just not like some cheerleader girl with pink ribbons in my hair and all that crap. It's weird. My mom and I fight and all that, but we are close. I am her only daughter, the only kid actually. And she tries really hard, you know."

All during this conversation, Elisa never said a word. But I noticed she was listening intently, nodding a bit here and there. I remembered the day I saw her crying with some guy. I wondered if that had anything to do with why she was so quiet.

"I like how the book talks about the girls. I like that these are real people's stories. Some of them are really sad though—almost pathetic. I mean, how does a person get to that place?" I said.

Then Tiffany looked at me and asked, "Well, have you ever made yourself throw up?"

"No."

Tiffany looked at all of us, as if she was deciding something. "I've done it. And after, like, the third time, I started to wonder if I was bulimic."

I'm pretty sure the rest of us just stopped breathing. I know I was stunned.

"Well, are you?" Grace asked. We all waited, and my heart was breaking for Tiffany.

"I don't know. I worry about it. Reading about these girls is good for me because I see a lot of me in them—well, some of me." Tiffany said. "I have not done anything like that for a year, but I used to back when we were freshman."

"Did you just want to be thinner?" I asked. "Because, Tiff, that is so crazy. You are so perfect. I would kill to have your body

"I think it was a lot of things, you know. I wanted to be so popular, and I wanted to have boyfriends. I had this idea of what high school was supposed to be like. And it wasn't. Instead I just felt scared to death all the time. I just don't know." Tiffany paused, and we waited because I don't think any of us knew what to say.

Tiffany sighed. "I still get tempted to do it now and then. It's been a lot harder to stop than I thought. It's easier when I eat well, you know? But when I eat too much, pig out on ice cream or something, that's when I want to do it. Just get rid of it, you know. But I tell myself, 'Hey, that's crazy. Do you really want to be crazy?' And then I just tough it out."

We must have looked a little skeptical, because Tiff dug deeper to try to explain. "It's like, I have to be OK with myself for overeating sometimes. It's really hard, but I tell myself that I'm OK – it really is OK. And I take that decision not to do it, and it's just like taking a wave, you guys. You see a wave, you choose it, and you don't look back. You paddle like hell, get your feet under you, and you ride forward. If you hesitate at all, you miss the wave. So when I get tempted to do the bulimic thing, I choose 'No,' and I paddle like hell. I get myself busy with other things, call someone, walk my dog, go on Facebook—no hesitation. Never look back. After a while, I realize I'm golden. I didn't do it." Maggie smiled at Tiff, letting her know she understood perfectly.

Tiffany continued, "And I *have* stopped doing it, and you know what? I just realized that I'm proud of myself for that. Reading about these girls," Tiffany patted the book with her finger, "that's where I might be if I didn't fight it. So, I guess I'm doing okay." And Tiffany smiled. I had tears in my eyes, and I wasn't the only one.

We moved on to safer topics—what we liked about the book, which girl in the book annoyed us—stuff like that. But all the while, I was thinking about Tiffany.

I think we all were.

February 14th

Mr. B decided to visit our group today and he began with a few questions.

"Who is Gloria Steinem?" he asked.

Blank faces all around.

"Feminine mystique?"

Maggie said, "Something about how women are mysterious?"

"Okay, how about something more basic like Woman's Lib?" I could tell Mr. B was toying with us. He knew we didn't know some of this stuff. He was trying to get us to realize we had a lot to learn.

"You guys need to put something together when you read *Reviving Ophelia*," he told us. "It was written in 1994, and that is a generation *after* the sexual revolution, the Pill, the ERA, and Roe versus Wade. So you girls need to ask yourselves a few things. Namely, how does the women's movement of the 60's and 70's affect girls today? Remember girls, you four, you are the daughters of that revolution. Your mom's might have burnt their bras, believed in free love, been to Woodstock…"

"You can stop right there, Mr. B" Grace smiled, "because *my mother* never did that. She was in China!"

We all laughed. Even Elisa.

"Well nevertheless, you are here now, and NOW is the name of the National Organization for Women. Gloria Steinem was the founder of NOW, the publisher of *MS Magazine,* and also a Playboy bunny!"

Maggie said, "Isn't that, like, ironic...or at least very strange?

"That is what you girls need to find out. What does the expression *glass ceiling* mean to you?"

"I'm all over glass slippers," I said. "You know, Cinderella."

Grace saved us, "Glass ceiling has to do with a job. It means that a woman can only rise so high in a business before she hits an invisible glass ceiling, right?"

"Yes, Grace, you have that right. Is this the way it is today, some 50 years since 1968? Have things changed much? So the next time you all meet, you need to know about some of the things I've asked you about. You are too smart for me to just tell you."

Then he left us to go pester another group. And we were left to research, I guess.

I did wonder why that stuff mattered—about the women's issues, I mean. Here we are reading about girls nowadays, not about the women's movement. So I asked Mr. B about it after class. He simply asked me, "Where is your mom right now?"

"At work."

"Yes. I suspect almost everyone's mom is doing the same thing."

"Yeah. I still don't get it, Mr. B."

"When does she get home?"

"About 5 o'clock."

"She must be awfully tired."

"Exhausted…usually."

"So, no mom in an apron baking you cookies and making your dad a martini after *his* tough day, huh?"

"Nope. And no dad either."

"Sorry, I did not know."

"It's okay. But I still don't get it."

"I suspect, Rhiannon, that you have to figure out a lot on your own—you and a lot of girls. It's not too easy being the 'second generation' revolution." Then he looked me right in the eyes and said,

"You are Ophelia, and I am very happy to know that you are not drowning."

If he only knew how sometimes…
I feel way over my head.

February 16th

OK, a lot has happened. I went on a date—a real date—to the Winter Formal with Donald. That is a huge story for a number of reasons. My mom was really happy for me and made a big fuss. I have to tell you it was the happiest I have seen her in a while. She did not seem in any way freaked that Donald is black. She went on and on about him being nice and sweet. She also went a little spastic about sex and drugs. I'm like, "Mom, gee, we are going to a dance *at school.* We are not going clubbing or some other weird thing. And Mom, we are going to dance—really dance. He is the best dancer and so chill, Mom. Chill, okay?"

So Mom and I did something we never do. We went dress shopping together! Now that is a story. She freaked out a little at the prices, of course. I was more concerned with the color and style. I wanted a "little black dress," the kind that is simple and elegant—and unfortunately costs a fortune.

In the end I found a "little green dress," dark green, sleeveless, satin-like, and very cute. Mid-length, cut a little above the knees. The back has a swooping curve. I found perfect dark green shoes (one inch heels so I won't kill myself dancing), and as a bonus, I found a matching purse and jade earrings. I put it all on when I got home and just stared at myself in the mirror. Mom just stared at me too. I kept thinking about how all this happened because Donald and I were just so into the swing, bopping to some 50's song. And here I am. I knew Donald was wearing an olive double breasted suit. I hoped people would be green with envy.

The Winter Formal was two days after Valentine's Day, so that was the dance's theme. I was a little surprised that Mickey and Maddie did not go—disappointed, really. I asked Maddie and she said that they were probably going to go to the prom, and so they were going to skip this dance. Pari said that nobody asked her, which sucks. I should have told Dan to ask her, but he is so shy—and she can be the same way.

I need to play the matchmaker later with those two.

The whole night was fun. We went to an Italian restaurant called Giuseppe's and it was romantic and not too expensive. The funny thing is when I told him we could split the bill (and he said no, and I said yes…), we found ourselves talking about the women's movement and woman's lib. I told him how women felt that if the guys paid for everything, then that's not equal. And that is when Donald said something like, "Look, let's not talk about the research paper, of all things. It is so totally not romantic!"

We split the check.

But more importantly, we split dessert—a killer pastry called a cannoli with dark chocolate chips in a creamy vanilla filling with more dark chocolate shavings on top. Boy, I needed to dance that off.

And the dance was fun, but they only played one swing song and that was because the students in charge of the dance insisted the DJ play something old-fashioned that kids could swing to. And more kids were out there dancing swing than I thought. I even saw Elisa and her boyfriend dancing. I waved to her, and we danced over and kinda talked while we danced. She seemed sort of happy but, boy, there was some strange vibe between her and this guy she was with. I think he was older, maybe a senior from another school. Of course, nearly all of the music was pretty much hip hop or pop. When they played a slow song, we were actually doing a fox trot. Donald held me the way Mr. B had taught him. We didn't care what anyone else was doing. We just were into each other.

We laughed a lot. I laughed more with him than I have ever laughed with a guy. And his dimples are so cute.

And he called me Rhiannon.

And he drove me home.

And he walked me to my door.

And I kissed him.

February 26th

Our group talked today, and talked and talked. There is another group in class reading *Ophelia,* and they were done in something like 20 minutes. Meanwhile we just kept talking. I finally asked all four of my book club buddies if they wanted to meet at the Metaphor Café tonight (just like Pari did with her book group a while back). And to my surprise they all said yes, even Tiffany.

Of course we told our parents we were working on school stuff. Study group, you know. And the funny thing was—we were a study group. But it was a crazy conversation. Crazy. So after we met, I got home and to the best of my recollection here is a summary of what everybody said.

Maggie laid it all out on the table: "Okay, women get screwed in the business world, still. They don't make as much money as men, and the ERA never passed, and feminists are called *fem-i-nazis* by this big dork guy. People blame women for everything, like the failure of the family, because women are out working. Never mind the fact that their money is needed to make ends meet. So I'm sitting here thinking, do I dare write a paper saying that the women's movement failed?"

"But it didn't," I said, "look how far we've come. There is Hillary, and there is Oprah, and a bunch of other successful women. I found an article saying that now there are more girls than boys in universities—first time ever in history."

"And girls have more freedom than ever," said Grace. "They choose their own careers and have more confidence. Like girls are asking boys out."

"And who did you ask out?" Tiffany asked her.

"But that is not the point." Grace smiled, and we laughed. "I feel I could if I wanted to."

"If you are willing to be rejected." We laughed again, but more of a nervous laugh. Then I realized it was Elisa who had spoken. Finally.

Maggie got back to the point again, "But look, we are not going to write some paper about women 30 years ago. We are going to write about how our world is now. This is the world our mothers, who are like 40 or 45 years old now, have left for us. And it sucks."

"Mary Pipher's big point," said Tiffany, "is how girls are valued only as sex objects..."

"We are valued for what we look like and how sexy we are," Grace clarified.

"That is why we have eating disorders and boob jobs. Seriously, I know a girl who had one *this year*," Tiffany whispered. "They are huge now!"

"I think I know who you mean," Grace said.

Suddenly the light mood ended with an announcement.

It was Elisa.

"I feel so much pressure, you guys." And she started to cry. We all sang a chorus of, "Oh, what's the matter?".

"My boyfriend and I got into a big fight, last week, and it is all about sex." The tissues came out. "He keeps pushing me, and I tell him I am not ready yet. But he keeps saying I'm a tease and that he is so frustrated. He says he'd rather break up with me than have me keep leading him on."

OK, I was a little surprised. First, to look at Elisa, you'd think she'd be the least likely one of us to be a virgin. She was dressed very sexy—tiny skirt, tiny top—just very skimpy all around. She was not in sweats and a hoodie like I was, for instance. I thought she must be freezing.

Second, she just gave off the vibe of being very mature, sexually. She did not come across as Little Miss Innocent. It was more like, "Hey baby, want some of this?" I mean, she'd smile up at a guy and tilt her head just so, and kinda tip her boobs out—sexy as hell. So all this was weird. Then it hit me.

"This is exactly what we are reading about, Elisa." I said. "You, me, all of us, we are so screwed up. Crap. Everything we see is us girls practically looking like porn stars. That is what our culture is selling us, you know. Every friggin' TV show, music video, clothing store—all of it," I said.

Grace followed, "And if we don't measure up, then we are losers. Or we freak out and start to not eat or hurl or…"

Tiffany cut her off, "Or we give in and have sex. I know about that too. You guys are going to think I'm such a screw-up. First the bulimia, and now this, too. I'm really not such a bad person. I'm a good person who just… Look, Elisa, if you don't want to do it, don't give in. Don't be like me! You can't take it back after."

Then Tiffany started to cry. But she kept talking too, so we listened.

"I was so stupid, really. I mean, I didn't even really like him all that much. We were at a party and I was pretty buzzed. And we went out to his car. I thought, 'Well, it's just biology. It's no big deal. Let's just do it. Get it over with.' So we did it, and afterwards I acted like it was no big deal. I acted like, you know, as long as I don't get pregnant or get some disease or whatever, it's no big thing. And we just went back in to the party like it was nothing." Then she took a breath. "But later I felt so stupid. He, like, never even saw me much anymore. Like the whole thing was just to get in my pants and feel like a man. He didn't even care it was my first time. I wasted my first time on that jerk."

Tiffany wiped her eyes and looked out the café window, "Well, I didn't get pregnant or anything because I'm on the pill. My mom made me go on the pill a while before because she was, like, really worried about me and some of my friends. I am so glad she did because I was so naïve. So stupid. So don't let him do anything to you, Elisa, that you are not cool with, OK?"

It was more a demand than a request.

Elisa nodded, and by then we were all crying. The owner of the café came over. He's a really nice old guy—Mr. Metaphor we always call him—but he is really Mr. Davis. He asked, "Girls, are you okay?"

We told him we were fine.

"You don't look fine. Don't tell me. This is about boys, right? You know, they are nothing but trouble," he cautioned. And he said it exactly the way Mr. B would have. *How weird* I thought.

We kind of laughed. Pretended all was fine. Smiled at him. Told him thanks for all the great coffee drinks. Hugged each other.

Then we left. I got in my Mom's car and turned on the radio and this Dixie Chicks song "I'm Not Ready to Make Nice" came blasting out. They were singing about being so mad that you just can't apologize for the crap that people do to you. And even though others say you should just get over it…you can't.

And I thought about Tiffany and Elisa and Grace and Maggie and boys and the crazy world that breaks hearts. Then the song ended; the cliché that *time heals everything* seems to be something they are waiting and waiting for.

Me, too.

And I walked upstairs to kiss my mom goodnight.

March 4th

We've all been researching like crazy. I don't want to numb you with all the stuff we learned—like the fact that one in four girls has a sexually transmitted disease (STD). One in four. Boy, is that depressing. I look around and I wonder which one of us has it.

I do know this: Dr. Pipher's book hit us just like the hurricane she describes at the end of her book. We girls are blown by forces that are so powerful that we are often swept away. We have nothing to grab on to, little to help us from being blown away by what she says is a toxic culture. Our parents are too busy. Our friends are just as bad as we are. Our teachers are overwhelmed. And often, we don't even bother to ask for help. So the hurricane sweeps us away.

Growing up is like being in New Orleans and not knowing that Hurricane Katrina is moving in. When you're a kid, you notice it's raining—you notice that the TV ads are trying to sell you stuff. As you become a teenager, our culture hits full force with wind and rain and unimaginable power on girls—and boys, too. Only we don't even realize it until it's too late. The media isn't just selling us stuff. It's selling *us*! And it doesn't matter how many iPods, cell phones, cars, jeans, purses, whatever, we buy at a mall. None of it really fills the void we feel.

To survive a culture hurricane, we need someone we can trust who's been through a storm or two. Someone who listens and who knows how we feel. Someone who knows what we can do about all this…and what we shouldn't do. And we need to ask for shelter from the storm.

Elisa fears rejection. What will she hang onto if her boyfriend dumps her while the hurricane winds howl?

Grace is blessed with confidence and she feels she can get what she wants. She's lucky to be on higher ground.

Maggie is more cynical because she has seen people swept away to their death. She has her mom though, and sometimes all you need is one good tree to hang onto during a storm.

Tiffany didn't recognize the hurricane in time and she has paid a price with her health, her virginity, and her innocence. But she survived.

And me?

I am a dreamer. Look, I don't want to be someone's Mrs. John Doe. I don't want to have my whole life hang on some man's vision of me. I certainly don't want a man whose big dream is to have some trophy wife. I will never be that "trophy" anyway (and I don't want to be).

I want to be Rhia. I want to take the risks, and I am willing to accept the responsibility that goes with them. I want ambition, yet I know I will endure rejection too. I know that my mother's marriage collapsed, but I don't believe that I'm genetically destined to share the same fate.

And I need my mom.
I need my brother Chris.
I need their strength, and they need mine.
I know I cannot go it alone.
I have needed Mary Pipher's advice.
People get through hurricanes by sticking together.
I was Ophelia, but I have revived and survived.

We girls are stronger from all that has happened to us. I don't know if I want to be a lawyer or a writer or a teacher or a business woman. I don't even know what college I will go to. But I know one thing now that I did not know before I read this book.

I am Rhiannon, and I won't blow with the wind.

Chapter 14: My American Pie

Pari's Hand

March 31st

A long, long time ago…

This is how Mr. B began class. He told us, "Don McLean's 1972 song, 'American Pie,' is a poem that eulogizes an America of bygone days, a country that is no longer as innocent and as carefree as in McLean's youth. He grieves for the America that he took for granted up until Buddy Holly's fatal crash in February of 1959."

I didn't know what he was talking about. Buddy who? I thought "American Pie" was a movie—a stupid movie, as a matter of fact.

He asked us if we had ever been to a funeral. Some hands were raised.

"Anybody speak there, at the funeral?" Well, of course somebody did. There's always a little sermon or speech at a funeral.

"I have spoken at someone's funeral. And let me tell you that a eulogy is not an easy speech to give. You have just a few minutes to sum up how you feel about a person and what impact they had on you and on others. I spoke about a wonderful woman, a secretary here at our school who really helped me when I was a young teacher. She helped everyone—the kids, the coaches; and the principal was probably her best pupil. We loved her.

"Well," Mr. B continued, "American Pie" is a eulogy. It is a song about a country we all thought we knew—only it may have been an illusion. Think about it. *Miss America?* Is she really a wholesome beauty queen? Or is she a botox-injected, buttocks-lifted, breast-implanted parody of wholesomeness? *Apple Pie?* Fifty-four percent of the calories are from fat. *Chevy?* American car sales have plummeted. Who wants a Chevy or a Ford or a Chrysler anymore? We lost our loyalty to American cars back when the Ford Pinto's gas tank would explode on impact, and Ford knew about the problem and sold the car to us anyway. *American ingenuity?* The O-Rings on NASA's *Challenger* could not handle a launch at certain temperatures, and the students of the first teacher/astronaut watched her die during take-off. *Corporate Responsibility?* Dow Chemical's "Agent Orange" was a defoliant that killed the trees in the jungles in Vietnam, but it also killed our own troops under those trees. But Dow Chemical (as the commercial said), 'helps you do great things.' Great things? We lost a president, lost a civil rights leader, lost a war, and lost a generation to drugs."

Mr. B was on a roll—and we knew it. Nobody interrupted or asked questions.

"So who were James Dean, Bob Dylan, Buddy Holly, Ritchie Valens and, Chuck Berry? Tell me about JFK's assassination in Dallas. When was the British Invasion? What were "fallout shelters?" What did Charles Manson do? Why was *fire* a symbol of the 60's? I'll tell you why. People burned ROTC buildings, draft cards, and bras, not to mention that after Dr. King's assassination, city's like Watts in Los Angeles and Shaw in Washington, DC, burned."

Mr. B paused, and said, "Remember, 'You don't know where you are *going* until you know where you've *been*.'"

Then he played the rest of the song—with slides of events that I either had no idea about, or if I did, it was only because I saw it in some *Time-Life* infomercial or on the History Channel or in some dusty textbook. Of course, I recognized the Kennedy assassination, the Beatles, the Vietnam War, and Martin Luther King, Jr. But Mr. B was not as interested in what we knew as much as in *what we felt*. He kept pushing one idea to us—"American Pie" was about the end of the innocence.

We were intrigued. Our next big assignment was that each student was to create their own American Pie. The bell rang, but not before Mr. B gave us a list of things to ask our parents about, or Google if we had to. Somehow, my parents didn't seem to be the type to ask about James Dean, hippies, Buddy Holly, or The Byrds—and wasn't that a typo?

To my surprise, my parents were about to end my innocence and explain their own Persian slice of American Pie.

Mickey's Hand

April 1st

After class today, I had a talk with Mr. B and then with Ms. Anderson. I discovered that Mr. B had already told Ms. Anderson about the book we were writing. Well, anyway, I wanted their permission to watch *all* the students present their American Pies—not just the students in my class. I wanted to write about them, kind of a tribute to my classmates. But to be honest, I also secretly wanted to experience the "writer's world" of researching and reporting. I wanted to see if I could capture the feelings that might bubble over during the presentations.

Both teachers were happy that I wanted to do this, but felt that they should have the ability to edit what I wrote if they thought something was too personal to be read outside of class. They explained that there was a trust among the students—that the kids believed what they said here *stayed* here. I agreed that I would not violate this trust, and that anything I wrote for our book had to be okay with all people, including the students who were revealing themselves.

Our American Pies would be different than the song. Don McLean was describing the America he experienced in 1971, but our assignment was to show how we see *our* America. I can tell you that for many of us, American doesn't seem so innocent. We are kind of numb to political corruption, sports scandals, and AIDS. These things don't shock us. They are just part of life as we know it. I guess it is like that song my John Mayer—we're just "Waiting on the World to Change."

Mr. B's American Pie project requires us to write and illustrate eight "slices" of American life, like the pieces of a pie. There'll be a slice about science and technology, a slice about politics, and a slice about history. For each of these slices, we have to show how whatever it is matters to us personally. Then there's a slice about a pivotal moment in our own lives. We get to do a slice about art or music, and a slice about a piece of writing we like. And finally we'll do a slice about a man and a slice about a woman that we admire.

Mr. B told us to put the project on a poster board or *anything* that seems appropriate, and to be as creative as we can with photos or even artifacts that symbolize our slices of American Pie. I wondered if he'd better be careful what he asks for. When we turn the projects in, we'll have to orally present at least one slice to the class. I have no clue yet what I'm going to do.

Later that night, we all met at the Metaphor Café, but a little later than usual because of my ball game. It's baseball season now, and I had this great baseball game today. You gotta understand that in some ways, I live for baseball. So if you're not a baseball fan, bear with me. My team had started out so well this season, winning 9 of the first 12 games, but we had been in a slump as we played schools in our league. I was pitching in relief, and being left-handed, Coach used me only to face other left-handed hitters. I felt I could do fine against right-handed hitters too, but our team had a lot of seniors, and I could tell Coach was trying to balance winning, being fair, and seniors' egos.

So today, I got to the field and Coach had a team meeting. He said that he had bad news. Our starting pitcher and shortstop, both seniors, had gotten food poisoning at some fast food place and they were both in the emergency room. Everyone looked shocked. He told us that the two juniors, me and Terrance, were starting in their place. We were the only juniors on the team, and this was a huge game. The shock turned to panic as I realized I was going to be the *starting* pitcher!

Everyone just looked at me like, *"Crap, we are so dead."*

That was when Coach just smiled and the entire team shouted, "April Fools!" Then the "sick guys" poked their heads up from on top of the dugout. After the surprise wore off, I busted up. *Really funny, guys.* I guess this was our initiation, and I've got to admit it was cool. Anyway we won the game, and Terrance and I both got into the game.

I even struck out someone—a right-hander. Coach gave me a thumbs up.

Maddie winked at me from the bleachers.

Ya gotta love baseball.

Madison's Hand

Pari was the last one to get to the Café tonight, and she was the one that surprised all of us for several reasons. She asked me, right away, to write down what she was telling us because she was having trouble getting it all into words. Her story spilled out all in a rush.

She started by saying she had been talking to her mother on *Nowruz*, the Persian New Year, two weeks ago. Typically her mother and father were very positive about both of Pari's older brothers, and her mother rarely confided that she was displeased with them. "Never to *me*, anyway," Pari said. But on that day, Pari's mom confided that she and her father were upset with her brothers. Apparently, the brothers were not going to finish college but were going to work full-time instead.

Then she remembered something her mother said to her on that holiday: "Parivash, you are our last child, but in you we are reborn."

Pari said, "I heard it, but I didn't really hear it, you know? I just figured she was being weird with the whole *Nowruz* customs. Besides, my brothers are always treated pretty special by both my parents, and I just didn't feel that I ever could be as important as my brothers in my parents' eyes. Not ever."

The three of us stared at her. Strange, I thought, because she is so talented and she never seems to think she is. This is one thing that makes Pari so different from other kids who are smart—she is the least conceited person I know. And I realized something else. Here was a person who seemed so distant and mysterious to all of us just a few months ago, and now we are the ones she's coming to. And she's coming to us not in the privacy of the journal writing she shares with us, but face-to-face in the soft evening light of the Metaphor Café. And I got it, and it made me smile at her. She trusts us.

"So anyway," Pari continued, "we were having dinner tonight, and my brothers were not there, again. I asked my parents some questions about when they came to America, and if they were around for the whole hippie-60's thing. And I even asked them if they knew the song, "American Pie." And my father looked up at me and said yes, he knew the song. I was not expecting this."

Nor was she expecting what came next.

"Parivash," her father began, "we are very, very impressed with you."

"Impressed?"

"Yes," said her mother, and her tone implied *well, of course we are.*

Her father continued, "I remember the song, although I didn't really understand much of it, however. It played when your mother and I teenagers...your age. We were still living in Iran. Under the Shah, it was very westernized and American music was very 'cool' to us. Anyway, America has its faults, no doubt, but your mother and I both came from families that valued education and progress. And America represented the most advanced nation in the world." Pari said her father always speaks in a formal way—she said it's kind of a Persian-father thing.

For a minute, Pari thought this was going into a long I-remember-the-day dinner speech, but suddenly her father turned it 180 degrees around: "Pari, we love your brothers, of course. But they just don't seem to have that passion that we have, your mother and I, that desire to learn and to grow..."

Her mother interrupted, "They don't really love school the way we did—the way you do."

Pari put her fork down and stared at them. She wasn't sure where this was going and she wasn't sure she really wanted to know. In a flash, Pari realized that in many ways it is easier to be the one that is not noticed, not expected to do great things. She held her breath.

"Pari, we know how smart you are, how determined you are, how good your grades are," her father said, "and yesterday your English teacher called us and personally told your mother and I how proud he is of you, and that you wrote the most outstanding research paper in his class."

"And he also told us about the book…" her mother gushed.

"Book?"

"Yes, yes, the writing you and your friends are doing." Pari said her mother seemed to be sitting up so straight with pride that she thought she was about to ignite like a rocket and zoom up through the ceiling.

Back in the Metaphor Café, there was a silence as we all took it in. Rhia finally said, "Oh, my God. What did you say, Pari?" Rhia's eyes were huge. Mickey and I knew about Pari's paper. We had proofread it and it was Terrific (yes, with a capital T). But we had no idea that Mr. B would mention anything about our book to our parents. It felt like a betrayal, or maybe just the idea that we had been found out stung us a bit.

Pari said she was taken so off guard that she didn't know how to react; she stumbled through words like, "We are just journaling. It's no big deal. Thanks for…." And she kind of faded out.

Pari's father said, leaning across the table, "Parivash, we want you at university. You belong there! Your brothers do not." He sat back again, and continued, "It is a new year, and it is about time we tell you what we think of you and that we know you have great ability. We do not care about the cost—okay, yes we do—but we are willing to do whatever it takes to get you to a university that suits you."

In the Café, our coffee drinks sat there untouched. "You guys," Pari said to the three of us, "my parents have never talked to me like that—like they talk to my brothers." We could see Pari struggling to understand it. "Actually, it was more than that. They were talking to me *not* like I was one of my brothers, but like I was something better than my brothers. I was…was…."

Mickey nailed it, "*You are what your parents are*—you are the one who can travel to a new world, like they did."

We were all quiet for a minute.

Then Rhia leaned forward and hugged Pari and said, "Happy New Year!"

Pari smiled and then laughed, but I sensed that the tears that were welling up in her eyes were not the least bit comical.

Mickey's Hand

April 8th

Boy, being a junior in high school just sucks sometimes. It is spring break, and what does that amount to? Let's see. Do we get to relax and go crazy? Nope. Try SAT test preparation, college discussions, homework that gets piled on during break, and AP tests just around the corner.

Yeah, we tried to pretend it was vacation, but I don't think any of us had too much fun. I had a baseball tournament for a couple of days, and that was a relief from everything. Just sitting in the dugout eating sunflower seeds, talking baseball, getting in a few games—it was all good.

But the thing we all promised each other was that we'd work on this book. We would re-read some of the chapters and clean them up. We agreed that we could procrastinate over lots of things, but not this—not if we were going to finish it on time. We know that much more than a book is coming together here.

We talked at the Metaphor Café about our American Pie projects. Rhia's pie was made out of an old Ben and Jerry's tie-dye t-shirt. She stuck all the "slices" of information on it with Velcro. Maddie was literally going to bake an apple pie with large toothpicks sticking out with flags holding all the info about her admired people and events. Pari's was really cool, too. It was one of those pastel-colored jewelry boxes in a hexagon shape. It was, as she described it, a "secret box" with all these hidden compartments that revealed each slice of her pie. I couldn't help but think how appropriate each one of their designs were. Being the biggest procrastinator of the group, I had not started yet.

I'd been more than a bit distracted by my own discussions with my parents. I just didn't want to tell anybody. I guess it is a guy thing, to keep things to yourself, huh? Probably pretty stupid.

Well, anyway, I texted Maddie after we left the Metaphor Café and asked her to call me when she got home. She wanted to know why.

I told her that I needed to talk to her about my parents and college and stuff.

"i m cmng ovr/sys" (I am coming over. See you soon.) That was all she said, and I could tell that that was that. Maddie is pretty stubborn.

It was 9 o'clock at night, which is pretty late for company, but Maddie is always welcome—my parents love her. They see her as the perfect student and a good influence on me, I guess. The funny thing is, apart from some really superficial things, they don't know her really. Sometimes I am not sure if they know me either.

Maddie quickly said hi to my folks who were watching TV, and I steered us outside to the patio where we could talk. As soon as we sat down, Maddie looked at me and asked, "So what's up?"

"Well, hmm. Okay. My parents are really into college right now. They want me to be as into it as they are, and they are so out-of-control, I can't even tell you."

"Yeah?"

"Yeah. It is about everything—I mean they are even talking about grad schools, business schools, law schools, East Coast, what universities are ranked in the top ten of this or that. It's too much, Maddie."

Maddie knew me too well. She narrowed her eyes and tilted her head at me.

"Are you sure there isn't something else, Mickey? I know your parents didn't start all this college stuff just now. They've been talking about this since you were a freshman." She took my hand and asked so softly, "So what is the real deal here?"

Moment of truth.

I gently squeezed her hand and let go, stood up and paced a little, gathering the words. She waited patiently. "Maddie, what do you do when you wake up and realize that what your parents believe, what they raised you to think, well, it's just not what *you* want? I mean, what I want is not what they even remotely think about." I looked toward the house, and then back at Maddie. "My dad is lawyer for a corporation and my mom is an escrow officer. They are so conservative. They are Republican through and through. My dad even wears a flag lapel pin sometimes. Our TV is permanently tuned to FOX News. Bill O'Reilly is practically a part of our family. My parents think that CNN is part of a left-wing conspiracy."

Maddie sat still. I know why. She is everything that my parents are not.

"Whenever politics comes up I cringe, Maddie. They think that Obama is too inexperienced and they say, 'What has he accomplished? He didn't serve in the military so what does he know?' They then go into their Bill Clinton rage with, 'He had no moral center.' And Hillary? Don't even get them started!"

"Well, they can't be too pleased with Bush."

"No. But they say things like, 'Well, have there been any attacks since 9.11? No, because now people know what we will do if they attack us. Bush needed to be tough.' They go into their 'best defense is a good offense' crap, and I just sit there so they think I agree. Finally, one time last week I asked them, 'Well, do you want me to enlist?' They looked at me as if I was crazy and said, 'Of course not.'"

"So then I asked them whose sons and daughters should pay the price for our freedom." Maddie looked surprised, and I said, "Yeah, I know. It was a loaded question. But they looked at me and said, 'You are so naïve. Fighting for your country is an honor and there are plenty of people who want to serve. You don't want to serve, and we don't want you to. That doesn't mean that their lives are worth less than yours. It just means that the military is not for everybody. We honor our troops.'"

"Maddie, it goes on like that with everything." I dropped back down in the chair, tired as tired can be. Maddie continued to wait for me. "When I dare to touch on any career that doesn't fit into their plan for me, they freak. Writer? 'That doesn't pay much.' Reporter? 'Well, only if you go to law school and then do something with it like Bill O'Reilly.' Teacher? Not a chance. They think teaching is so demeaning that they can't even talk about it except to say something like, 'Mr. B is the exception, Mickey. Most of the teachers are just so mediocre and have no ambition.' My father always says that teachers often can't even afford to live in the neighborhoods where they teach."

I leaned back to look at the stars. Maddie took hold of my hand again. "I don't know, Maddie. I feel like one day I'm just going to blow up at them. And I don't want to do that. I don't want to hurt them. I mean, most of the time I just ignore it and leave. But how can I ignore what schools they want me to apply to or where I want to go? Can you imagine if I told them I wanted to take a year off before college and go build homes for Habitat for Humanity? Or what if after college I go into the Peace Corps?"

I knew Maddie could do things like this. Her parents loved Jimmy Carter and heard him speak at their church. They had planned to go next year to repair homes damaged during the wildfires last year. Her father didn't need to wear a lapel pin with a flag because he wore a uniform with a flag stitched above his heart. Maddie's parents didn't care what she did as long as she was passionate about it and did her best. They seemed to listen to her. I got the feeling that even if Maddie turned out to be very different than them, her folks would accept *her* even if they disagreed with *her views.* I know that Maddie's folks can't afford to send her to the really expensive colleges that she could probably get into, but they will do their best. And that is enough. They are happy together.

"When will my folks ever be happy, Maddie?" We watched some clouds move past the moon, and she moved closer to me. I put my arm around her and she felt so soft and fit so perfectly in my world.

Finally, she spoke.

"Mickey, here is what I think. I think someday—soon—you have to tell them how you feel. Maybe not about everything, but about important things. You need to hope that they understand. If they don't, then you have to ask them to respectfully disagree. And then you have to make *your* choices."

She let that sink in, and then continued, "If they don't support you, well then, you will have to ask yourself how much *you believe in what you want.* And if you really *do* believe in these things, then you may have to go it alone."

The implications made my heart stop. Pay for college myself? Make my way in the world totally on my own? And yet, I could see it. It would take me longer. I'd have to work full-time and go to school at night—figure out how to get grants and loans. It certainly wouldn't be easy. And I might make some mistakes along the way. But it could be done.

Maddie wasn't finished yet. "One more thing, Mickey. If you pretend now, while you're in high school, when does it stop? When do you allow your folks to see the real you? I'm not sure it gets any easier as you get older."

She was probably right about that. Maddie straightened up and looked right at me, bright-eyed and hopeful. "Besides, your parents just might surprise you."

That is why I really like her.

She is my Emily Webb.

Mickey's Hand

April 17th and 18th—The American Pie Presentations

I had my notebook in hand, and Mr. B explained to everyone that I was taking some basic notes for him so he could pay closer attention to people when they spoke (which was true, but I also went back later and showed people what I wrote and asked their permission to share these stories). For the next 110 minutes, each person showed off their version of the American Pie. One by one, my classmates spoke from the heart. I had no idea how rich and hearty their servings of "American Pie" would be—and for me and my classmates, how difficult they would be to digest.

Here, then, are some of my journal entries:

Elisa

The first girl is petite and outgoing. Elisa seems confident, in touch with the fact that every guy is staring at her. She was in Rhia's book club reading Ophelia. Then she begins: "I am most inspired by Jesus Christ and I am a Christian." She is uncomfortable stating this out loud. I would not have pegged her as overly religious—the exposed midriff, strapless tops, and flirtatious attitude do not fit the stereotype. However, that is exactly what this is about. "I have picked a piece of white lace to symbolize this part of my American Pie. It represents that…when I get married…I want to be a virgin…." Her final words are the kind you struggle to get out, choke on them, stammer. Elisa's face flushes, and her eyes burst like balloons. She leaps behind her poster to hide her face. The class is as frozen as am I. Then a boy floats over to her, and gallantly places in her hands the class' tissue box. He takes a bow. We all laugh. The tension relaxes our throats.

"I am so sorry. I can't even believe I am crying. It is so stupid. I am sorry." Her face reappears from behind her poster, and then darts behind out of embarrassment. "It's just so hard, you know. The pressure to give in to boys—and—I don't know—to myself. The idea that, 'Well, everybody's doing it!' I am sorry, but I can't stop crying. I just…."

I feel the urge to rescue her. Mr. B pipes up: "Elisa, you are doing great. Do you want to wait?" Suddenly a deeper resolve propels her, as if she has finally come out from her closet to reveal her true self—a girl who could be having sex with boys so easily, but a girl who ultimately views herself as traditional. And she steadies her ship.

Bradley

I used to know Brad when we were little kids, playing baseball. He is big and tough—not football tough, but the hard shell of a guy molded by events out of his control. I did not really know him anymore. He sat on the other side of the room. It's funny how desks can separate you in a room. He spoke softly: "My slice of American Pie I want to speak of is music. Actually, it is a Jackson Browne song. Yeah, I know, this is Mr. B's kind of music. But Jackson is cool. His songs are about things I feel, you know? Anyway, there is this song about a house he remembers when he was growin' up. I'll never forget that song. I used to listen to it all the time after my dad left us. My mom and my sister and I were just blown away when he left. He just left. No warning. Gone. My mom, you know, she is a 3rd grade teacher. Well, we didn't have much money. We had to move out of the house. It was fast, like within a week of my dad leaving, we had to pack up—move to this cramped apartment. I drive by that house and I get angry. I am still so angry. I hear that song, and it reminds me of how much I had, and how much I lost. An old house, you know. It was great. My room…." I glanced over at Rhia, who was wiping her eyes, trying to hold it together.

Phong

"My slice of American Pie isn't very American," he begins. Phong's pencil thin mustache bends around his upper lip like a strand of angel hair pasta. His jet black hair is slicked back and becomes my focus as he bows low to speak. H keeps his eyes screwed into the desk top.

"I choose to talk about my personal history." A long breath. "I am from Vietnam, and I wrote about it. My family came here when I was eight. It was not very easy. We were in prison. First my dad, then our whole family. They kept us together, except for my dad. I guess they thought we were against… we were against the government because my dad helped the Americans in Saigon. You didn't really know because they didn't say anything. Then they let us go. I don't remember too much, but that it was dark and we were hungry.

My parents were so strong. I know a lot of you guys have problems with your folks, but I just respect mine. My dad still doesn't talk about it. He doesn't talk much at all. I don't want to let him down, I guess, now that we are in America."

We look at Phong with the wonder of someone who's barely avoided a terrible car crash. Amazed. Appreciative. Another girl in class, Suzanne, asks him which prison. She is also Vietnamese, and she was in prison too. The class and I sit stunned. But Phong has his head held high now.

Teri

"God, I feel so lucky. This is a picture of my parents. Aren't they cute?" They are. So is she. Her American Pie poster is cut in the shape of a heart.

"They are so much in love—still. And we just bought a new house. It's huge. Things have gone well for them, financially—and I feel so blessed. I am so amazed because I have heard your stories, and I feel for you guys, but I cannot relate. I was kind of afraid to say this to you because I did not want to make you guys think I'm a spoiled brat and all."

"My parents are strict—well, stricter than some of my friends. And sometimes I get mad, but really it is their values that they have put in me that helps me the most. They love me and I love them. God, now *I am* getting emotional!"

"You know, when Mr. B taught us the swing dances, my dad got so into it that he got out the old albums and we danced and danced. He was… He was so smooth—and then my mom danced with him. They were into it—like they had danced every day of their lives. I want that, I guess. I want that feeling, too. I do. I really do."

Lisa

She begins with a big smile that lasts for seven words. "My mom is my most admired person." And there goes the smile. "Oh, crap…I knew this would happen. I can't help it. You guys, my mom is so strong, and I just can't tell you…." Pools of water fill her eyes so quickly that they pour down her cheeks. The anguish and the pain make her bend at the waist like a soda can with the air sucked out—imploding. "Oh, man, I need the whole box of tissues. I need to breathe."

We all laugh nervously. "Okay, anyway my mom is so strong. There are the three of us now. My sister was a sophomore, but I was just going into high school. My dad, he decided to move to New York. And he left us…." We wait. Wait. I can feel my heart beating. Lisa is a perky cheerleader, but she is so volatile—quick to judge, immature at times. Yet at other times, she is the shoulder others cry on. I guess she's had a lot of practice.

"We were so poor. My mom had nothing, except two scared daughters. And we had to pull together." More tears. The tissues are forming a baseball in her hands. "I will never understand how my mom did it. She is my inspiration. But it is very hard for me…for me to trust people. I can't believe I am telling you all this, blubbering like a baby. I am sorry. I'm sorry." She needs a father so badly that it just hurts to watch.

Long

Long was in Maddie's book club reading about the Vietnam War. He starts quietly: "I am sorry…my English not so good. Anyways, I choose for personal history my flag. I am from Cambodia. I was with my parents and my grandma. I really love my grandma because she do everything for me—make my breakfast, wash my clothes—all that stuff. My parents both farm on the land we own. I would help and go to school. I love the farm. I had places to go and explore things. But, so, one day my father says, 'Long, you will leave to go to USA. You will go in three weeks. You will stay with uncle.'"

"I say, 'Why? I don't want to go. Why?' I was 13."

"He say, 'Because you must get education.'"

"I told my grandma what he say. She knew. I ask her if she will come with me. She say, 'No, you go alone, Long. You are a boy, but soon you are a man, too. You go alone.'"

"I was so shocked. I had no idea I was to be alone in America. I have been here four years now. I have no grandma to make breakfast, wash clothes, talk to. Three weeks ago, my mom called me from Cambodia and say, 'Your grandma is dead. She had brain cancer.' I am so alone here. I never said goodbye."

I hope that after today, Long won't be so alone. I hope some of us, one of us, will reach out to him—today, tomorrow, the day after. I hope Long finds a friend in one of us. I hope.

Maddie

My Maddie. She is a mess before she even starts. It is such an emotional day and Maddie has a tissue balled in her hand, two on the floor, and a box on her lap.

"Okay, well, this has been emotional. I guess I am not going to make it any better. I want to talk about my grandmother who passed...."

That is about all she gets out. Maddie is one of those girls that really, really makes you want to cry. She cries from someplace much deeper inside her, and the pain of it is so intense you think she is going to break apart. But she doesn't. Maddie is tough.

"I want to read this letter she wrote me. It is my written word slice...okay...breathe...okay. 'Dear Madison...'"

It was clear that Maddie isn't going to be able to read that letter out loud on this day. Mr. B asks if it would be okay if he reads it to the class. Maddie nods, grateful for the help.

"'I want you to know you remind me so much of me as a little girl,'" Mr. B. begins. "'You are a little spitfire out there on the soccer field, and you speak your mind. People always told me I was too opinionated. Well, I just think that is too bad for them. I tell them if they can't stand the heat, then get away from my fire. I like that you have that same spunk in you. I wish I could see you get to go to college and get married and all those grand things, but I know what I would see—and I am sure proud of my little Maddie.'"

Maddie then musters up the composure to breathe out, "I really miss her."

Donald

Donald is, I think, dating Rhia. Well, they are a couple ever since the Winter Formal. Today, he is the opposite of everyone—cool, calm. That becomes so ironic as he explains: "Five years ago, when I was, what, 12 years old, my mom was diagnosed with a brain tumor. Okay, chill, you guys. She is alive and well. It was operable and all, and the operation was a success. Maybe I was a bit too young to really grasp it all then. Yeah, of course, I was scared for her. But I really did not get death then. I am not sure I even get it now."

"I kept her wristband as a symbol of what happened because I want to say that technology and medicine is what I want to focus on. The fact that we now know even more about the brain, and we are saving people like my mom—it's amazing. I think it is why I want to be in the medical field. A doctor even, maybe—I don't know. But I definitely want to go into medicine."

For the first time in the day, Rhia is beaming.

Allison

Allison is a dancer, like Pari. She is from Alabama and she has a big-time Southern accent. When it's her turn, she asks if she can play a bit of a song for the class because it represents so much of who she is. Then she fires up *Sweet Home Alabama*:

"You guys, when my parents moved us out here from Alabama after 8th grade, I was crushed. You all are really great and I love this class, and I have made great friends. I dance at the same studio with Pari, and I love the dance troupe here at school. But I made a deal with my parents that every summer I would go back to Alabama to see my best friend, Kelli. When Kelli and I were little kids, we were inseparable—and we still are. We talk almost every day or text or whatever. And we just know we are goin' to always be like sisters…"

Allison takes a long breath and looks down.

"It really hurts to think of all the things we miss together. It hurts to hear about her life and not be there. It…I don't know if you can understand…I want to be her maid of honor, you know. I am just…a country girl and…I just miss her."

Bastel

Bastel is, by far, the smartest math student in the school. He is very cool—but rarely speaks. Today he changes that.

"I am from Pakistan—but not really. I am really from Afghanistan where my dad was a detective for the police. He is my most admired person. Um, when the Taliban came to Afghanistan, my dad knew right away this was going to be bad. So he told my mom we were leaving to go to Pakistan. But nobody then could just leave, like you can here. It was bad. So my dad decided he would figure a way out. Basically, he knew that he could get across the border alone saying he was on police business. So one night, we drove toward the border, and he put me and my mom and my brother in the trunk of the car when we got close to the checkpoint. He told us to be really quiet—really quiet. My brother and I were so scared. You know, like those movies you see, like *Hotel Rwanda*, where you just don't know what will happen, or if you will die or something. Well, that was our family. We made it."

"When we got out of the trunk, my mother and father hugged, and then we all four hugged so hard—you guys—I almost knocked the wind out of myself. Yeah."

We just stare at him. None of us has any idea what to say.

"Yeah, so my dad is, like, my hero. And it all reminds me to not screw up now that we are here. Sorry I spoke so long, Mr. B."

Mr. B simply smiles and says warmly, "Bastel, don't worry. You just knocked the wind out of us, that's all."

Kelly

"I am a cutter."

That is how she starts. A cutter. Kelly? She is blonde, fun, popular—well, in the surfer crowd and she is friends with Tiffany.

Before Kelly says much more, the tears and the mascara are running. "Some of you know my folks got a divorce and we moved from Las Vegas. Anyway, my dad is in jail and he writes to me. My mom is kind of a mess. My friends' moms all watch out for me a lot. I don't know why I cut myself. I have stopped, but I know that sometimes I want to start again. But I don't. Mr. B, I think you are the reason I have it more together. I know how totally cheesy this is going to sound and all, but like, the lessons, and the sermons you give—they are…they help so much…and I know they help others. And I promise I will not cut myself again…okay…. "

Rhia runs up to her and hugs her, and they escape to the bathroom.

Later, when they return, I watch Mr. B talk to Kelly and give her his business card. He hugs her, and I can tell he is a little shaken.

Me

I decide it is easier to explain what I have to say by telling a story which is a metaphor for what has shaped me. So here is what I say:

"I won this medal here—it is a part of my personal history—I won it when I was like 10 years old. We won the Little League championship. It was so great. I was on the same team with Terrance, and I think Brad was on our team. Anyway, we were this kind of crazy team. Our parents were so into it and sometimes the pressure of it all made some of the kids cry or want to quit. In fact, one did quit, at least for a while. Yeah, I know, Little League—you would think people would just let us be kids."

"So thing is, it was the last inning and we were down by a run. And one of our best hitters was up with two guys on, and they decided to walk him and load the bases so they could pitch to me. Well, as most of you know, I am a pitcher—and not the greatest hitter. So with two outs, and the bases loaded, and the whole championship on the line…I was up. My dad just looked at me—he was an assistant coach—and he said, 'Tell me what you're gonna try to do.'"

"I told him I was gonna hit it between third and shortstop."

"He just said 'Good.'"

"So the first pitch was like a foot over my head, and I swung and missed. But all my teammates were cheering, and I just didn't think about anything except where I wanted to hit it."

"And then on the next pitch, I swung and it went right where I imagined—a line drive. I just put my head down and ran and ran and ran."

"Somewhere around second base, I saw our coach bouncing toward me from the third base line and I didn't get it. It was over. We won. Coach grabbed me, and the kids dog-piled me, and it was so cool. So cool."

I look at Mr. B and then at Maddie.

"Yeah. My dad hugged me, and he said no matter what would have happened, he was proud of me. And then my mom and grandparents waved. And then we shook hands with the other team and got medals, and went out for pizza. We were so innocent. Sometimes, Mr. B, I just wish the innocence never ended."

Mr. B looks at the class and responds: "You trade some innocence for wisdom, Mickey. Just don't let that wisdom sour into cynicism."

So, in two days' time we had plenty of pie. It was amazing. All the stories, some ordinary and others extraordinary, but all were important in their own way. We were stuffed, but satisfied.

Tonight, I was downloading music and I found out that Don McLean, the guy who sang "American Pie," had written a lot of great songs. But then I read where this other songwriter heard him sing in concert and wrote a song about McLean. The chorus of that song was so appropriate for our experiences of the last two days: after all, McLean was killing us all—softly, with his song.

Chapter 15: *Pleasantville*, Parents and Proms

Madison's Hand

April 26th

It is all flying by so fast. Time is my nemesis. I'm staying up late, waking up early. I've got this thing to do for an AP test; that thing to do for a scholarship. I think about college, think about my parents, think about Mickey, think about the book, then there is Math, French, Chemistry… Ouch, my head is spinning.

Okay, Maddie. Deep breath. Back to our story.

Over the last two days, our class watched the film, *Pleasantville*. Mr. B says it's an example of "magical realism," which just means that it's a realistic setting, but magical or utterly fantastic stuff happens there. He said it's a cult film, like *Big Fish* (which Mickey and I saw but few others did), or *Field of Dreams* (which everybody saw and Mickey constantly reminds me, "If you build it, they will come…they will most definitely come"). Mr. B told us we need to suspend reality, but only just a little, to see the parallels between the Pleasantville of the 1950's and our not-so-Pleasantville of today.

I had seen *Pleasantville* before, and so had Pari. But none of the others in our expanding circle of friends new anything about it. I knew that seeing it with Mr. B would be cool. When I saw it before, I laughed and everything, but it seemed either too corny or too weird. I can't remember.

Anyway, Tobey Mcguire (pre-Spiderman) and Reese Witherspoon (pre-June Carter-Cash) are the stars of the movie. They were very young then and believable as two teenagers (brother and sister) sucked into an alternate world inside their TV set. They get transported from their 1990's dysfunctional family with an unhappily divorced single mom into a TV Land "perfect" town of the 1950's called Pleasantville.

Everything in Pleasantville looks like an old black and white TV show, only everything *really is* black and white and shades of gray – no real colors. Even people are shaded a pasty black and white (and by the way, there are no black people to be found anywhere). This 1950's TV town has a basketball team that has never lost—or even missed a basketball shot! The big emergency for the fire department is a cat stranded in a tree because nothing catches fire in Pleasantville. And naturally, every mother stays home to prepare a scrumptious dinner for her family and a martini cocktail for her loyal, wholesome husband who opens the door, places his hat on the rack, and cheerfully calls his wife *Honey* and announces he is finally home from another grueling, man-in-the-gray-flannel-suit day.

Needless to say, this is not our world—but it was once someone's idea of paradise.

Pari's Hand

All four of us—and the whole class, really—was curious about many things the film promoted: open enjoyment of sex, free thinking, artistic expression, rebellion against established values… and most obviously the use of color, all sorts of colors, in a black and white world. What did it mean?

Right after the film ended on Friday, the bell rang and the class had no time to ask Mr. B questions. And we had lots of questions, especially since we knew we were supposed to start reading *Catcher in the Rye* next week. Just as we were leaving, Mr. B stopped me and handed me an envelope.

"If you guys are meeting this weekend at the Metaphor Café, then open this envelope, and read my questions one at a time, okay?" I think, now, that he was frustrated that he couldn't help us answer our questions about *Pleasantville,* so this would have to do for now.

Unfortunately, then, I only stammered something like, "Of course, Mr. B." I was taken off-guard. He is very warm, but also intimidating, at least to me. When I showed the others what he had given me, we agreed *for sure* to meet Saturday night at the Met Cafe.

When I got there, I ran into Rhia at the counter waiting for her drink. When she heard me ordering yet another latte, she chided me about being stuck in a rut. She said why not try a frozen drink since it was a beautiful spring evening. So I did. After I got my frothy, pink smoothie complete with whipped cream, I settled in at our usual table and pulled out the envelope. I unfolded the piece of paper inside and saw that Mr. B had written a little paragraph and three questions. I reminded everyone that he said to take the questions one at a time. And as I read the first part out loud to the others, I wondered where this was going:

> *In the Bible in the book of Genesis, Adam and Eve eat from the tree of the knowledge of good and evil. Eating the tree's forbidden fruit is*

considered by some to be the Original Sin. Was it God's intention that Adam and Eve stay in Eden and remain untroubled? Or did God know that they would eventually fail the test and eat the fruit?

Is mankind worse off having been evicted from Eden, or better off?

I read it three times. We all looked at each other wondering what this had to do with the film. Maddie was the first to offer an explanation.

"Well guys, in the film, remember where that girl offers Tobey Mcguire's character, Bud, the apple at Lover's Lane? That's pretty Biblical, don't you think? And it's got to mean something that when Reese Witherspoon's character, Mary Sue or Peggy Sue or whatever, comes on to that cute guy in the car, everything is already changing. He sees the red rose—and it's real red, and people literally start changing color."

"Yeah, why do they change color?" Mickey asked.

"Hold on," Maddie interrupted, "so as Pleasantville starts changing the way it thinks and acts, people start rebelling, questioning authority…"

"Or simply questioning just why they do things at all—like the hamburger guy who wonders what is the point of making burgers," Rhia cut in.

"Do you think the whole people-changing-color thing is a civil rights and racism thing?" Mickey kept asking.

"Well, color isn't about sex, because sex alone doesn't mean squat. Mary Sue has way more sex than the other people, and she is still in black and white," Rhia declared. "But what does all of this have to do with the question Mr. B asked?"

That is when I joined in: "Guys, let me tell you something about the Muslim view of creation. At least I'll tell you what I understand as the Quran explains it."

"You mean you learned a different Adam and Eve story?" asked Maddie.

I replied, "Well, the creation story in Islam has lots of similar stuff. It's just that there are six days not seven, and man gets made from clay instead of a rib, and Eden is paradise but it's not "earth" exactly. But here is the key thing I see: the angels look at man and wonder why God would create such a weak, imperfect creature. The angels even ask God why he would create something with the capacity to disobey him."

"Yeah, well, what did God say?" Mickey leaned forward, all attention focused on this question.

"Well, God replies something like, 'I know what you do *not* know.'" I paused to set Mr. B's paper on the table. "And that makes me think that maybe God knew that man would disobey Him one day. He gave man free will and knew that the evil angels—Satan—would succeed in tempting Adam and Eve. But do you think that maybe God wanted man to work for salvation, and to enjoy the highs and lows of what life has to offer?"

"Then why bother with the whole Garden of Eden thing at all? God could've just created them in Cleveland or something, couldn't He?" Mickey cracked.

I laughed, "I don't know, Mick."

Maddie jumped in, "Look, if Adam and Eve had stayed in the Garden of Eden where nobody and nothing dies, and everything is perfect, then there is no challenge, no effort—like Pleasantville where everything is always…"

Rhia cut her off: "Ta daaa! There's the connection." We stared at her. "That's what Mr. B is getting at here—with that first question." We smiled and nodded, pleased with ourselves. Rhia continued, "But in Eden, there is no sex. They don't need to have kids. Why? Because they are immortal. Adam and Eve didn't even know they were naked, right? So what is the point?"

"The point of what?" I asked.

Mickey picked up on Rhia's idea, "What good is good when there isn't anything bad? What is happy without sad? Eden, or Pleasantville for that matter, has nothing scary, nothing bad, but nothing exciting or risky…"

"Or sexy!" Rhia concluded. "Guys, I figure Adam and Eve made the right choice, or at least I think God knew what He was doing putting them in that garden with the snake."

I added, "Adam and Eve made the human choice, the predictable choice. But with the joy comes the sorrow. And in our world, that means wildfires, cancer, car crashes, war,…"

"But that is the *real* test, isn't it?" Mickey was excited now. "Survival of the fittest. All those things mankind had to face to survive made us use our minds and our courage. And to thrive, we had to pull together. Remember when Mr. B said that 9.11 was our generation's Pearl Harbor? He said something else too. Something like what makes us stronger is that we 'struggle for victory even in defeat.'"

"But look at what suffering happened that day. Those terrorists caused the suffering. There's no denying that this world is full of suffering. Not all of it is caused by terrorists, of course. But is that God's will, too?" I asked them. "I hear that all the time. For instance, can it be God's will for a little child have cancer?"

It was then that Maddie happened to glance at the paper on the table and said, "Wait, listen to this. Here's his second question:"

Why do people suffer?

Rhiannon's Hand

Everything comes easy to me, especially compared to my brother Chris. A lot of things are nearly impossible for him. He tells me that he reads something or hears something, and then it just disappears from his mind. I ask myself *why?* We come from the same place, the same "gene pool." Why does he have to suffer like he does?

I'm glad he is who he is though. I simply can't imagine my family without him. And the funny thing is that he is so popular. Everybody loves Chris. He is warm, kind, funny, willing to do anything for you. He'll get his hands dirty and do the things nobody else will do. He is such a good guy. I've never heard him cuss out anybody or just be crude—especially to girls.

So does he suffer because of his disabilities? I mean, I know he does. People have teased him (such jerks!). But we all get teased at some time, right? We endure, and so does he. I have to say that Chris lives his life with joy most of the time. He makes other people happy. I think being around Chris brings out the best in most people. I wonder if it's a fair trade-off. Everyone loves Chris, but will he go to the prom? I hope so. What does *suffer* mean anyway? And between Chris and me, who is the lucky one, really? Maybe we both are.

So all of this was flying through my mind as we read that second question and pondered suffering. I looked at them and said, "You guys, did you ever hear about how some cancer survivors say facing cancer made them better? That they have no regrets? Maybe we suffer because it just makes us stronger."

Mickey looked at me. "Kind of like scar tissue being tougher than the original skin."

"But what if they don't survive?" Pari asked. "What if they don't make it?"

"Well, think about it. We all die someday," said Maddie. "We all suffer, you know? Isn't it about what we make of whatever life we get? It's like Emily Webb said in *Our Town*, remember? She said something like, 'We waste time like we have a million years,' and she asks, 'Do we really appreciate life?' Maybe the 'saints and poets' are really the people who grew and suffered?"

I thought of Chris. He is a saint.

I don't know why we have to suffer, really. I guess we never will know why—not in this life, anyway. All I know is this: What is the point of moping around and wasting what little time we are given?

Pari asked all of us, "I wonder what this has to do with *Pleasantville?*"

Mickey said, "Yeah, I was thinking about that. Remember how at the end of the film, Tobey Mcguire's character comes back to the present time and sees his mom crying in the kitchen? But first, he turns off the TV because he doesn't want *Pleasantville* anymore. He wants reality. Okay, well, he goes and talks to his mom and she's crying and saying how her life is so messed up. She says this isn't the way her life was supposed to be because she figured she had all the *right* things--the right house, and the right husband, and the right kids and all. And Tobey Mcguire looks at her and says something like, 'Nope, Mom, there's no *right* house, or *right* man, or even a *right* life.' Well, his Mom just stares at him and seems blown away by his sudden wisdom and asks how he got so smart all of a sudden. And all he says is that he figured the best way he could explain it was that he had a good day.

Mickey looked up at us then and, in the same way said, "So I'm thinking what the movie says is that some of our best days come from some of our worst days. Maybe."

I wondered then when Mickey got so smart.

But there was one last question in the envelope:

What makes people "colored?"

Mickey's Hand

"It's all about the courage to change. The willingness to face your fears and act on new ideas." I looked at Maddie. I knew what she was thinking. *As long as I don't face my folks and at least talk to them about how I see the world differently from them and how I have to lead my own life—as long as I don't do that—well, I am never going to be colored.*

But it is hard, you know. We can say we are our own selves and have our own identity. But when it comes down to it, facing the people you love and telling them you don't want to lead the life they've created for you... Well, I can see how heartbreaking it would be for them, and how it would just suck for me. I don't know if they'll understand, or be disappointed, or just think I am naïve and immature, or think I'm wasting opportunities, or whatever.

Well, anyway. Pari and Rhia both nodded when I said what I did about the question. I guess they think I'm smart.

Yeah, right.

Madison's Hand

May 4th

Today is Sunday. So much has happened in class and out of class that I need to work backwards. After seeing *Pleasantville,* we began reading *Catcher in the Rye.* Mr. B said he has mixed feelings about the novel, but that its stream-of-consciousness style and the fact that it was the "teen angst" book of the second half of the 20th Century made it worth the time. Besides, he added, "Holden Caulfield is alive and roaming around schools everyday...if you look for him, or her." And it didn't take long for the story to hit home with us...

Or rather hit us at home. That brings me to Mickey.

Back on April 28th

Mickey had just lost a game—his first loss of the season. He'd come into the ball game when it was tied. When he came out, he was fit to be tied. The homer hit off of Mickey went over the fence and bounced so high off the road that it kangarooed all the way to the gym. Yikes. His coach had let him face a right-hander who, I guess, was really good—as in, he was the league's player of the year last year as a *junior!*

OK, so Mickey had a bad game. But that was just the start. I guess he shouldn't have lost his temper coming off the field after the game, but he did. And I was there to see it all.

It began with his dad saying something to him about why he was even facing that hitter, like, "Doesn't the coach know you are supposed to face lefties? And besides that guy is so good."

Mickey looked at his dad and said, in what has to be described as a very pissed off way, with a look and a tone I have *never* seen or heard from him…ever. "Gee, Dad, thanks for the vote of confidence; I really appreciate it! Oh, and by the way, *I told* coach I could handle him. Me, Dad. *I* made the decision and he thought I knew enough to do it! And *I sucked!*"

His mom and dad were mortified. People heard Mickey yelling at his folks, and turned away to give them some privacy. I was embarrassed, too. I knew this was coming. But it was coming in a public place and it was such an ambush for his folks. For them, it was right out of the blue with no warning.

Mickey's dad spit out through gritted teeth something like, "Son, I don't know what's eating you, but you have no right to talk to us that way. This is just a game, and we are your parents." Angry as Mickey's dad was, he was right, technically. Then there was just Awkward Silence—capital A, capital S. You could feel the heat coming off father and son. Mickey stared at the dirt, and his dad looked everywhere but at him. Then Mickey's dad said, "Mickey, whatever is *really* bothering you is something we should be talking about right when we get home…" And his mom added, "And when you calm down…both of you."

Mickey was supposed to take me home, and I felt like an intruder, so I said something to Mickey about calling my folks to get home. Mickey said no and told his parents he was taking me home first.

He did not say a word to me all the way to my house. We hardly looked at each other. When I got out, I turned to him and tried to say, "Good luck, Mickey," but somewhere between the "*luck*" and the "*Mickey*" I just choked up. He turned to me and hugged me, and I started crying.

That was the first time Mickey ever said, "I love you, Maddie."

And the first time I ever told him that I loved him, too.

He said, "I will call you later."

"I don't want you to call me, Mickey. I want you to *see* me." We looked at each other. We both had so much to say, but there weren't any words for it. We simply understood.

My Mom made this great dinner that night, but I never ate a bite. I lied about my stomach hurting. My dad knew better.

Mickey's Hand

Why are some things so hard? Why is getting it out from my guts to my voice and through my teeth so damn hard? If you explode, then it's easy. You just *tell 'em off,* right? But this was not about telling off some jerk. These were the two most important people in my life and they were *so not ready* to hear what I wanted to say. And I wasn't sure I had the courage to say it.

That was all I could think of on the way home after I dropped off Maddie. Maddie. Her perfume was still in the cab of my truck. I thought of her mascara running down her adorable cheeks. When she wished me luck, her eyes were focused so deeply into mine. She knows me, and she knows that all I want to do is please everyone, including her. I thought of my folks, and I was literally shaking.

I guess you could say it was a bad day in the big leagues.

When I got home, I took a deep breath and headed into the house like I was facing my execution. My last thought as I crossed the threshold was that at least the waiting was over. There was some comfort in that. My folks were waiting for me. I think my mom had lectured my dad about not getting mad at me. He reminded me of a big bear, pacing back and forth. He stopped pacing when I walked in. My mom asked me if I wanted to change out of my uniform first, maybe take a shower.

"No. I just want to say what I want to say." No way I was going to stop now, and besides the uniform felt like a security blanket. "Look, I am sorry I got so mad at you guys. I'm sorry I blew up at you like that in front of everyone." They nodded, accepting the apology.

Deep breath. "I don't know how to say this, so I'm just gonna say it. I just want to make my own choices, okay? I don't think I want to go to the colleges you want. I don't even know if I wanna go to college right out of school." My teeth are chattering when I am talking. "Heck, I might want to join the Peace Corps, or whatever. And I don't want to be a business major or engineer or lawyer or whatever *you guys* think I would be good at…"

My dad tried to interrupt, but a stern look from my mom froze him.

"And I might want to be a writer or a teacher. I don't know. And I am not going to register as a Republican. And I hate the war, and I hated Bush, and I know that you guys are not gonna agree with me…" I stopped. That was the gist of it.

That's when my mom spoke. "Honey, we know all that. Really, we do." I wasn't sure I'd heard her correctly. I frowned and she continued, "Do you think we don't have a sense of your politics and what you believe in? Mickey, your father and I are not blind. We live with you." You could have knocked me over with a feather. So I sat down.

My mom took a deep breath and looked at my dad. "I know you see us as trying to dictate your life to you. I'm sorry if you feel that way. Maybe we come across too pushy. We've lived longer than you, and we want to pass on what we've learned, like shortcuts, so you don't have to waste your time learning the same things. But in the end, we only want you to be happy, and we only want to support you."

"I know that, Mom." Silence. It was my dad's turn. I waited as he took a deep breath and then sighed, looking at his hands.

Then my dad looked me right in the eyes and said, "Mickey, I have always tried not to be the father-who-lives-through-his-son. I never wanted to be like that. Maybe I screwed up and got carried away anyway. I don't know. I guess I just want what's best for you…"

So I got my courage up and said gently, "Yeah, but that is the point, Dad. *I* don't even know what's best for me yet. So how can you or anyone else know? I just gotta figure it out for myself. And when you said that after the game, I just felt like you were saying, again, that it was somebody else's fault that I failed. Or that I was just not good enough. Or, even worse, that I needed to be protected."

He started to reply, but I held my hand up. "Well, it isn't anyone's fault but mine." It felt good to say that. "And you know what, Dad? I can handle it. I gotta fail sometimes, and I gotta be pissed off and I gotta just…I don't know." They waited.

The tension was evaporating from the room, and I felt a whole lot better, so I kept going, "Look, I want to make everyone happy. Sometimes, I just forget about me and I fake it to keep everyone happy. And I don't wanna be like that anymore." They didn't say anything, but they didn't seem angry either. I said, "I don't know if this is making any sense at all."

"Mickey," my dad stood up, "I'm going to tell you something. I never had the courage to tell my dad or my mom what you just said. I wish I had. Those were different times, different parents. Your mom and I promised ourselves we would not be the people our parents were." This was news to me, but now it was time for me to wait and let him talk.

"There is this famous book I read a long time ago called *The Road Less Traveled,* and the writer said that the best parents get their kids to evolve past them. That has been your mom's and my goal, Mickey. And what you just told us tells us that you are becoming exactly what we wanted you to become."

My mom looked at my dad then, and I saw her pride in him…and then she looked at me with the same look.

Then my dad grinned and said, "Your mother and I actually considered voting for Obama."

Yeah, right. It made me laugh so hard that I started to cry.

Who said there is no crying in baseball?

"I think we need to send this pitcher off to the showers," my Mom said.

Madison's Hand

He came over and we went to the Metaphor Café, naturally. But before we went anywhere, I reached right over and pulled his face to me and kissed him like someone who was just so thirsty and only his lips could quench my thirst—my desire to hold him and have him hold me.

When we got to the cafe, I wanted to hear it all, and I was amazed because I guess we sometimes underestimate our folks. Maybe we see so many of our friends with parents that are so messed up that we forget how truly lucky we are. Maybe all that *No Spin Zone* conservative stuff that Mickey says his parents obsess about is just not really all that important to them. Mickey was so relieved that he just flopped into the chair and grinned at me. Then I told him my part of the night.

Right after dinner, my dad asked me to help him wash my mom's car. And as soon as we had it good and sudsy, he cut right through the "bullcrap" as he calls it in the military. "So did you and Mickey have a fight?"

"No."

"'Cause I saw what you looked like after he dropped you off. Looked like a fight to me."

"Yeah. I was a mess. But the fight isn't with Mickey."

My dad waited with his eyebrows raised as he looked at me over the hood.

"It's Mickey and his folks. They are so conservative, and they want him to go to some business school, you know. We've talked about this, and Mickey had decided to be honest with them, but…"

"But…?"

"He kinda blew up on them at the game, and it wasn't totally fair and he needs to tell them how he feels and stuff."

"And that is what caused you to cry and not eat?"

A long pause from me. I scrubbed the fender more than it needed.

"Dad, I really like Mickey. Really. I am about to say something so cheesy I can't believe I am about to say it. Wasn't there some song called, 'How Do I Know,' as in how do I know when I'm really in love, or something like that?"

"Whitney Houston—but I think the title was more like, 'How Will I Know,' as in 'if he really loves me.'" My dad had that smirk on his face which I recognized as the cosmic look of a father who understands his daughter. "But I have a sneaky feeling that you already know how Mickey feels about you, so that title is maybe not what you are troubled by."

"Oh, Dad. I think I am just so in love with him. And I can't believe I am talking about this...to…."

"Your military dad and not mom, huh?" He smiled and picked up the hose.

"Yeah. I guess so. Do you get closer when things get harder? Is that, like, the way it is with you and mom?"

"Yep. When I leave for tours, it is hard. We never get used to it and we are always really tight then." He stopped, thinking about it as he rinsed the roof and back window. "Sometimes our feelings are so powerful that it's better not to talk about it. We don't need to say anything."

"Yeah." Long pause. "Dad, that is kinda just what happened with me and Mickey. I wanted to tell him something and I just couldn't…"

He handed me the hose so I could squirt the front of the car. "Words didn't work, huh? It ain't about *words*, Maddie." He smiled at me, and sighed, his eyes all crinkly at the corners. He picked up our old chamois and began wiping down the roof. "But I will tell you one thing. I missed a lot of days and nights with *you,* too. And when I came home on leave, I would race your mom up the stairs to talk to you because I missed those times. I don't want to miss much more because you are growing up so fast. And, heck, here you are falling in love." He glanced my way as he worked.

Long, long pause. I turned off the hose and started gathering the sponges and stuff.

"We aren't gonna have a sex talk are we, Dad? 'Cause I…"

"No, we most definitely are not. The Commander in Chief–Mom–is in charge of that." I smiled, but he wasn't finished yet. "I still don't think we've gotten to the bottom of this."

Then I plopped down on the grass beside the driveway and said what I had balled up in me. "I am afraid of the future, of what I feel. I'm afraid of stupid stuff like, will we stay together, or what college will I go to, and if he will be a zillion miles away… I don't know, Dad. I shouldn't be so worried about everything."

He squeezed the water out of the chamois, and kept drying the car. "Maddie, you can't plan out your life and have no messes. You're going to have some messes in your life. You gotta just keep your eyes open and enjoy the adventure, honey." He stopped and looked at me. "Mom and I got your back. We always will, okay? Dang,… you know I love you."

But somewhere in between "*love*" and "*you,*" the words never quite made it out.

"Now, go inside so Mom can have another sex talk with you."

I laughed.

Mickey laughed when I told him.

Then Mickey kissed *me,* and it felt different than any other kiss.

Pari's Hand

May 2nd

Prom. It is a four letter word that strikes fear into the hearts and souls of teenage girls. May 31st is the day of reckoning for us this year. We know where it is, when it is, but we don't *if* it is. I never wanted to go before—really, it wasn't a big deal to me. Until now. Until the dance in Mr. B's class. Dan-ce. Dan. Hmm.

Prom came up tonight at the Metaphor Café. But no matter how much we talk about it, for now it is *a story without an ending.* (I stole that line from *Casablanca.)*

We were supposed to be meeting about *Catcher in the Rye,* but first we needed to gossip. We concluded that the best thing to do was go to prom as a group. That way Mickey could talk to the guys *we* wanted to go with and not have the whole tragic-drama scene. We wanted April, Maddie's friend, in our prom group, and of course Donald and Dan. Tiffany would be fun. So would Brad and, well, the list grew exponentially. So we figured we would spread the word and see how it all falls out over the next few weeks.

I just want to go and have fun, and dance, and get dressed up, and go to a nice restaurant, and be with my friends. Oh my God, listen to me! I used to sit by myself and sip café mochas, and read my books, and only think of school and college and my religion. I was always feeling like an outsider—and I thought I liked it.

I remember studying the immigration chapters in Ms. Anderson's class and thinking, hey, that's me—the token Middle Eastern girl. I wouldn't think of being a cheerleader, or a Prom Queen, or the star athlete. And then Mick saw me alone in the Café that night, and Maddie and Rhia swept me away. And here I sit, scheming and dreaming.

An American dream.

Chapter 16: Holden's Hands

Rhiannon's Hand

May 5th

I really like Holden Caulfield. I do. I know some people in class think he is a loser or a whiner or some depressed punk, but I get him. I think he is one of the most real characters I have read in books, at least in books at school. He reminds me of Huck Finn, except he is a city boy—a rich one but just as lost, you know?

So we have gotten to the part where Holden leaves the crappy prep school he is getting kicked out of (again) because he is failing. Not one person asks him why he's failing. Instead they feed him lame lines like his old fart teacher Spencer who says, "Life is a game, boy…you have got to learn to play by the rules."

I agree with Holden. That is such a bunch of crap. What "rule" says it was okay for my dad to leave my mom and me and Chris? What part of the "game" says people don't have to play fair? What part of growing up says it's okay for a daughter to be abandoned by her dad? And what happens when that dad calls and asks if it's okay if he gets re-married to some woman who thinks she can actually be my stepmother?

I am just so mad, and so sad, that I just don't know what to say—but writing this down helps. I feel like I'm going nuts. When my dad called, I just did not know what to say to him. I don't know if he has even told my mom yet—or Chris…

And why the hell is he asking me for permission? Is he trying to get me to like him again by offering to care what I think? Doesn't he get it? I know that he is a rat. It's like what Holden says of his stupid, selfish roommates who are such jackasses. He thinks that when you grow up like a jerk, you never change being a jerk. I wonder if my dad just fooled my mom all those years before he took off so she couldn't see what a rat he was. Holden says there are morons and phonies in this world. Well, it's awful for a daughter to say this, but my dad is both.

I don't know when or if I can ever completely close this wound. I wanted so badly to stop him and his phony bullshit on the phone and just say this:

> *Dad, you are such a liar. You have hurt us more than you can imagine. There is no forgiveness when there is no atonement. You are selfish. You make me want to hate you, and I promised myself that I would never hate anyone. I just never thought you could be this stupid. No, I never want to see you again. No, I never want to see this new woman. No, I don't even want you at* my *wedding. You cannot give me away… because you already have. So just go away, and stay away. And by the way, don't tell Mom about this new marriage. You have already damaged her, and she doesn't deserve to have one more teardrop spill on her chessboard.*

That last part about the chessboard is from *Catcher.* The scene is where Holden's real love, Jane Gallagher, starts to cry because her stupid boozer of a stepfather hassles her. As she cries, a teardrop falls on a red square of the board.

That scene kills me. Holden is starting to rub off on me.

Yeah.

May 7th

Class today was really interesting because we talked about the ducks on the pond in Central Park and what happens to them in the winter. And we talked about Holden's brother, Allie, and Holden's stupid roommate, Stradlater. We talked about why Holden freaks out and tries to beat up Stradlater when he finds out the jerk is going to try to make it with Jane Gallagher in the backseat of his borrowed car. That's Holden's Jane, no less, although I'm not sure if the two of them have really dated yet.

So Mr. B asked me in class where the ducks go. I said they fly south.

"What if they don't make it? What if they are too young, too old, too weak, or just too unlucky?"

Mr. B's question prompted silence from the class.

"They die." It was Pari.

"So does anyone protect them? After all, isn't that what *Catcher in the Rye* is all about?"

Another silence. Maddie said, "So we 'catch' people who are falling. We're catchers. Is Holden falling, then?"

"What do you think?" Mr. B asked.

"I think so. I mean isn't he, like depressed, and maybe suicidal…?" Maddie replied.

"He says he would be if he wasn't a chicken." It was Donald from across the room.

I said, "But he wasn't a chicken. He knew Stradlater was going to beat him up if he got in a fight with him. He was defending Jane's honor, protecting her—like she's a duck on the pond. I mean, isn't that right?"

Mr. B smiled at me like he was really proud of me, and I have to tell you that it made my day.

Then he said, "Rhia, tell me the scoop on Allie, Holden's brother."

"Well, he died when he was like 14 or something from leukemia. And he was smarter than Holden, and Holden really loved him. And when he died, Holden went into the garage and smashed out all the windows of the car until be broke the knuckle on his fist."

"Ever been that mad?

"No," I said to him. I lied.

"Well, gang," Mr. B said, "some of you have been that mad. I think we get the angriest at situations we are powerless to change. There's nothing more frustrating than something really bad happening when there's not a thing we can do to prevent it." Long pause. "So why do people get leukemia anyway, Mickey?"

"No one knows. Genetics. Bad luck."

"So why do bad things happen to good people, like Allie? That's what is killing Holden. Especially when people like the Stradlaters, who prey on the innocent, get to live. It just doesn't seem fair."

"Do the Stradlater's ever pay a price?" I asked Mr. B. I kind of surprised myself. I think it was the first time I'd ever asked him a question in class.

"Ah, well Rhia, that is a profound question. Me, I'm a believer in the idea of what goes around comes around. Karma. If you try to do good in this world, good things come back to you. If you are a rat, eventually you get what you deserve. At least I like to think this is how the world works. But I think Holden is wondering whether or not this is true. He's wondering if the rats sometimes win." Mr. B leaned against his desk and continued, "I can tell you this. You will discover that the people you love the most and care for the most are givers, not just takers. And the takers usually get caught. Then they move on like all con artists. But in the end, I believe, the takers have empty souls and lonely lives. It's not worth it."

I didn't know what to think of this. Everything we were discussing kept crashing into my thoughts of my father and his needs, and my anger …and even my needs. I was all jumbled up. Then out of nowhere, I had a thought…

Maybe I am not supposed to know what to do yet. Maybe that's okay. Maybe I don't have to "do" anything about my dad's phone call—except be honest about how mad I am so I don't bottle it up. Just give myself time to heal, you know?

Just then Mr. B moved to the sound system and pressed play, and we heard the voice of Avril Lavigne's singing "I'm With You:"

It's dark, it's raining and it's cold. She's just all alone and waiting for someone to take her hand. She's confused and things just have just been breaking up inside of her; she is searching for a friendly face, a place that's safe. It doesn't really matter where, as long as she's with you.

For a minute, I felt like I understood everything. Holden wants his brother, Allie, to come back to him, to not die. If Holden could have one wish, it would be for Allie to come take his hand and lead him home, to get out of the rain and the cold and the pain.

But Allie never comes.

Neither does my father.

But you know what? Someone always does come. Maybe not the one you want, but someone. And it feels good. For me, the person who comes to get me out of the dark rain might be Chris, or Maddie, or Mickey, or Pari, or Donald…

And there is always, always my mom. Even if no one else comes, my mom will always say, "I'm with you." And I'm with her. I am not alone.

And the next thing I knew, the bell had already rung.

Mickey's and Madison's Hands

May 14th

We decided to write this together—kind of a new experience for us. We argued a bit about who does what, but in the end we just thought this next sequence would be best told from the guy's and girl's perspectives. Maddie is in regular font and *Mickey is italicized*, just so nobody gets confused.

We are deeper into the novel and lot has happened, but the key is how Holden sees people. They are either phonies or morons. There are also perverts. There is a lot of truth in the whole thing about people. I mean, from our perspective, it's 55 years later and high school is still filled with drama, manipulation, users, posers, and just about every other stereotype you can think of. We are not saying all those people are bad, necessarily. It's just that, well, Holden is right in that a lot of kids, parents, politicians, ministers, sports stars and such are just not what they say they are. Or worse, they are corrupt liars and cheats. Steroids didn't exist during Holden's time. He didn't see the lies on TV or on YouTube.

And then there are the perverts Holden refers to who do bizarre things. What could be more sad and perverted than the scene with Holden and the prostitute, Sunny? And how about her moronic pimp Maurice, who also beats up Holden? Holden just wants someone to talk to and kind of falls into having Sunny come up to his room. He just wants to talk to her—to anyone with a sympathetic ear. But all Sunny wants to do is turn the trick and get it over with.

That is when he notices Sunny is about 15 years old. She's younger than he is! And that is so depressing to Holden that he can't stand it. How could someone so young sell herself? Why?

Is she yet another person who cannot fly south for the winter and is forced to survive any way she knows how? The last thing he can think of is sex—with her. But it's sex and Jane Gallagher that made Maddie and I decide to write this part of the chapter together. Jane is Holden's dream. That is exactly how I feel about Maddie. And so I totally get it when Holden tries to hold her and protect her.

When Jane cried and the teardrop fell on the red square of the chessboard and she tried to instantly rub it out, I felt myself reach out with my thumb and try to help her make it disappear. But for girls, the hurt and the tears don't always dissolve without leaving a mark.

And Holden hugs her and kisses her nose, her eyes, her forehead, but not her lips.

No. Because that would be a betrayal to her—to all girls who open up to a guy and reveal some of the pain.

And then Holden asks her to go to the movies. I would do the same. Sometimes just going with Maddie to the movies, just the two of us, is exactly what I want to do.

Me, too.

And they hold hands. Holden does this great monologue about holding hands. He describes how Jane is so perfect when she holds your hand—not all nervous or sweaty or squirmy.

There are just some times when Mickey's hand fits so perfectly into mine and I feel like Holden does—safe and comfortable…like I belong.

But then there is the sex-maniac part. Holden thinks girls just drive guys crazy. And it is confusing. Really.

It's just as confusing for girls, Mickey. We have all this pressure on us to be "sexy," like some Victoria's Secret model, and to give in to boys…

Holden thinks that girls lose their minds when they get all passionate.

I don't lose my mind, Mickey. But I admit I love kissing. I do.

Ah, but the point that Holden makes is that when a girl says for him to stop, well—he stops. Every time, he always stops. He figures it's unfair since girls get so passionate. He would be so guilty if he pushed her…

Like Stradlater does when he rapes (or comes close to raping) that one girl when he and Holden are on a double date.

Yeah.

Yeah.

Anyway, later he feels like he did the right thing. But, boy, he gets frustrated. Sexually, I mean.

Do you? Get frustrated with me, Mickey?

Well, no. I mean, well, sometimes. I don't know, Maddie. I mean…I understand.

I am sorry if I drive you crazy, Mickey.

[Really, really long pause here.]

So anyway, last weekend we went to the movies, just me and Mickey.

And I held her hand…the whole movie.

Boys, …they drive a girl crazy. You know?

Pari's Hand

May 21st

"I was wondering, Pari, if you would like to go to the prom with me? And, you know, with everyone else too, but, like, with me still, you know, because it would be fun…"

Dan gave me a small bouquet of flowers.

It was lunch. He caught me walking with Rhia, and she immediately disappeared. Once I told Dan I would love to go with him….and our whole group, Rhia reappeared from nowhere. How does she do that? Anyway, Dan had waited a long time to ask me since the prom is only two weekends from now. But Mickey assured me that Dan was just shy, and that he thought maybe I wanted to go with someone else, and so he was worried or whatever.

I had already spotted the dress I wanted to wear, and I'd put it on hold just in case. I guess for a while, girls live on hold, you know? My mom was in charge of buying the dress as soon as I called her. She said she'd go right over and get it. Thanks, Mom. I think moms have to be "on call" for girls 24-7. Anyway, I had a great lunch today.

Today, we also finished reading *Catcher*. What a strange ending. I like it and I hate it. Maybe that is how I feel about the whole book. I guess it's because I just want to help Holden, and I'm so frustrated with how detached his parents are from him—and all the adults, in general. Why didn't the school inform his parents of how he was doing? Why didn't his parents ever call him? How could they not realize that he was so desperate for help? It seems obvious to me that failing out of two schools and seeing a boy jump from a window to his death would traumatize Holden. How come his 12-year-old sister is more concerned and understanding than his parents? How could his only trusted teacher be so stupid as to *pat* Holden's head when he is sleeping in his apartment? What was that supposed to fix? After all, Holden just told him all his troubles and the teacher, Mr. Antonelli, had just warned him of a *fall* he was likely to take. How could adults be so lame?

But I guess that is the point. In our own class, in speech after speech during the American Pie presentations, kids talked about the crazy, thoughtless things parents had done to them or their siblings. Mickey told you some of them. But believe me, there were other stories, like fathers or mothers in jail, or kids who hadn't seen one parent since they were infants only to be contacted years later. There were parents who were so frustrated with their kids or with their own lives that they beat their kids. There were parents who were alcoholics or drug users just out of rehab. I couldn't believe what craziness kids in my own class were living with day in and day out.

Mr. B once quoted someone who said that being born without parents is like being born without skin. In that case, there are an awful lot of kids walking around my high school without skin. Funny thing is that Holden's world of the 1950's was a world of fewer divorces and more material wealth (at least in *his* family). Imagine what he would think of today's world.

For example, Holden goes to his sister's school and sees *F-you* written on the walls. He gets mad because he says that it's obscene that little kids have to see that. Holden thinks *F-you* is so mean-spirited, and he asks how you even explain it to little kids. It makes him crazy. Well, imagine Holden today. When I walk from one part of campus to another, I hear the *F-word* and all sorts of curse words come out of everyone's mouths. Cursing is so common that I wonder if it's just part of the natural vocabulary. People are calling girls *bitches* and *'ho's*. And believe me, the girls are just as bad as the guys. The amazing thing is that the kids who curse the most are the youngest. So I guess Holden would be so blown away that he would figure that all the *F-you's* have finally taken their toll. We've all just gotten mean.

Anyway, the book ends with Holden sitting in the rain with his red hunting hat watching his sister, Phoebe, riding the carousel. He says he is finally happy. I guess I believe him. I assume he goes home with Phoebe and finally tells his parents that he is failing school, again. The next thing you know he is sitting in the psychologist's office as he finishes rehashing the whole story. That was why they sent him to California to some rehab place to talk out his troubles. I think he is lonely. He doesn't know if he can do better, or feel better. He just ends the story. What a weird way to finish a novel.

At the Metaphor Café, we argued about whether this was a happy ending or a sad one. I guess it depends on your view of life. Are you a romantic or a realist? We also decided that another way to look at it is whether Holden is the crazy one or the only sane one.

Rhia said the ending was definitely optimistic. "Holden had to grow up faster than any of us. He sees things we just ignore, and he can't stand the lies and the cheating. I think we're immune to it, or we just accept it too easily. So I think he just needs to chill out and get some balance back in his life."

Mickey wasn't so sure: "I hope you're right, Rhia. But he still has a long way to go. And did you notice that in the whole book the doctor guy never speaks or offers any help? I think Holden still doubts that the rehab place isn't just filled with phonies, too."

Rhia said, "But it does help, Mickey. It helps to just get it out of his system. He tells us, at least."

"You have to assume the doctors will help him cope," Maddie said.

I sipped my café mocha and listened for a while. Happy ending or sad? Is Holden going to be okay or not? There were no definitive answers. I thought about how Holden says at one point that when he loves a book, he wishes that he could sit down and talk to the writer.

Too bad Salinger isn't going to drop by the Metaphor Café. We'd have some serious questions for him. But if Salinger could come here, I think he'd see just what he'd wanted to see. I mean, here we sit arguing about Holden, hoping he will be okay eventually.

Finally, I looked at the three of them and said, "Guys, here's the thing. Holden just has more to catch than he is prepared for. Holden's hands are just too weak or too broken to catch all that he sees falling. See, we all see others running from one place in life to another, and we want to stop them because they cannot really see what they're doing. The rye fields are so high that they cannot see the cliff coming and they fall. It was like you said, Rhia, about *Reviving Ophelia.* There is a hurricane blowing us, and sometimes it blows so hard we lose our footing and fall.

"But we are all supposed to catch each other—to break the fall. That's what growing up is all about – becoming the catcher in the rye."

The others looked at me and smiled.

What they didn't know is that all three of them had done exactly that for me.

Chapter 17: The Season Finale

Madison's Hand

May 30th

This week has been crazy. Tomorrow is the Prom. I feel like I am seeing things with a new set of eyes—we all are. Let me get you caught up.

May 23rd

First, there is the bad news. April's father was injured last week, and he was flown back to the States this week. He is in stable condition, but he suffered a concussion (his second one) from a blast on the street that threw him against a wall and knocked him unconscious. In a way it is a relief because, hopefully, he will not be deployed to Iraq again. But his family was frightened; so was ours.

April's father is older—44 to be exact. With that and all the other factors that come into play, it looks like he will be re-stationed here. In the meantime, he will be hospitalized back in Virginia for a while. I remember the junior papers that dealt with the Walter Reed Hospital and all the controversy about our soldiers' treatment there. Well, April's father is at Walter Reed. So that's still a worry.

April called me and told me everything. I went over immediately with my mom and dad. Here is the crazy thing—she called me on Memorial Day, the 26th. We had our flag out, our barbeque on, and some friends and relatives over. But none of that mattered because in military families when something like this happens, we all stop whatever we are doing and pull together.

We said a prayer for him and tried to do anything we could. My dad made sure April's mom could get on a flight the next day to Washington, and he drove her to the airport. April stayed with us while her mom was in DC.

It was the very least we could do. We watched CNN and saw the President speak and lay a wreath at the Tomb of the Unknown Soldier. What was unspoken between us was that April's father had come so close to death. He was anything but "Unknown" to April.

Once it was apparent that April's father was going to be relatively okay (he still has some hearing loss and headaches), her mother insisted she still go to the Prom. We all insisted that April and her date join up with our group—the more the merrier. We are all looking forward to it. None of us had been to the Prom before.

Mickey's Hand

May 26th

Our baseball season ended. We were so close to making it to the finals…so close. We lost in the semi-finals, and it was a heartbreaker, especially for the seniors playing their last game.

We'd qualified for the playoffs, barely, by upsetting two teams to reach the quarter-finals. Then we played the game of our lives to get into the semi-finals, beating a team we'd lost to three times this season. We used nearly our whole team in that game. Coach said, "Look, there is no tomorrow, so we cannot hold anything back."

In that quarter-final game, we had a one-run lead from the first inning on and miraculously held onto it for the next several innings. I came in to pitch with two outs in the 5th inning, and I successfully got my one hitter out. Then I was done, but the game wasn't over yet. We hadn't won a 1-0 game all year, and somehow it seemed like it would be impossible to hold on.

In the last inning, they loaded the bases with two outs. We held our breath, preparing to watch it all slip away. Then our senior closer just reared back and struck out their guy! We all jumped out of the dugout like we had just won the World Series! We dog-piled the pitcher and were jumpin' all over. The coach told us to chill out because he didn't want us to show up the other team. They were so bummed because they were the defending champions, and even though they were not as good as last year, they'd been favored to get to the finals. Instead, we were going to the semi-finals and they were leaving the field empty-handed.

So we had all this momentum going for us into semis. But we also had pitchers with sore arms while the other team was throwing their ace. We hung with them and, like I said, we were close. In the last inning we were down 4-1 when we got back-to-back singles. One of our best hitters, a senior named Sam, was up and he hit that sucker so far—we all thought, "Dude, he just tied it up!"

Then their guy snagged it right at the wall. Game over. Season over. And for the seniors, baseball itself over.

It was a bummer. And this time, they were the ones jumping around like they'd just won the Series.

Coach called us all over after the game. I gotta hand it to him. He said some things that came right out of the *Mr. B Book of Life Lessons:* "Guys, this is why we play the game. (Silence.) You know how baseball has no clock? The games just take as long as they take, right? That's because baseball is timeless. And the lessons that baseball teaches us are timeless too. Guys, you did everything I could have hoped for and more because you had your heart in it… and it hurts. I know. But this game pushes us, all of us, to challenge what we think are our limits. And when we keep pushing back, the competition makes us stronger. And in the end, the champions are all those who become better people because of the game."

I saw Maddie standing with Rhia and Pari and our other friends, and I knew what Coach was saying was true. If you're going to play the game, you have to accept the fact that you're going to lose sometimes. But at least you're playing. You're not on the sidelines wishing. You're in the game. And that says something about you.

"Guys, I wouldn't want to coach any other team but you. You made my year and I am proud of you."

My dad was in the outer circle of parents watching Coach, and he was beaming. You would think we'd won. Then Coach said something that explained why. "Guys, Mickey's dad collected some money from the parents, and we are stopping at In'n'Out for burgers—their treat. Eat to your heart's content. The bus driver has been bribed, too. So let's go, dudes. I am starving."

My dad winked at me and, dang, if my eyes didn't water.

Then I remembered… there is no cryin' in baseball.

Pari's Hand

May 27th

We had an amazing experience today, and we all were both intrigued and frustrated. In class, Mr. B showed us a PBS *Frontline* documentary called, "The Merchants of Cool," by a writer named Douglas Rushkoff. Mr. B told us when he first showed this to his classes, they were really angry with him. He said, "I guess I had 'found them out' and made them look into the mirror. They did not like what they saw."

In a nutshell, "Merchants" is about how the media machine has taken over the teen world according to one of the college professors interviewed. Business people know that they desperately need to market to teens because we have more disposable cash than any generation before us. They use all the tools of the media: movies, music, TV, anything that kids watch to get us to buy what they are selling. They want us to believe that if we buy these things, then we are *cool*.

These huge media corporations, like Viacom or Time Warner, own almost everything we see—like MTV and all the other music stations out there. These companies even hire "coolhunters" (former cool kids now working for advertising agencies). These coolhunters become "culture spies" who creep around finding kids who seem cool. They photograph the cool kids and sell the pictures for thousands of dollars so corporations can see what today's *cool* looks like. Then they sell that image back to us. But that is not the really creepy part.

These companies actually *create* kids so they know exactly who they are marketing to. They create boys who Rushkoff describes as *mooks*: vulgar, immature, sex-obsessed, jackasses. Sorry for the pun since *Jackass* is the ultimate TV show for mooks. They also push *WWF Wrestling* and *Ultimate Fighting*—all for the purpose of selling the idea that cool popular guys are into fighting and violence.

Meanwhile, the media also creates a girl version of the mooks, called the

midriffs. The midriff girls use their body to sell themselves, even if they don't understand they are just using sexual teasing as their new *cool* identity. Britney Spears was the classic midriff. She got 14-year-old girls dressing like sluts and singing about being "not that innocent." And we saw 13-year-old girls in the documentary being paraded to the media in bikini talent shows. These girls desperately want to be the next Britney. They welcome being sex objects, and they don't even realize (or maybe don't care) that they are disposable as soon as the next batch of midriffs shows up.

One of the professors said that media just drags standards down. After a while, the kids being marketed to literally became what the corporate machine is spitting out—mooks and midriffs who consume and consume. They push their parents to give them more and more guilt money. Teenage trends come and go, and *cool* keeps changing. But that makes the whole marketing world happy because there is a new cell phone, iPod, DVD, watch, purse, whatever, to buy.

The freakiest part was watching even those who reject the coolhunt get pulled into it anyway. For instance, we saw the band called Insane Clown Posse (ICP), who were so grotesque and hideous that I wanted to hide my face, creating a kind of rage rap rock where they attacked women, gays, and anything mainstream. And I mean they attacked—calling women every disgusting thing you can imagine. Limp Bizkit was another band into the whole rage rock scene screaming lyrics about skinning people with chainsaws, or something like that. Arguably, these guys may have inspired a riot after Woodstock '99, which left four girls raped. I thought these bands were like lightening rods for negative energy. They rejected the corporate media machine (which I can understand), but they also seemed to want to hurt and destroy people. They seethed with both violence and ignorance.

So what happened to both bands in the end? Both of them got big recording and multimedia marketing contracts. They sold out. They became the very thing *they said* they despised—a tool of the media. Maybe that was the plan after all. Who knows?

So when Mr. B turned off the TV, we were all thinking the same thing: Where does that leave us? Are we like that? Mr. B asked us as much, and comments started flying around the room. Of course not, we say. We insisted that we know when we're being sold something. Then the debate started. Do we *always* know when we're being sold? Are we just some sort of media-manipulated new *cool*? Is there anything real and authentic about us?

Then we were quiet for a moment. I think we all wanted to feel in control of this whole media scene, but as Maggie finally said, "We just didn't know the tentacles had become so widespread and powerful. It *is* everywhere you turn."

Mr. B nodded, "M-hmm." He turned and looked at the floor for a moment. Then he looked up and asked us what was the newest "rage rock."

Donald surprised me saying the politically incorrect thing: "A lot of the new *cool* is Gangsta rap—the whole 'ho's and ghetto scene. I mean that is the ultimate rebellion. Kids like us, growing up in the suburbs, can listen and download the bad boys from the hood and pretend we are home boyz. It is kind of funny when you think of it because most of us are, like, so *not* going to drive down there and mess with any of these people. But we listen to it, and we buy it."

Rhia seemed unconvinced, "But a lot, I mean a lot of us, are like so past all that. We don't care about that stuff. We like the beat of the music and we dance to it, but we get how all that Gangsta and stupid metal is just so dumb."

Mitchell snorted, "Not everyone agrees with *you*, Rhia!"

"Okay, so we *do* buy the trendy clothes, and we *do* want more and more, and we compare who has what cell phone and all," Maddie said. "But that doesn't make us mindless idiots like Britney."

From around the room, I heard all sorts of opinions. *This show is out-dated.... We are not like that anymore.... We knew this.... What do you want us to do? That stuff is everywhere.... I didn't realize it was so bad.*

After some more denial and disagreement, Mr. B calmed us down and asked us, "How do you escape? How are you *authentic*?"

We were quiet again. Then Tiffany spoke up. "We don't—or won't—let the brands, or the movies, or the songs, or whatever, tell *us* who we are, Mr. B. We know they're all watching us, I guess. But I don't care what others think. I just want to do and be what feels right for me. I ...what do you call it, Mr. B? I just want to follow my own North Star."

I was very proud of her at that moment.

Mr. B still pushed us: "So popular does not matter? What everyone else buys doesn't drive your decisions? You are not mooks or midriffs?"

Quiet again. But it wasn't a bored quiet. Oh, no. You could literally see people setting their shoulders, lifting their chins a bit, or maybe tightening down their eyebrows a little. There was determination in our attitude.

I finally answered him: "*We* aren't, Mr. B. The media's goal is to make money, pure and simple. And they don't care by what means they do it, either. We understand that. But here's the important thing. You have taught us to pay more attention to what *we* believe about ourselves because, in the end, *that* is all we can control." And since I'd gone that far, I decided to say what I was really thinking.

"That is the *cool* you sell, Mr. B."

Rhiannon's Hand

May 31st—The Prom

We did all the things you are supposed to do at the Prom. And it was great fun. But something happened that made the night so special that, well, it was very romantic and a bit hard to believe. I'll get to that in a minute.

First, our group kept growing until there were about 14 of us. All the parents got together and rented us a limo-bus-van thing and it was very cool because we didn't (and they didn't) have to worry about driving and all that stuff. The group was mostly all kids from our class except for some dates.

We all met at Mickey's house for pictures with parents. OMG! It was like the paparazzi! Parents were snapping away, lights flashing, pow-pow-pow. I have to say it was so cool since all of them were so proud of us and all. My mom was so cute! She is terrible with cameras, so Donald's dad—complete with the coolest dreadlocks—took pictures for her and was making copies for lots of parents. (I found out that Donald's dad is from the island of St. Thomas in the Caribbean, and he says it so cool…*Ca-ribbb-e-on.*) Anyway, my mom started to cry a little. I know she was wondering how this would have played out if my father had still been with us. I am sure she felt weird being there without a husband. I know for me, it felt like something was missing. But I wasn't going to let that ruin the Prom—no way.

Everyone was beautiful. Maddie wore an off-white lacy dress. She looked so elegant. Mickey cracked me up since he wore the same thing as Rick in *Casablanca*—you know, the white dinner jacket and bow tie with black pants. Pari went in the opposite direction. She wore the classic "little black dress" that cost a lot, I bet. And Daniel also wore a black tux. I decided to be sensible and wear the same jade dress I wore to the Winter Formal (I loved it anyway) and Donald had a black tux but with a matching green cummerbund and tie. We were all laughing and hugging as we greeted each other. It was just such a great way to start the evening.

We all agreed on a not-too-expensive-but-really-cool Italian restaurant downtown called *Café Tuscany*. Mr. Buscotti actually gave us the idea. Italians!

The Prom was at the Roosevelt Hotel, which I found out was named after President Theodore Roosevelt (not Franklin or Eleanor, as I first guessed). It was old, but very formal, and…well, woodsy. Okay, I know that is a dumb way to describe something. But it was so different from all the modern hotels with all the glass and escalators and sleek lines. The Roosevelt had an old-time elevator with a man who operated it in an open cage. The stairs and banisters were wide, dark mahogany wood. Gorgeous. I think the hotel was built in the 1940's and there were pictures of Presidents, actors, golfers, and all kinds of celebrities who had visited. The Grand Ballroom was exactly that—Grand. The chandeliers were huge and, more importantly, the dance floor was big!

The teachers who were there were all commenting on how much *this* was the ideal setting for a prom. And it was. We saw Ms. Anderson there with her husband and they looked wonderful. She obviously loved seeing all of us dressed up. And she seemed to like finding out some of the latest gossip. We asked about Mr. B and his wife, but Ms. Anderson said he didn't come to the Prom very often. She said maybe he would be there later though.

Our DJ was pretty good. The music at our dances is always a source of frustration because we argue and bicker about what kind of music to play. Teachers always frown at us when they see us dancing, too. You can hear them saying stuff like, "That's not dancing. They're just grinding against each other" or, "It's like sex with clothes on." And I guess it is a little. But it's fun, and it's us, and I bet their parents hated the way they danced, too.

The room got very hot with all that dancing, and we all were sweating, so the three couples (Mickey and Maddie, Pari and Dan, and Donald and I) decided to walk around the hotel for a bit. That is when we realized there was music coming from another direction. Live music. We were drawn to the music because it was a song we all recognized. We followed the sound upstairs to a lounge.

A small band was playing. Most of the musicians had gray hair, but they looked like they were having fun. A few couples were dancing on a small floor in front of them. The singer softly, deeply echoed the theme song to Casablanca—"As Time Goes By."

And there they were.

Mr. Buscotti and his wife, dancing.

We were so surprised. We just stood there watching them. Mr. B had spoken of his wife and his great love for her so many times. There she was. Petite. Dark hair. Sweet face, you know? Fitting her head under his chin. Moving like they had never lost a step or missed a beat. Romantically swaying back and forth. It reminded me of a song he taught us months and months ago called "Perfect Love." As we stood there, Maddie's head dropped softly onto Mickey's shoulder. Donald gently put his arm around my waist. It was a perfect moment.

Then the song drifted off. Soft applause. Mr. B didn't notice us. The band picked up the pace, playing "It's Only a Paper Moon." We all decided that this was a fox trot we could handle, so we marched to the dance floor, hoping we weren't invading Mr. B's privacy.

Then he saw us. "Oh, my," he said. He looked truly surprised, but happy too. He introduced his wife, Deborah, to us and we all continued dancing. Mr. and Mrs. B fox-trotted as smooth as silk, smiling and talking to each other. We were laughing and trying to remember all the steps he had taught us. But it wasn't long before we got the knack of it again. It was so much fun. It was another world from the jam-packed Grand ballroom. As Donald led me around the dance floor, we were transported back in time when, with a simple touch, a man and a woman could communicate so much, and look so deeply into each other's eyes.

And, of course, when the song ended…

We kissed.

And the rest, as they say, is history.

Chapter 18: Graduation

Madison's Hand

June 12th

I have a lump in my throat. So much has happened and some of it is inevitable, some of it sad, and some of it inspirational.

Some of it scary. I guess change is that way.

Today is graduation for the seniors. It is sad to see them go because I did not realize how much we, as juniors, relied on them. We have big shoes to fill. But that is only a small part of the anxiety and stress. This week has been finals. Some teachers require we remember absolutely everything from their class— impossible!

Mr. B and Ms. Anderson, as usual, were creative. We performed readers' theater that turned out to be 12-minute dramas that we read out loud and, in a way, acted the parts. They were like mini-plays, but we didn't have to worry about sets and staging. Each readers' theater was written by group of students who focused on a particular decade or time frame.

Rhia and I were in the 20's *Gatsby* group. We had fun re-creating Jay and Daisy and Nick along with some of the historical characters of the time like gangsters, flappers, and jazz artists. It was really cool when Donald did a monologue on Duke Ellington.

Mickey was in the 60's group and he played Tom Hayden, one of the Chicago Eight at the Democratic Convention in 1968 where there was so much protest and violence. Mickey was perfect!

Pari was in the last group that focused on the 90's until today. They were so clever, turning their Readers' Theater into an episode of *Oprah* with Pari playing the role of Mary Pipher, the psychiatrist who interviewed all those girls in *Reviving Ophelia.* Tiffany was one of the interviewed girls, as was Maggie. It was really dramatic because they played girls that were very much like who they are.

Yeah.

It was cool because we performed by candlelight (well, battery candles) and the room was very dark. Scary, dramatic, fun…and just a bit nerve wracking. But as Mr. B said, "You are supposed to study drama in this class, so we might as well create it and perform it!"

In my opinion, that is a real final exam.

When the last group had finished their performance, Mr. B had his own candle and he said these words to us:

"Listen, gang, we, Ms. Anderson and I, are the merchants of *uncool.* We make no profit on you. Everything we do is free. We just try to get you folks to think. To dream and hope. To write and sing and dance. To experience new things and understand more people. To understand that you don't know where you are *going* unless you know where you have *been.* But most importantly, we want you to *read.* Reading takes you places you can only dream about. Literature and art helps you to see life in color. And I can only hope that wherever your journey takes you, wherever your ship sails, that you hold the rudder with a clear eye gazing northward to the sky."

OK, so that got me even more choked up.

Pari's Hand

And for me, it is a rollercoaster of emotions.

Dan kissed me at the prom.

I had never kissed a boy before. We have gone out two times since. My parents like him—they don't even make mention of him *not* being Persian.

Then, they told me we were going to Iran for four weeks in July.

I did not know what to say. I had forgotten in all the excitement and stress and Prom madness that they were making the arrangements. I am such a mess right now. Yes, I want to see my cousins. Yes, I have not been back since 8th grade. Yes, I do love Iran—at least the Iran of my youth…of my family.

But I am lost. I finally have Maddie and Rhia and Mickey…and Dan…and Mr. B and my senior summer. There is the beach and the movies and just hanging out with each other.

But what I will miss the most is the Metaphor Café.

You see, this week we all found out the Metaphor Café is closing. We were there one night and the owner came by and told us he was retiring and looking to sell the business, but that he most likely would have to close the café.

"Too much competition from the big boys," he said, wiping down the counter. He said that he loved how the Metaphor was a place that people just met and talked. He had a distant look about him.

"My wife and I want to travel and see our grandchildren before they become too old, like you all," he mused.

All four of us just sat there stunned.

Closed. Where would we go next year? That's when Mickey spoke up.

Mickey's Hand

"Mr. Davis, if you sell the place, can we buy something from you?"

"Do you want to buy the place?"

"No. I wish we could, but no, Mr. Davis. If you close it, we would like to buy a…a…memento or something to remember the Metaphor Cafe. And it would be a gift for someone."

Mr. Davis really liked us. As a matter of fact, he knew we were writing this book. He often overheard us talking about a chapter or sometimes reading a new part to each other. We were clearly his best customers. He agreed with my proposition.

But that isn't the only thing that has all of us so emotional right now. You see, we are done.

This is the end of the book. It's like Holden Caulfield's last lonely chapter. It's Huck's, "Chapter the Last," where he heads West. It's the closing moments of *Pleasantville* when you hear the Beatles singing, "Across the Universe." It's Nick Caraway's somber words at the end of *Gatsby* telling us all that we march on beating against the wind and the world. It's Rick and Ilsa at the Casablanca airport, and we all feel like Ilsa as she leaves to get on that plane because if we don't, we will regret it, too.

We have lived with this book—with Mr. B and Ms. Anderson—for 182 days and we *so* don't want it to end. On the last day of class, Mr. B played one last song to us. It was by Jackson Browne. He told us he hadn't played one song from him, but he felt that he was one of the best writers of melancholy songs, and that, "this is a melancholy day." It was called, "Sky Blue and Black." It was about memories. Songs on the radio. Being younger. Simple times.

Promises. Holding on to the people you love in good times and bad…blue skies or black.

He told us that although the song was written years earlier, some folks thought it was dedicated to the survivors of 9.11. And that brought all of us back to that day with Bruce Springsteen and "Mary's Place" and "The Rising" and "The Land of Hopes and Dreams." And we knew that we were finishing that ride as part of what Mr. B called "The E Street Nation" and that we were all so grateful that we had climbed aboard.

I looked at the girls and lots of them were crying as the song played. They hugged each other—we all did a lot of that as the class was ending and the last minutes of "the show" were coming to a finale.

That was when I stood up, walked to the front of the room, and made my speech:

"Mr. Buscotti and Ms. Anderson, the class pitched in and got you a gift. We wanted to buy you a Porsche or some cool gift that you get on *Oprah*—and even send you there, Ms. Anderson. Or we wanted to send you, Mr. B, to see Springsteen." The two teachers looked at each other and smiled, raising their eyebrows to silently say, "Oh, yeah."

I continued, "But we are poor. So… As you know, some of us have been meeting and studying and sometimes writing at the Metaphor Café. What you might *not* know is the Metaphor Café is probably closing since the owner is retiring. Mr. Davis agreed to sell us these two signs, the original plaques from the Metaphor Café that he had made in 1977 when he opened the place. There's one for each of you to hang in your rooms."

Maddie handed me a big box that she'd grabbed from outside where her mom was waiting. I pulled out the two signs and continued with the speech:

"We wanted you both to know that the Metaphor Café is not a place that can ever close—not really. You have taught us that life is a state of mind—like slavery was, and freedom is. And as long as we keep our minds open and our eyes focused on our own True North, then whether skies are blue or black, we will never be lost."

I made up that last part on the spot. I couldn't believe the words came out so easily for me. And then the class applauded. Ms. Anderson got a little emotional. She thanked us. "This reminds me of a gift my class got me when I got married. Thank you all very much," she said, holding the wooden sign. "I do *get* the symbolism of this."

Mr. B, for once, was speechless.

But I'm not.

Mr. Buscotti, you rock my world.

I hope one day you get to meet Bruce Springsteen—or rather, he gets to meet you.

--Mickey

Rhiannon's Hand

And this afternoon Chris graduated. I thought I was all cried out after Mr. B's class, but I cried so much at Chris' ceremony that I think I lost weight.

I remember when he was so frustrated because he wanted to read things that I could, but he just couldn't. I remember reading to him at night, whether it was picture books or every chapter of the latest *Harry Potter*. He could read it, he pleaded with me, but, "It's so much better when you do it."

I remember when he protected me from some bully boys.

I remember when he tried to protect me when our dad left.

And there he was. Huge smile. Red graduation gown, goofy hat. Waving at us as he marched onto the football field for the last time. He was also excited about senior grad night tonight. I am so proud of him. I have learned, though him, that nothing ever comes easy. There are always great challenges and obstacles, but it is all about rising up and dancing to your own beat and never giving up just because it will be hard.

The singer at the graduation chose a song that had special meaning to me. She sang it beautifully with confidence, called "I Hope You Dance."

And I remembered the Dance of the Decades. And Donald. And blurting out, "God, I hope you aren't already going with someone to the Winter Formal!" I remember his answer. I remember us laughing and getting all tangled up in some crazy swing move.

I am sure glad I never, never sat out that dance.

Mr. B, promise *me* that you will dance with me someday at my wedding.

--Love Always… Rhiannon.

Pari's Hand

I was in the Junior Honor Chain that leads the seniors on to the field that night. I saw Mr. Buscotti sitting in the front row of the teachers and I waved at him. When we came to our seats he did the most unusual thing. He walked over to me and handed me two cards in envelopes and whispered, "Parivash, your dad wrote to me yesterday. Please give him the blue envelope. Yours is the yellow one." Then he winked at me. He knew I would read it during the graduation—I had to!

What had my father written to him? My father rarely got involved with teachers or school. That was my mother's job. I was mystified. When I opened the yellow envelope, there was a card that had a picture of the Eiffel Tower in Paris. Inside the card was a folded paper, handwritten, and I immediately recognized the penmanship.

Dear Mr. Buscotti:

How can I thank you for all you have done for my daughter, Parivash? She has always been bright, but I felt she was also a lonely soul. I cannot blame her since I have moved her from one home to another and yet another. For some reason, she felt that she was not as "good" as her brothers, or that we did not think as highly of her compared to them. You have helped change all of those attitudes. She loves your class and she loves her friends. He mother and I were so proud of her when we came to see her dance at your Dance of the Decades. And when she attended the Prom with a young man also from your class, well, my heart swelled.

You have inspired her to come out of her shell and embrace this new homeland. She is even fighting with us about our vacation to Iran—she doesn't want to miss her friends. We have decided to take Pari and her friends to a wonderful Persian restaurant before she leaves, and we would like to invite you and your wife to join us. Words simply cannot express our respect for you.

Please share these thoughts of gratitude with Ms. Anderson, whom I know Parivash also admires greatly. I have also invited her and her husband.

Sincerely,
Anwar and Yasmin Said

Then I read my card. On the inside a simple message was printed:

We will always have Paris!

The *s* was crossed out, and in Mr. Buscotti's handwriting there was this message to me:

> *Don't be sad. See the world. We will all be eager to see you when you return. You, Mickey, Maddie, and Rhia, have been the most wonderful gifts a teacher can receive. My wife and I will be honored to join you and your family for dinner.*
>
> *- Mr. B*

I closed the card and squeezed it shut. I just couldn't believe all this was happening to me. I looked in the stands for my parents, but it was just a sea of faces. The teachers' seats were nearby and when my eyes met Mr. B's, he smiled at me.

One time I remember him reciting a line as the Stage Manager from the play *Our Town* in which he said something about how you have to live your life to find out how to truly *love* your life.

Thank you, Mr. Buscotti, because you have taught me to love my life.

--Your Act Three Emily Webb... Pari

Madison's Hand

Okay. Big breath.

This all started last Thanksgiving when I got the idea of writing this book.

Now I am sitting here in my bedroom with about a hundred balled up tissues all around me and my laptop. Pari just emailed her entry to me and I am a wreck. Mickey told me I have to be the one to write the final words.

I wonder what Mr. B and Ms. Anderson will think of all this. I am sure we have made a gazillion grammar mistakes. I am also sure that there is no such word as gazillion. I know we are just 16 going on

17, and we don't all have our driver's licenses yet, and we don't know if or when there will be peace in the Middle East or if the price of gas will ever come down. There is so much we may never know. I guess that is what keeps life interesting.

Yeah.

Anyway, I know this book was something we *had* to do!

I cry whenever I watch *The Wizard of Oz* when Dorothy has to say goodbye to her beloved companions—the ones who guided and helped her on her journey. She loves them all, but she says she'll miss the Scarecrow the most.

Well, Mr. B, I will miss you the most.

You will always and forever be my…To Sir…with Love.

--**Maddie**

The Afterword

Mr. Buscotti's Hand

It is the notes that always get me. Whether they are handwritten or typed or attached to the photo of two young people in their best Prom outfits, it's those notes that make the difference for me—and for them. I usually read them over from time to time, and particularly before school begins anew—like today. Why? Because of the fear that builds up in me. Do I have the energy to lead another campaign? Can I reach them? Is that connection still there? Will the songs, the literature, the history still have relevance to them? However, the letters always make me smile. Some of the faces are now in their 40's; they have children, and sometimes their children are a part of my world now. Second generations.

But what these four young people did for me is, without question, the greatest reminder of why I do what I do. I am honored to have been their teacher. I will miss the four of them. That's the funny thing about being a teacher; young people get on the ride, learn and grow, and then get off. But you remain there, spinning on the carousel of time.

But I have always felt that I was also *on the ride.* Teaching is a stage and the spotlight is not for the timid. There is great responsibility and great risk. These letters and notes on my wall take me back: the girl who needed me to stop what I was doing and find out why she was homeless; the boy who had to tell me that he finally got over his anxiety and depression; the girl whom I chased into the parking lot because I forgot to tell her something that later made all the difference between sadness and relief; the boy who cried over his sister's abortion; the teacher who cried because she thought she had failed her kids; the kids at graduation who cry and hug their teachers because we believed in them—what a cast of characters this play reveals!

But as Maddie, Rhia, Mickey and Pari have demonstrated in writing this narrative, they have overcome the obstacles and climbed this mountain…only to learn there are mountains that follow. Mountains and memories. From those vantage points, there is no telling where their adventures will take them. But I know this—their compass is pointed to "True North."

I love them all with all my heart.

Goodbye and God Bless…from the Metaphor Café.

Songs and Notes from the Metaphor Café:

These were all the things Mr. B and Ms. Anderson taught us, and all the material we looked up during the year. We all thought you should know that we didn't make all this up!

Prologue

- Lulu: "To Sir with Love" from the film of the same title. Also mentioned is the 10,000 Maniacs' version.

Chapter One

- Jewel: "My Hands" from *Spirit*
- Billy Joel: "The Stranger" from *The Stranger*

Chapter Two

- Bruce Springsteen: "The Big Muddy" from the album *Lucky Town*
- Bruce Springsteen: "It's Hard to Be a Saint in the City" from *Greetings from Asbury Park*
- The Doobie Brothers: "Black Water" on the album *Best of The Doobies*

Chapter Three

- Bruce Springsteen: "The Rising" from *The Rising*
- Bruce Springsteen: "Into the Fire" from *The Rising*
- Bruce Springsteen: "Empty Sky" from *The Rising*
- Bruce Springsteen: "Countin' on a Miracle" from *The Rising*
- Bruce Springsteen: "You're Missing" from *The Rising*
- Bruce Springsteen: "Mary's Place" from *The Rising*
- Bruce Springsteen: "Land of Hopes and Dreams" from *Live from New York City*

Chapter Five

- 10,000 Maniacs and Natalie Merchant: "These Are the Days" from *Our Time in Eden*
- Green Day: "Good Riddance: Time of Your Life" from *Nimrod*
- Marc Cohn: "True Companion" from *Marc Cohn*

- Five for Fighting: "100 Years" from *The Battle for Everything*

Chapter Six

- Ernest Hemingway's short story: "Hills like White Elephants"
- The Verve Pipe: "The Freshman" from *Villains*
- Jewel: "You Were Meant for Me" from *Pieces of You*
- O. Henry's short story: "The Gift of the Magi"
- Marc Cohn: "Perfect Love" from *Marc Cohn*
- Joseph Dever's short story: "50 Missions"
- John Denver: "Leaving on a Jet Plane" from *Rhymes and Reasons*
- Bruce Springsteen: "Point Blank" from *The River*

Chapter Seven

- F. Scott Fitzgerald's novel: *The Great Gatsby*

Chapter Eight

- John Steinbeck's film: *The Grapes of Wrath* (with Henry Fonda) 1940
- Woody Guthrie, in one of his *People's World* columns (1939-'40), reprinted in Woody Sez, New York, NY, 1975, p. 133.
- Bruce Springsteen: "The Ghost of Tom Joad" from *The Ghost of Tom Joad*

Chapter Nine

- Bruce Springsteen: "Let's Be Friends: Skin to Skin" from *The Rising*
- Cole Porter: "Begin the Beguine" (1935) from Great American Composer Series
- Michael Buble: "Fever" from *Michael Buble 2003* (Original by Peggy Lee, on the *Mad Hot Ballroom* soundtrack)
- Glenn Miller and his Orchestra: "In the Mood" (1940) words by Andy Razaf, music by Joe Garland, as recorded by The Andrews Sisters.
- Cherry Poppin' Daddies: "Zoot Suit Riot" (1997) from album *Zoot Suit Riot*
- Frank Sinatra: "I've Got You Under My Skin" from *Classic Sinatra 2000*

- Dean Martin: "Sway" from Dino: *The Essential Dean Martin 2004*
- The Arthur Murray Orchestra: "Ole Guapa" *from The Ballroom Mix 3*
- Johnny Mathis: "Silver Bells: from *Merry Christmas*
- "The Charleston," lyrics circa 1923.
- The Bee Gees: "Night Fever" from *Saturday Night Fever*
- Danny and the Juniors: "At the Hop"
- Bobby Darin: "Beyond the Sea" from *That's All*

Chapter Ten

- *Casablanca:* (1942) directed by Michael Curtiz.

Chapter Eleven

- Melba Beals' memoir: *Warriors Don't Cry*
- Roger Wilkins: "The Throwaway People" PBS Frontline 1990.
- Jim VandeHei and Peter Bake: "Critics Say Bush Undercut New Orleans Flood Control" The Washington Post Friday, September 2, 2005; Page A16

Chapter Twelve

- Tim O'Brien's book: *The Things They Carried*, Houghton Mifflin, 1990.
- Bob Dylan: "The Masters of War" from *The Freewheelin' Bob Dylan* 1963
- *1968- documentary:* The History Channel
- *Robert F. Kennedy*, Wikiquote.
- "Soldiers Face Neglect, Frustration at Army's Top Medical Facility." Dana Priest and Anne Hull. *Washington Post.* Sunday, February 18, 2007; Page A01
- Joseph Stiglitz and Linda Bilmes: *The Three Trillion Dollar War. 2008*

Chapter Thirteen

- Dr. Mary Pipher: *Reviving Ophelia*: saving the souls of teenage girls. 1994.
- YouTube: *Reviving Ophelia*: saving the souls of teenage girls. www.Mediaed.org

- An interview with Mary Pipher, Ph.D. author of *Reviving Ophelia* on www.Commitment.com
- The Dixie Chicks: "I'm Not Ready to Make Nice" from *Taking The Long Way.* 2006

Chapter Fourteen

- Don McLean: "American Pie" from the album *American Pie.* 1973
- Lynyrd Skynyrd: "Sweet Home Alabama"
- Roberta Flack: "Killing Me Softly with His Song" from the album of the same title.

Chapter Fifteen

- *Pleasantville:* Directed by Gary Ross. 1998.
- The Quran: 002.030 Behold, thy Lord said to the angels: "I will create a vicegerent (man) son earth." They said: "Wilt Thou place therein one who will make mischief therein and shed blood?- whilst we do celebrate Thy praises and glorify Thy holy (name)?" He said: "I know what ye know not." Wikipedia. "Fall of Man"
- "In Christianity, the Fall of Man, or simply the Fall, is believed to refer to the transition of the first humans from a state of innocent obedience to God to a state of guilty disobedience to God. In the origin stories of Christianity, the first humans, Adam and Eve, live at first with God in a paradise, but are then deceived or tempted by another creature to eat fruit from the Tree of Knowledge of Good and Evil from which God had forbidden them to eat. After doing so, they become ashamed of their nakedness and God consequently expels them from paradise. The Fall is not mentioned by name in the Bible, but the story of disobedience and expulsion is recounted in both in different ways." From Wikipedia. Fall of Man.
- M. Scott Peck: *The Road Less Traveled.* 1978.

Chapter Sixteen

- J.D. Salinger: *Catcher in the Rye.* 1953.
- Avril Lavigne and The Matrix: "I'm With You" from *Let's Go.* 2003.
- Harper Lee: *To Kill a Mockingbird.* 1960

Chapter Seventeen

- Douglas Rushkoff: "The Merchants of Cool" part of PBS's *Frontline* 2001.
- Brittney Spears: "I'm Not That Innocent."
- Limp Bizkit: "Hard Stuff."
- Dooley Wilson: "As Time Goes By." From the film *Casablanca*
- Nat King Cole: "It's Only a Paper Moon" by Billy Rose, Harold Arlen and "Yip" Harburg

Chapter Eighteen

- The Beatles: "Across the Universe" from *Let It Be.* 1970.
- Jackson Browne: "Sky Blue or Black" from the album *I'm Alive.*
- Lee Ann Womack: "I Hope You Dance" from the album of the same title. 2000.

Robert Pacilio was born to teach. He's been teaching high school English for 30 years, and was awarded San Diego County "Teacher of the Year." He is a regular presenter at various educational conferences and school districts. **Meetings at the Metaphor Café** is his first novel. He is the author of several plays and readers theaters performed in high schools. He lives in San Diego with his wife Pam and his children.

He can be reached at **robertpacilio@gmail.com**

Made in the USA
Lexington, KY
25 November 2009